The Magician's
Daughter

Books by Judith Janeway

The Valentine Hill Mysteries
The Magician's Daughter

The Magician's Daughter

A Valentine Hill Mystery

Judith Janeway

Poisoned Pen Press

Library of Congress Catalog Card Number: 2014951265

ISBN: 9781464203381   Hardcover
      9781464203398   Trade Paperback

Poisoned Pen Press
6962 E. First Ave., Ste. 103
Scottsdale, AZ 85251
www.poisonedpenpress.com
info@poisonedpenpress.com

Printed in the United States of America

To
LUKE
In my heart
every day
forever

Chapter One

I pulled a skunk out of my hat and looked shocked. The children squealed with laughter. I'd tried four times with intentionally escalating failure to produce a rabbit from my top hat. Making animals appear, even the plush-toy kind, wasn't my favorite kind of magic, but the exhilaration of making it happen seamlessly ended up being all that mattered to me.

At ten in the morning outside the Golden Pirate Casino, the clumsy magician-in-search-of-a-rabbit routine acted like a magnet for children and their parents. The casino liked it because it attracted the child-free adults to the blinking and blaring slot machines just through the open doorway behind me. Eddie the Wiz liked it because I advertised his afternoon and evening shows in the casino theater. And I liked it because I needed the money my audience dropped into the other top hat strategically placed in front of my immodest The Great Valentina banner.

I tossed the skunk onto the pile of rejects at my feet and jammed my top hat onto my head. "Not to worry," I told the audience while looking very worried. "There may be other forces at work here. Possibly there's another magician present who's working against me? Hmmm?"

I took my time to scan the audience, even though I'd been doing it automatically all along. I didn't like the looks of the guy in the torn jeans who kept oozing out of sight into the crowd every time my gaze locked onto him. I did another quick visual sweep. No sign of Jeff. I was winding down my performance and people had already dropped bills and coins into the hat as they moved on into the casino. Jeff should've been there watching the hat and looking out for the questionables like Torn Jeans.

I pretended to scrutinize the children standing closest to me for signs of magical ability. I narrowed my eyes at a little girl in jeans and pink tennis shoes who giggled and gripped her dad's hand with both of hers. "Could it be you?"

She shook her head emphatically. "No."

I moved my gaze past a few more children. A boy, maybe nine, took a half step forward.

"Aha! It must be you!" I whipped my cape close to my body as if trying to protect myself.

"No." His eager look said "choose me."

I would have chosen him, if a group slumming from the Bellagio hadn't tried to break up my show—a gray-haired man with an improbably boyish face, a blonde with equally improbable breasts, a big guy showing a lot of muscle, and a teenage girl looking like an escapee from a Japanese anime convention. She had short purple hair frozen into permanent windswept spikes above a polka-dot blouse, short plaid skirt, and white knee-high socks with lace around the top. The men wore designer sunglasses and expensive casual clothes that made the Golden Pirate folks in my audience look dowdy. They didn't join the audience but stood to one side watching both the crowd and me.

Anime-Girl said in a loud voice, "See Dad? I told you," and pointed at me. The audience shifted their attention to the girl.

The dad ignored his daughter. He pulled his sunglasses down his nose to stare at me with a flat gaze. I'd had a lot of experience with drunks and hecklers so they rarely fazed me. I'd even had a couple of stalkers, one of the reasons I gave Jeff a percentage of the hat. But this guy wasn't the stalker type. No, he snapped his fingers and people came to him. Why had he trekked over to the Golden Pirate to give me the once-over?

"I wanna see the rabbit," a child whined. People shuffled their feet and a few at the fringes drifted off without leaving anything in the hat. I'd lost my rhythm and was about to lose my audience. Time to take the situation in hand. I had no idea what the party-crashers wanted, but no way would I let them break up my act. Time for improvisation.

I tossed one side of my cape back over my shoulder and announced, "I, the Great Valentina, sense the presence of another force, a dark opposing force." I spoke louder and faster. "This dark force is hiding, but it can't hide from…"

I gave a flourish with my right hand and a wand appeared in my left, "the Great Valentina's dark force locater." I pointed the wand toward the audience and moved it slowly to the left and right, making eye contact with as many people as I could. As I swung my arm at the intruders, the wand took on a life of its own, jerking my arm toward them and dragging me to where they stood. While the audience focused on the twitching wand, I palmed the flat circle of my collapsible snake from the inside of my cloak. A little marvel of sheer silk over a one-ounce titanium spring that I always kept handy as an emergency backup.

I flicked the wand back and forth between the girl and her dad. "The dark force is…" I paused dramatically "here." The trembling wand pointed to the dad. "Don't blame yourself," I said quickly. "The dark force is cunning. But with my help, and with the help of this brave girl, we shall all be safe." I stepped toward the dad and his daughter. A big man with them growled and moved to block my advance, making it clear that he was a bodyguard. I fixed my gaze on the older man. Who was this guy?

His fingers signaled his bodyguard to let me approach. The bodyguard backed off. I stepped between the dad and the daughter, jostling him slightly as I did, so he didn't notice me drop my snake in his jacket pocket.

"We shall appease the dark force with a gold ducat." I turned to the girl. "Give this man the gold ducat," I commanded, pointing to her father.

"What gold ducat?" she asked.

I extended my hand toward her hair. "May I show you?"

She hesitated, then said, "Yeah. Okay."

I snatched a golden coin from her hair and held it high for the crowd to see, then turned back to her. "Now take the gold ducat." I pressed the coin into her palm. "Do you have it?"

She nodded.

I closed her fingers over it. "Are you sure you have it?"

"Yeah, I'm sure."

"There are strong opposing forces at work. Promise me you won't let go."

"Okay."

I couldn't wring more cooperation out of her than that. "Excellent." I dropped my hands and took two steps back. "Now show it to everyone."

She opened her fist and gaped at her empty hand. "I know I had it. Where'd it go?"

The crowd pressed forward to see. I had my audience back where I wanted them.

I shook my head at her in exasperation. "You promised you wouldn't let go. Did you carelessly drop it into his pocket?" I pointed to the dad, who stared at me fixedly. He straightened and glanced at his daughter.

"No way. I had it in my hand."

"You'd better check his pocket. But be careful." I took a step back. "Go on."

She stuck her hand into her father's jacket pocket, pulling out the flat disc which immediately exploded into a six-foot snake. She cut loose with a glass-shattering shriek and threw the snake. People in the audience screamed. I grabbed the snake before it hit the ground and shook it slightly, making it writhe convincingly. I staggered, finally wrestling it into submission. I dropped it to the ground where it lay still, turned and shook my finger at the girl. "I warned you to be careful."

The audience laughed.

"And now that I have conquered all opposing dark forces," I whipped my hat from my head and paused dramatically. The audience held their collective breath.

"We can now have the rabbit!"

I reached into my hat one last time, and with a grand gesture, produced a three-foot tall rabbit—another one of my titanium-spring wonders. The audience gasped, oohed in appreciation, and clapped.

"Thank you. You've been great." I bowed and scanned the crowd. I spotted Torn Jeans still moving along the perimeter, but no Jeff. He should've been here picking up my paraphernalia before the nosy audience looked it over too closely. "Don't forget that you can experience the amazing magic of Edward the Wizard in the Golden Pirate Casino theater." I waved toward the wide casino doorway with one hand and bent down to retrieve the snake and the rabbit with the other. Stuffing them hastily out of sight into the bag behind my banner, I beamed at those who stepped forward to drop money in the donation hat.

Anime-Girl and Dad approached me, with the boob-job blonde and bodyguard close behind. "You're very good." Dad gave me a full blast smile, but no money in the hat. I couldn't guess his age—over fifty but with very well-tended skin and hair. "Do you have a card?"

If I'd gone with my gut response, I'd have said "No." But Aunt June's number one rule had been "don't lie," and I'd promised I wouldn't. So I evaded. "I'm glad you enjoyed the show. Are you booking acts or looking for an act to do a private party?"

"Neither, actually." He shifted the smile to a boyish grin that probably got him his way—most of the time.

I turned to stow the rest of my gear.

"Ask her about Beth Hull, Dad," Anime-Girl said.

I froze in the middle of rolling up my Great Valentina banner. Beth Hull, aka Elizabeth Hill. Aka my mother. Hard to believe that Elizabeth would still rely on such an old alias. Beth Hull was her version of a soft-spoken, well-bred lady. When I'd last seen Elizabeth she'd been playing Liz Heldin, the exuberant, fun-loving babe in Miami. That was nearly nine years ago, and I was twelve, fourteen, or sixteen, depending on which date of birth Elizabeth thought most useful for the current con. She changed my age, her name, and our residence as often as most people change underwear. She went by Hill only when incarcerated. I'd been searching for her for five years.

"Hey, he's got your money!" the girl yelled.

I spun. Too late. Torn Jeans had already snatched up the hat and taken off at a sprint. I took three steps and stopped. Everyone else stood rooted to the ground, watching next week's rent disappear down the street. I'd known that guy was trouble. I couldn't catch him now, but I was going to kill Jeff when I got my hands on him. I turned back to packing my gear, jamming it in.

"Should we call the police?" the girl asked.

"No point," I said.

"So I take it that you do know Beth Hull," the dad said the way other people said "Gotcha."

"Take whatever you want. Everyone else has," I said without meeting his gaze.

"You know, you look just like her," he said.

I did know. Even nine years ago our eyes were the same pale blue, noses the same straight line, and ditto for jawlines. Both blondes, too, only my hair was frizzball and hers straight. What I didn't know was what this guy wanted. I could only guess that he wanted Elizabeth because she'd made off with the family silver and bankroll. He could get in line, because she'd taken more than that from me.

"You do look like her. I mean totally like her," the girl rattled on. "When I told my dad, he like, didn't believe me. He had to see for himself."

"Ash!" Her dad cut her off. I glanced up in time to catch the look he gave her, and it hit me why my gut had taken against him. Elizabeth used one of two kinds of men in her life, the Uncles and the Creeps. Uncles were marks, and Creeps were boyfriends. Creeps were never nice people. Deliberately and happily not nice.

Ash crossed her arms and gave her dad a sullen look, but she kept quiet. So did I. The last thing I needed was another one of Elizabeth's Creeps. Particularly not one she'd conned and robbed. I finished packing up.

"I'd like to talk with you for a few minutes," he said.

"I have to get to work." I picked up my gear.

"I'll make it worth your while."

"No thanks." It was easy to turn him down. Sure I needed the money, but money from Creeps always came at too high a price. Even those who didn't have a revenge agenda.

He would've persisted, but his cell phone beeped. When he pulled it from his pocket to check the number, I hoisted my bag onto my shoulder and marched toward the casino entrance. I faced a dilemma. I didn't want to talk to one of Elizabeth's victims, but I couldn't pass up the chance of getting on her still-warm trail. So as I passed by the daughter, I said, "I see you're into Japanese anime." That got her attention.

"Yes, I really love cosplay. How about you?" She fell into step next to me. Her dad watched us walk away, but kept talking into his phone.

Cosplay? I guessed that meant dressing up like an anime character. "A little." In fact, all I knew I'd learned when I'd done a street performance outside an anime/manga expo, but I needed to find out what she knew about Elizabeth. "You're called Ash?"

"Actually I'm Ashley, but Dad calls me Ash." We entered into the casino's sensory overload of frigid air conditioning and beeping, clanging, and light-flashing slot machines.

"I think Flame fits your persona better than Ash," I said. She flashed a brief grin, pleased. I hated being manipulative, but this was the closest I'd come to tracking down Elizabeth in five years. "Nice to meet you. I'm Valentine Hill."

Ashley's face fell. "Hill, not Hull? I thought for sure you were related to Beth."

"Definitely related. Her real name is Hill. How long has it been since she disappeared?"

"What do you mean, disappeared? She's in San Francisco."

I stared at her. "Are you sure?"

"Sure I'm sure. We saw her the day we left. She's my dad's girlfriend."

"So the blonde with him is just a Vegas moment?"

Ashley wrinkled her nose. "That's Marcie. She's his private girlfriend. Beth's his public one. It's complicated."

"Why does he need a public girlfriend?"

"He's Bobby Kroy. You know, Kroy's Doors and Windows? They have commercials on TV?"

She raised more questions than she answered. Like, why would someone who sold doors and windows need a bodyguard? What was public-girlfriend-Elizabeth really up to? The overriding fact was that finally I knew where Elizabeth was.

We reached the door marked Employees Only, and I turned to Ashley. "I have to go to work now. But can I ask a favor? Could I get Elizabeth's address from you?"

"Sure. I have it." She pulled out a cell phone and pushed some buttons.

I turned, grabbed a pencil and a ticket from the nearest Keno stand, and pivoted back to Ashley. "Okay, I'm ready."

Ashley held her phone against her chest. "First, tell me how you're related."

"Okay. But promise not to tell your dad or Elizabeth?"

"Why?"

"I want to surprise her when I get to San Francisco."

Ashley's face lit up. "Okay, I promise."

"She's my mother." And she'd be surprised to see me, but not happy surprised as Ashley assumed.

"Your mother? And you don't know where she is?"

"It's complicated. Like your dad and his public/private girl-friends. We can talk about it if I see you when I get to San Francisco."

"Okay, deal. But promise you'll come see me."

"I'll try. Very hard. That's the best I can do." I held the pencil over the paper, waiting for her to give me Elizabeth's address.

She frowned. "Don't you want to put it in your cell?"

"I don't have it with me."

"Forgot it, huh? That sucks."

"No, she didn't forget it." Jeff's voice came from behind me, "The Great Valentina lets her entourage—namely me—take her calls. She can't be bothered with non-magic-related technical details."

I whirled around to face him. "Where were you?"

"You're not going to believe it." He draped an arm around my shoulders.

I flung off his arm and glared at him. "I lost the hat, thanks to you. And you're not my entourage. You're my hat man, remember? Correction. Make that, you were my hat man." I'd definitely been too easy-going with Jeff in the past, but he'd been reliable for months before he started showing up late for my show.

"Sorry about the hat, but it's all cool. I got a gig." He turned to Ashley. "I'm in a band."

Ashley looked impressed. With his "I'm in a band" line, his long hair hanging in his eyes, his jeans' waistband at his crotch, and the natural charm of every narcissist, Jeff easily scored with naïve young women. He'd been persistent in hitting on me too, but I'd repeatedly made it clear I wouldn't have sex with him.

"You mean, you used to be in a band," I said. "You haven't worked as a musician for a year. Now stop hitting on an underage girl and go away."

"I wasn't hitting on her. Come on, Val, you know you're the only one for me."

"No, I'm the only one who won't sleep with you."

"That's not it. You have standards. I respect you for that. But it's all going to change now. It's like we talked about. I'd get a gig and you'd come with me. But we have to leave like—now."

"*You* talked about it. You never listened when I said I wouldn't sign on for it. And why would I? Because of you I lost next week's rent."

"Why are you stressing about the rent? You're not anywhere near broke and you know it."

I gritted my teeth. Why had I confided in Jeff about my safety net stash?

"And," he added, "you won't have to pay rent if you come to Berkeley with me."

"Berkeley?" Ashley put in.

"Yeah. And get this—I'll be playing with Ghoul Food. Can you believe it? They have a gig in a really cool club. And my sister lives in San Francisco, so we can stay with her."

"Omigod," Ashley said. "It's like karma or something."

"What is?" Jeff asked.

I put out a hand to stop Ashley, but she was swept up in the whole karma thing. "She's already going to San Francisco to find her mom. And then you get a job there. Wow."

"For real?" Jeff asked. "Wait—find your mom? Not your dad?"

"I have to go to work," I said.

Ashley stepped closer. "You don't know where your dad is either?"

I shook my head. I didn't want to talk about this with either of them.

"Yeah," Jeff said. "Her dad's a magician, too."

"Really?" Ashley asked, wide-eyed. "What's his name?"

"That's the problem," Jeff said. "She doesn't know."

"Then how are you going to find him?" She raised her eyebrows at me.

"I'm sorry, Ashley," I wanted to stop the questions, "but I really do have to go to work now."

"Valentine, please." Jeff gave me his best puppy dog in the pound look. "You know how I feel about you. This is our chance. It's like she said—karma."

"No, Jeff. Karma is you finally getting a gig but not having any money to get there because you didn't show up for the job you already had."

"Babe, don't do this to me. We're meant to be. You know we are. Why do you keep fighting it?"

I narrowed my eyes. He was being way too persistent. Then it hit me. "How were you planning on getting to Berkeley or San Francisco or wherever you're going?"

He brightened, apparently taking this as encouragement. "There's a flight out tonight. I can just make it and be in time for the show. I know you can't fly, but you can take the bus and meet me there tomorrow."

"And who's buying the tickets?"

"You front me the money, and I'll pay you back." He didn't blink. "But here's the deal. I told them I'd make it for tonight's show, so we got to go."

I stared at him. "You expect me to pay your way after you cost me a whole week's rent? You're delusional."

"You're not listening. I'll pay you back. I'm going to make a lot of money. This is my big break. And you're going to San Francisco anyway, so it's like we're meant to be. You know you care about me at least a little. You know how I feel about you."

"Sure. You feel like I'm an easy touch, which I'm not. Go hit up someone else for your plane fare."

"I can't believe you're doing this to me—to us."

I folded my arms. "Will you go away, or do I have to call security?"

Jeff held my gaze for a few seconds, turned away, then turned back. "I know you don't really mean it." He walked away.

Ashley stared at me. "You're not breaking up with him, are you? I mean, you're going to make up, right?"

I shook my head.

"But he loves you. Don't you feel anything for him?"

"He doesn't love me. He just can't face the fact that there's even one woman in the world who won't have sex with him."

"Why not? He's hot."

"Hot or not, he's a musician. You know what they call a musician without a girlfriend?"

Ashley shook her head.

"Homeless."

Ashley cracked a faint grin.

"Trust me, he was hoping I'd go with him so I'd pay to get us there. Forget about him. You were about to give me Elizabeth's address?" I held up the paper and pencil again.

Ashley read out the address from her cell.

"Thank you so much for this. You don't know what it means to me. And please don't tell her or your dad? I want to surprise her."

"I won't. But take down my cell number. Call me when you get to San Francisco."

I added Ashley's phone number. "I really have to go. I'm late for work. Thanks again."

"Call me."

"I promise that I'll try. Bye, Ashley." I hurried through the employee's entrance and up the stairs to the theater's backstage. I was late but Eddie was later, so no one knew.

The problem with being paid under the table is that you have no recourse if your employer stiffs you. I waited until after Eddie gave me my pay post-performance before I told him I was leaving. As I'd expected, he didn't take it well and vowed he'd never hire me again. An empty threat, since he was an unreliable drunk, who ran through assistants the way he ran through bottles of vodka. But if I got what I needed from Elizabeth, I wouldn't have to work off-the-books again. I'd be a regular tax-paying citizen at last.

I'd be lying if I said I wasn't excited as I made my way home. I'd been trying to find Elizabeth since Aunt June died. Once I'd even hired a private detective, but he was too expensive and never turned up anything. I jogged up the stairs to the apartment where I rented a room from Diane. As a Vegas showgirl she made much more than I did but rented out rooms because she was forever saving for her next plastic surgery. She always complained about the unfairness of my having breasts almost as big as hers that I didn't pay for.

The apartment lay in darkness. Diane and our other roommate were still out doing a late show. Lucky me. My rent was paid through the end of the week. I could leave her a note and not have to explain why I left so suddenly.

I felt my way through the darkened living room. Diane was hypervigilant about the cost of utilities, so we never turned on unneeded lights. I pressed the light switch in the hallway, started toward my room at the end, and stopped short. My door, my always-padlocked door, stood open. Diane was the only other person who had a key, because she'd insisted "in case of emergencies."

I ran into my room and hit the light. My room had been ransacked. Diane would never do such a thing, but Jeff would. He must've rushed here and talked Diane into letting him into my room.

The room was such a mess it took me a few seconds to register the real disaster. My beautiful Chinese wooden inlay box lay in splinters in the middle of my bed. The precious box that Aunt June had given me because it had not one, but two secret compartments. It had taken me five minutes to figure out the clever tricks to open the compartments, and no one else who tried had been able to open it. I sank to my knees next to the bed and fingered the shattered pieces of wood. To lose this special gift from the one person in the world who'd loved me was crushing, and to lose the two thousand dollars I'd hidden inside the box was almost as unbearable.

A letter scrawled in Jeff's handwriting lay on the bed. I snatched it up, my hand shaking with rage. The stupid, worthless jerk. How could he have done this to me? His letter began with an apology but quickly moved on to recrimination. It was all my fault for not believing how much he loved me. So he'd decided to take our destiny into his hands. I could find him and my money at his sister's house San Francisco. He was "holding it hostage" and would give it all back as soon as I arrived.

Yeah, right. He'd give it back minus his expenses after I'd had sex with him. The rotten scum. He knew I couldn't call the cops.

I closed my eyes to think. I had my night's pay from Eddie and a few dollars in my pocket. I could probably wangle a ride to San Francisco on a gamblers' express bus. Then I'd find Elizabeth. After that I'd find Jeff, get what was left of my money, and even though I'd promised Aunt June I wouldn't get into fights anymore, I was going to punch him in the nose. Twice.

Chapter Two

I gazed at the pillared façade of the Pacific Heights apartment building and wiggled my left toes against the comforting thickness of the forty-three dollars I'd stuffed in the bottom of my shoe. Except for three bucks and change in my pocket, it was all I had to my name, thanks to Jeff. The jerk. Once I'd faced Elizabeth, I'd track him down at the address he'd left.

In spite of the pillars, the building managed not to look pretentious. It wasn't more than three stories, not new, but with everything in view fresh-painted or polished. Just right for someone trying to pass herself off as ultra-respectable, not to mention well-off.

I shifted the strap of my duffel to ease the strain on my shoulder and climbed the steps to the front entrance. Hard to believe I'd found Elizabeth at last. Now all I had to do was convince her to tell me the truth for once. That would be harder than finding her, because Elizabeth had never in her life told the truth when she could tell a lie.

I scanned the printed white name cards lined up in shiny brass holders next to a row of doorbells. The seventh one down said "B. Hull #301."

"Are you looking for someone?"

I turned around. A fiftyish woman in a mauve wool suit and matching shoes fingered her key holder, her eyebrows raised, waiting for an answer. I could tell by the way she eyed my worn jeans, black wool Army Surplus sweater, and ancient duffel bag that she didn't think I belonged in this upscale San Francisco neighborhood.

I straightened my shoulders. "I'm Elizabeth Hill's daughter." Aunt June's Rule Number One: Always tell the truth—although Elizabeth would hate me for it.

A small frown formed a double line between the woman's carefully drawn eyebrows. I stood still and let her look.

The woman turned, fitted her key into the front door lock, and spoke over her shoulder. "My goodness, her daughter. She's so young-looking, you could be taken for sisters."

And would be, if Elizabeth had anything to say about it. I followed the woman through the doorway and turned toward the wide carpeted staircase to my right.

"There's an elevator down the hall," the woman said.

"Thanks, but I prefer the stairs." Easier to put it that way than to say flat out that I was allergic to elevators. I hitched my duffel so the weight of it rested on my back and headed up the stairs. Two flights of stairs offered a much shorter hike than the trek I'd made up the steep hill of Pacific Avenue to get here, but my breath came in bigger gasps with each step. Now that I'd come this close, I was as scared as the first time I'd gone busking solo. Just a street corner gig, but my legs had felt like cooked spaghetti until I was halfway through my routine.

I straightened and gripped my duffel strap tighter. I was the Great Valentina. I'd faced jeering kids, drunken hecklers, and apathetic passersby and won them over. I could face Elizabeth. I said it over and over in my head to the rhythm of my steps. Not that it did any good. My knees didn't believe me.

I reached the third floor and walked down the wide hallway. Three-oh-one was easy to find because the door stood ajar. It wasn't like Elizabeth to be so careless. I rapped on the door and tried, without pushing the door any further open, to peek through the gap into the room beyond.

A man jerked the door open. I jumped back. He had a thick, muscled neck. I'd bet the muscles went all the way up to his buzz cut. He wore a car mechanic's blue jumpsuit with *Dwayne* sewn on the left front pocket in red thread. Not at all Elizabeth's type. Aside from the workingman look, he was younger than she was. Elizabeth had always targeted men in their fifties and sixties.

I waited for him to say something, but he just stood in the doorway and stared at me with his close-set eyes, so I said, "Hi, Dwayne, is Elizabeth here?" Which, it turned out, was the first of several mistakes I made that morning.

Dwayne grabbed me by the wrist, jerked me over the threshold and tossed me still clutching my duffel into the middle of the room. "How the fuck you know my name?"

I rubbed my wrist. I'd been right about the muscles, thick on his arms, shoulders, neck—and between the ears. What had I walked into? A quick scan of the room showed no Elizabeth. I tensed and readied to fake to the left, run to the right and out the still open door, but I hesitated. My second mistake. But I was so close to finally finding Elizabeth I couldn't make myself run. "Elizabeth?" I called. "You here?"

"She's in there." He gestured toward a doorway. "Getting her coat," he added with a sneer and kicked the door shut.

Elizabeth didn't answer. We stood staring at each other for a long two seconds. In the years I'd served as her accomplice, Elizabeth had never lived in a place with only one exit. Two would serve; three or more was ideal. I could see the thought coming to him. No sudden illumination, but gradually, like a light bulb on a dimmer switch.

He grabbed my wrist again and dragged me with him to the bedroom doorway. I dug in my heels and tried to hook my duffel on the doorframe. He hauled me after him anyway and in the end it was my shoulder socket that decided I should let him. He pulled me across the empty room and kicked open the door of the bathroom. It slammed against the wall and bounced shut again. Naturally he gave it another, harder kick—with the same result. At least he could be sure she wasn't hiding behind the door. On the third kick he put his hand out and stopped the door from closing. The bathroom was quite small and Elizabeth wasn't in it.

He moved to the bedroom window, still towing me along. He yanked the curtains down, curtain rod and all. We both stared at the fire escape on the other side of the open window.

"Fucking bitch." He released my wrist and stuck his head out the window.

As soon as he let go, I ran. I made it as far as the living room before he caught up with me. He grabbed me by the back of my sweater and hoisted me off my feet. "Where'd she go?"

The neck of my sweater pressed against my throat like a noose. I pulled at it with my hands. "Can't breathe," I gasped.

He let go of my sweater, and I jolted to the ground. "Now talk," he said.

I had to think fast, talk fast, and move faster. "Okay, I'll talk. I want to talk. I'm glad to talk. I'm looking for Elizabeth, too. She's hard to find. Hard to pin down. But maybe we could work together?" I edged a quarter step away from him.

Dwayne stared at me, maybe trying to take in my rapid speech.

"Yes," I said, as if he'd agreed with me. "We could work together and find her. She can't have gone far, right? I mean, I know all about things appearing and disappearing. Like this quarter." I produced a quarter as if out of thin air. "I mean, it's there. But then," I flipped the quarter into the air, and it disappeared. "It's gone."

Dwayne scowled at the empty air and I edged a little further back. He stood between me and the door, but there was a chance I could get by him, if I could get out of arm's reach.

"Then look!" He looked where I pointed. Taking another surreptitious step to the side, I reached up and snatched at the air. "Here it is." I opened my hand and showed him the quarter. "Elizabeth's like that, right?" I smiled my best aren't-we-having-fun smile.

Dwayne didn't smile back. Instead he closed the small distance I'd made between us and leaned his face close to mine. "Stop fucking around and tell me where she is."

"But that's what I'm trying to tell you," I gave each word deliberate weight so they might sink in. "I don't know where she went."

He slapped me. "Don't lie to me, bitch."

"Okay, okay." I put my hands up, palms outward. I couldn't stop a goon like Dwayne, but I could buy a few seconds to get past him and out the door. I made direct eye contact and held his gaze. "I'll tell you the absolute truth. I never lie. I never swear. And, I never hit, unless someone hits me first." With those last words, I stomped on his instep hard and raised the knee of the other leg toward his groin. It's a good move because men so instinctively bend forward and cover their privates with their hands. Dwayne did just that, and I gave him the straight arm directly to his solar plexus, the force of my blow amplified by his forward movement. He grunted and froze in his bent-over position, hands still crossed over his crotch. I immediately punched him directly on the nose and ran for the door.

Dwayne might be mentally slow, but his reflexes were rapid. He grabbed me by the sweater a second time and before I could wriggle out of it and get free, he tossed me to the floor. I screamed as loud as I could. That was my third big mistake, because, as I found out, Dwayne really hated screaming women.

"Shut up." He kicked me in the ribs.

I screamed louder.

"Stop screaming." He kicked me again. I felt something in my side give.

I rolled into a ball and kept on screaming. The next two kicks landed on my back. Shock waves of pain radiated over me like an electric current. Someone had to have heard me. They'd at least call the police, even if they wouldn't confront Dwayne themselves.

"Just shut the fuck up."

I gasped for more air, let loose another screech and tried to roll out of the way of his feet. It didn't work. The next kick landed on the side of my head. Lights out.

〉〉〉

A woman's voice woke me. "No, oh no."

Elizabeth?

"Oh my God." Anguished tones.

Not Elizabeth, then. Anguish had never been in her emotional vocabulary. "It's okay," I tried to say, but it no sound came out. My throat hurt from all the screaming. "I'm all right," I said in a hoarse whisper, opening my eyes to prove it. There wasn't anybody leaning over me. Must've dreamt it. I inhaled an acrid odor. Seemed familiar for a second—then I couldn't smell it anymore. Must've dreamt that, too. I closed my eyes. Maybe I could go back to sleep and dream that my head didn't hurt.

The beep-beep sound of cell phone dialing had my eyes open again immediately. I slowly turned my head. A woman with short dark brown hair wearing gray tailored pants and jacket knelt next to a man lying sprawled on the floor. Not Dwayne. This guy wore a suit. I couldn't see his face because she blocked my view. The woman spoke into her phone in a low voice. I couldn't make out the words, just that they were clipped and urgent. I tried to sit up. Big mistake. I groaned.

The woman turned her head. "Wait a minute," she said into the phone. She covered the mouthpiece. "Don't move. Let's check you out first."

She averted her head and spoke rapidly into the phone again. She didn't say good-bye or wait for the other person to say anything, just hung up, slipped the phone into her pants' pocket, and moved to my side all in one fluid movement. I tried to see beyond her to the man on the floor, but she stayed right in my line of vision.

"I'm okay." I slowly moved first my arms then my legs. "Just a cracked rib, I think. And my head hurts." I fingered a lump on the side of my head. "Who's he?"

"Can you identify the man who attacked you?"

"It wasn't him. He was wearing a blue mechanic's outfit, not a suit. His name is Dwayne."

"Dwayne who?"

"Dwayne, short on brains, long on muscle. Dwayne, who kicked me when I was down. That's all I know."

"Do you think you can stand up?"

"Sure, just give me a minute. Why don't you see if you can help the guy over there?"

She gave me a steady look. "I can't. He's dead. Let's go next door to my apartment."

"Dead?" I struggled to a sitting position, even though my side screamed at me to stop. "Are you sure? Maybe he's just unconscious."

"He's dead. He was shot."

I stared at her. Dwayne had had a gun? Why shoot that guy and not me? "Where's Dwayne now?"

"Good question. He's gone. I checked the other rooms. Let's get you out of here." She moved to a crouch, facing me. "Put your arms around my neck and hang on."

I did as she said. She looped her arms under my armpits and stood up bringing both of us to a standing position. It didn't hurt as much as I thought it would, but then she'd done most of the work. The room tilted a bit, then righted itself.

"Which side hurts?"

"The left."

She shifted to my right. "Just keep your arm around my neck. You can put your weight on me."

I risked turning my head to look at the still form sprawled on the floor with his head turned away from me, profile outlined by a pool of blood. I stared at it, and then at the spray of blood that speckled the carpet and furniture beyond. So much blood. More even than the time the coyotes had broken into Aunt June's chicken coop. But that was just chicken blood. This was a person. And that acrid smell. I'd recognized it. The same smell of Aunt June's shotgun when she'd fired uselessly at the coyotes running away. The room did its tilting act again. I must've suddenly leaned more weight on the woman, because she bent her knees and braced herself to take my weight.

"It's just a short way. Think you can do it?" Something in her crisp matter-of-fact tone told me she wasn't really asking. She aimed to get me out of there.

I wanted to leave, to get away from the crumpled body, the awful blood. But it didn't seem right somehow. I didn't even know who he was. One of Elizabeth's friends? Or had he heard my screams and come to help? "Shouldn't someone stay with him?"

"This is a crime scene. The only help we can give Eric now is to preserve the evidence needed to jail his killer."

"Eric? You know him?" I dropped my arm from her shoulder and pulled away. I was just a little dizzy. I could stand on my own.

"Yes, I knew him. Come on now. I'll explain when we get to my apartment." She didn't make any effort to take my arm or compel me to go with her—no physical effort, anyway. But her determination that we should leave the apartment was a force in itself.

"I need my things." I gestured to the contents of my duffel that were now dumped in a pile on the floor. When had that happened?

She shook her head. "Have to leave them until the evidence recovery team's been here." She moved toward the door and gestured me to follow, which I did by the time-proven method of putting one foot in front of the other. After a couple of steps the dizziness disappeared. I passed through the open door of the apartment, its lock smashed. It had been kicked in.

The hallway was surprisingly empty. Where was everybody? You'd think with all the screaming I'd done, not to mention the gunshot I'd been too unconscious to hear, there'd be at least a couple of people. Maybe they were cowering behind bolted doors.

In a matter of moments, the woman guided me through the doorway of her apartment. It wasn't what I'd expected. Elizabeth's apartment had been decorated with tasteful furniture and neutral colors, in keeping, I was sure, with her current scam. Elizabeth's taste always matched who she was pretending to be at the time. This woman's apartment was a bower of chintz. The small love seat and the two upholstered chairs across from it each wore a different pattern. The pillows stacked on all the furniture sported different flowery material, although everything blended in shades of pink and lavender—even the curtains. Why would a woman who wore no makeup and dressed in tailored gray flannel decorate her apartment like this?

"Have a seat." She gestured to a tiny sofa that had so many pillows piled on it, it wasn't clear where anyone would find room to sit down. "I'll make us some tea, unless you'd prefer coffee?"

"Tea's fine." I sank down gingerly on the sofa and gazed around the room. Every wall held glass-fronted cabinets with the largest display of ceramic figurines I'd ever seen. All of them pale elongated figures glazed in pastel shades. I recognized them. One of Elizabeth's many husbands, "Uncle" Artie if I remembered right, had had figurines like these on display in his living room. His dead wife had collected them. Like the flowered décor, they just didn't match their owner. "You have an amazing collection of Hummel figurines. Have you been collecting Hummels for a long time?"

She put her head around the corner of the kitchen door. She had her cell phone to her ear again. "What did you say?"

"All these Hummels." I gestured toward the figurines. "Must've taken a long time to collect them."

"Yes. Quite a long time," she said. "Would you like something to eat?"

"No, thanks."

I waited until she retreated to the kitchen, and I heard her clinking some dishes. I stood up, my knees shaking. The figurines were Lladrós, and she was a liar, in on a con with Elizabeth. Or worse, in with destructive Dwayne. I had to get out of there fast. I headed for the door.

She must've heard me even though she was still murmuring into her cell phone, because she came out of the kitchen. "Where are you going?"

"Downstairs to wait for the police. So I can let them in when they get here."

She moved quickly and intercepted me before I could get halfway across the room, pocketing her phone as she moved. "That's not a good idea."

Even without a broken rib, I wasn't a physical match for her. I'd have to talk my way out of this one. "I think it is, and I'm going."

"I can't let you do that." She approached me, and I backed away until I bumped against the little sofa. "Let's sit down, and I'll explain."

"I think I'll stand."

"Suit yourself. Look, I'm supposed to keep a lid on this until my boss gets here, but I'm going to have to trust you'll keep what I tell you to yourself." She paused for a moment, as if debating whether to continue. "I'm with the FBI."

I just managed to keep my face straight. I'd known more about running cons when I was five years old than this woman would know in her lifetime. Her line was classic, her delivery flawed. My only hope at this point was to play along. "Do you have some identification?"

She reached into an inner pocket of her jacket, pulled out a leather folder and flipped it open. I gazed at her likeness and the official seal. I'd never seen a real FBI agent's identification, so I didn't know how good it was, but it would convince anyone who didn't know better. "You're Eugenia Philips?"

"Call me Phil," she said with a lopsided grin. "Please."

I revised my opinion. That "call me Phil" along with the grin was good. If I didn't know better, I'd fall for it, and the story that she'd spin, too. "Okay, *Phil*, what's the confidential reason you can't let me go downstairs to meet the police?"

She gave me a sideways look, as if she suddenly had doubts about revealing the big secret. Maybe I should've acted more impressed by the FBI agent bit. "First, tell me who you are, and why you were in Beth Hull's apartment."

I could say let's wait until the police come, and I'd tell them both at once, but it was pretty clear at this point that she hadn't called the police. I needed to convince her that I wasn't a threat just long enough to get out of there. "I'm Valentine Hill, Elizabeth's daughter."

"I know her pretty well, and she never mentioned a daughter."

"Must've slipped her mind."

"You go by Hill?"

"It's Elizabeth's real name, but you know that, right?"

"You call her Elizabeth?"

"Except when I call her Mommy Dearest."

That gave her pause. "Do you have any identification?"

I lowered my gaze. My search for my identity had brought me into this mess in the first place, but there was no need to spill my guts to this imposter. I had what passed for my official identification in my back pocket, but it would be wiser not to give Phil, or whoever she was, any more information than absolutely necessary. "You told me I had to leave all my stuff next door for the crime scene guys." I shifted my feet. It wasn't exactly a lie.

"You look a lot like her."

"Looks are all we have in common."

She hesitated, giving a good show of making up her mind to tell me what she'd planned on telling me all along. "You can't tell anyone."

It took an act of will not to roll my eyes. "My lips are sealed."

She narrowed her eyes at my flip answer, but she knew, and I knew, that she had to go through with the script. "Beth—or Elizabeth, as you call her—is working with us. Through her, we're going to get evidence to convict a major bad guy. Someone we've been watching for years, but have never been able to get anything on. Nothing that would stand up in court, anyway."

Elizabeth was helping the FBI. Yeah, right. I would've laughed out loud, except it hurt to laugh. "This 'bad guy' is what, a mobster?"

"No, that's part of the problem. He's a highly respected member of the community. No one would ever believe what he's really into."

Now I got it. Elizabeth, with Phil's help, was running a blackmail scam on a wealthy mark. It wasn't too clear how she was playing it, but with Elizabeth, the more twists and turns, the better. But what did I care how she planned to work the con? I just needed a way to get past Phil. Now that Phil had revealed the "secret" to me, she had a good excuse not to let me go, even if I took a blood oath never to tell. What could I possibly say that would convince her?

The sound of the downstairs door buzzer stopped me. Maybe the neighbors had called the police? Phil crossed to the intercom. "Philips here."

A man's voice said something succinct. I couldn't make out what, though. Phil pressed the downstairs door release button and turned back to me.

"Is it the police?"

"Not yet. Our people have to take care of some things first."

"What things?"

"Crime scene. Loose ends. And we need our liaison in place."

She couldn't have been more vague. Why answer in the first place? It was all a fairy tale, anyway. I could only hope that she hadn't guessed that I knew it was a fairy tale—one without a happily-ever-after for me.

"Would it be all right with you if I stretched out on your bed while you tie up those loose ends? I'm feeling pretty bad."

She blinked a few times, as if bringing me into focus. "Sure. Of course. You got pretty banged up, didn't you? Go ahead and lie down. We'll need to interview you before you talk to the police. But, I'll make sure that you're seen by a paramedic as soon as possible."

"I'm sure I'll feel fine if I can just lie down for a few minutes." I turned and headed slowly toward what I knew to be the bedroom, because Phil's apartment was a mirror image of Elizabeth's. Just as I entered the bedroom, I heard a knock on the front door. I pushed the door almost shut, stood behind it and strained to hear what they said. Phil greeted them with "Hey guys" so there had to be more than one. I heard a man's deep voice saying something about "containing the situation." That was one way to speak of the dead man lying next door. Deep Voice must've asked something about me, because Phil told him I was lying down.

The door closed. No more voices, but I heard someone moving around. I tiptoed over to the bed. First, I'd make it look like I was lying down. I stuffed pillows artistically under the bedspread—an old trick, but with any luck it would work. I crept over to the window and peeled back the curtains to get a view of the fire escape. A great way out, if only I could get to it. But the windows in here, unlike the ones in Elizabeth's bedroom, had new locks on them. Keyed locks. Phil, or more likely whoever really lived in this apartment, wasn't taking any chances with thieves making off with her Lladrós. Bad luck for thieves. Worse luck for me.

I turned and leaned against the wall. If I didn't have a broken rib, I'd have risked trying to outrun Phil, or one of her posse of goons. Had Elizabeth recruited this team herself? When I'd lived with her, she'd sometimes work with one other person—usually me. Twice she'd had others in on the con, but not often.

The window was locked, the front door guarded. I'd run out of options.

"Just stay in the doorway, Phil. We'll wait for the ERT Unit." Deep Voice again.

At the sudden sound of voices, I ducked behind the bed. I crouched there, heart thumping, until I realized that the voices weren't coming from the living room. Weirdly enough, they were coming from the walk-in closet.

I eyed the closet, its door halfway open, and shuddered. I'd spent a life-defining forty-eight hours locked in a closet when I was a child and hadn't had much tolerance for closed-in spaces ever since. I dragged reluctant feet over to the closet and opened the door wide.

"What the hell's keeping them?" That was Phil, and with the door open not only could I hear the voices better, I could also see right through the back of the closet to another closet—Elizabeth's. They'd cut an opening the size of a small doorway through the wall between the two apartments. So this was Elizabeth's real escape route, with the window open to the fire escape to mislead. The fire escape might've been just for show for Elizabeth, but it was a real way out for me, if I could only make myself walk into the closet and out the other side.

It took me a good thirty seconds to work up the nerve. I held my breath like someone jumping into the deep end of a pool, walked into the closet, and ducked through the low doorway. The light from behind me shone dimly, so it wasn't completely dark. I'd never have made it if it was, but I had to get out of the closet soon, no question about that. Just being in there made my heart jump around in my chest and my hands sweat. The voices weren't coming from the bedroom. I pushed the door fractionally open to check. No one said anything. I pushed it open a little more, just enough for me to slip out. I had to cross the room to reach the window. If someone in the front room looked this way, I'd be toast. *Go now!* My feet stayed glued to the ground.

"What's that stuff?" Deep Voice again.

"Belongs to the girl."

Who was she calling a "girl?" I was a grown woman. I was…I straightened. I was the Great Valentina. Magician extraordinaire. Capable of amazing feats. I could make myself invisible. I could disappear into thin air.

I scanned what I could see of the bedroom. Since, in fact, I hadn't managed to make anything as large as a person disappear into thin air yet, I'd better go for the alternative—duck and run. I dropped to my knees and crawled out of the closet. The bed would hide me from anyone not actually in the bedroom. From the bed it was a quick angle to the upholstered chair. I crouched behind the chair and looked at the window. It was open much wider than it had been when Dwayne had dragged me in here. Dwayne himself must have used it to get away. At least I could be sure that the fire escape worked. I listened for voices. Nothing. I counted to three and made my move. One step to the window, one leg over the sill, other leg following immediately and ducked down below the window sill onto the metal bars of the fire escape. No one yelled out. They hadn't seen me. Maybe I was better at the invisibility thing than I'd thought.

Luckily heights never bothered me the way closed-in spaces did. The fire escape was at the back of the building, but with all the neighboring buildings stacked so close together, fifty people could've seen me if they'd looked out their windows. I made my way down the rungs of the ladder to the second floor and then the first. A drop to the ground, thankfully not cement, but soft dirt neatly planted. Dwayne had already stomped on some of the flowers.

The sight of the large footprints stopped me cold. What if Dwayne was still around? No, that was crazy thinking. He'd have taken off as fast as he could, which was just what I needed to do. I found my way around to the side of the building and tried to look casual when I reached the sidewalk and headed down the hill—like a woman out for a morning walk.

Chapter Three

Once I'd contacted the police, I'd expected to talk to the cops and have to explain a few things, but what was up with having me sit in the cop car outside of Elizabeth's building just waiting? Not that I wanted to go inside and view the body—again. But Officer Newman, who'd answered the 911 call I'd made from a coffee shop five blocks away, had asked few questions, driven me back to the scene (as he called it), and kept me waiting in the car while he stood around talking to the other cop-types who showed up.

I needed to get my stuff so I could find Jeff and reclaim my money. If I didn't, I'd be sleeping on a park bench tonight, and the way my side hurt, I wouldn't be getting much rest on a bench. I felt my ribs tentatively. Pressing on them hurt. Not pressing on them hurt. The only thing that didn't hurt was holding my breath. Not much of an option.

I scanned the onlookers who'd slowly accumulated since I'd arrived. The cops had herded them onto the sidewalk across the street. I counted seventeen. No, make that sixteen. The woman walking her corgi must've decided that she'd seen all there was to see, because she let her dog drag her away. People had come and gone and others had come to take their place, except for five of them—Shaved Head, Anorexic, Green Sneakers, Lies-About-Her-Age, and Truant. They'd hung on the whole time, waiting for something ghoulish to come into view. Like a black body bag. Or a shirtless suspect in handcuffs. Sometimes they swiveled their heads in my direction and quickly looked away if I returned their stares.

I fished a quarter out of my pocket and tried a simple routine of palm and pass, French slip, and thumb palm vanish. Even at half speed, I felt the quiver in my left hand in rhythm to the pain in my side. The third time through the set, the coin slipped from my palm. I shoved it back into my pocket. Street performing had always been my fail-safe backup plan. Until today. What would I do for money if I couldn't find Jeff?

Elizabeth must have already caught a plane to someplace far away. Not that I could've counted on her for a loan, but I'd at least have had a place to sleep tonight. The forty-three dollars in my shoe wouldn't cover a night in any hotel in San Francisco. And, unless I found a magic healing potion, I wasn't going to be doing any street performances today. I had to find Jeff. That was all there was to it.

I checked the uniformed gathering in front of the apartment building. Two more cop cars and some official-looking unmarked cars had arrived while I waited. A parade of uniforms and suits had entered the apartment building. Three, including Officer Newman, had stayed outside to keep people away from the building and traffic moving on the street. And maybe to keep me waiting in the car.

I'd had enough of waiting. I reached for the door handle, but before I could open the door, a uniformed policeman emerged from the building. The other cops gathered around him, listening intently but keeping their eyes on the crowd, the street, and me. Officer Newman nodded his head several times in response to whatever the other cop was telling him, turned and hurried to the car, got in and started the engine.

"Where are we going?"

"Just into the garage here." He drove ten feet into the driveway next to the apartment entrance. The garage door lifted and he steered the car down the slanting driveway. The garage area looked like it filled the entire basement area of the building. We stopped near the elevator on the far wall, where a man, who had to be a cop, stood.

"What's the rush all of the sudden?"

"I have orders to keep you out of sight." Newman switched off the engine and got out of the car.

Before he could circle the car to my side, the waiting man came over and opened my door. He was about forty, thick-bodied, his short black hair going gray. He wore khaki pants, a tweed jacket, and a look that said he'd seen it all. "Please step out of the car."

I got out slowly. After sitting still for so long my bruised muscles had stiffened up, and I had to grab the top edge of the car door to lever myself upright.

The man watched without comment. "May I see some identification?"

"Are you with the police?" Everything about him said "cop," but the rules stated that he was supposed to identify himself to me first. And I like to go by the rules. I also needed to stall a bit to think, since the issue of identification always created problems for me.

He reached into an inside coat pocket, pulled out a leather holder and flashed a badge at me.

"I'd like to see where it gives your name."

He flipped the wallet over and held it up so I could read it.

"Inspector Hector Lopez, Homicide Division," I read out loud. "Okay." I pulled my own ID holder from my back pocket and held it out to him.

"Please remove your driver's license."

"I don't have a driver's license."

"What form of identification do you have?"

I unsnapped the wallet and tilted it. The long plastic strip of cardholders spilled out. I had to raise my arm to keep the end from dragging on the cement floor. People usually laughed when I did this, or at least looked surprised. Lopez's expression didn't shift out of deadpan. He hooked the strip with his hand and examined some of the cards.

"You got anything besides expired library cards?"

"The last one is current. The head librarian's name and phone number is on the back. She'll vouch for me."

Lopez released the strip holding my library cards and put his hands on his hips, pushing his jacket back as he settled his hands at belt level. The right hand came to rest just above his black holstered gun. "You don't want to play around with me. Do you have any current identification?"

"My name is Valentine Hill. I've been working in Las Vegas for the last four months. I just got here this morning to see my mother. Instead I find a guy in her apartment. He beat me up and knocked me out. When I came to, there was a dead guy I'd never seen before and a woman pretending to be an FBI agent, who wouldn't let me call the cops. I had to sneak down a fire escape to get away and call 911. If I weren't who I said I was, I would've just kept walking, right?" I refolded my library cards and pushed the wallet into my back pocket.

"You go by any other name than Valentine Hill?"

"No."

He shifted his gaze to Officer Newman. "Run the name."

Newman slid behind the wheel of his car and started punching keys on the computer keyboard.

"What made you think this woman in the apartment was impersonating an officer of the law? Didn't she show you some identification?"

"You guys and your obsession with identification. She showed me something, but do I know what official FBI identification looks like? I went by the fact that there was this dead man, and she wouldn't let me call the cops. And besides that, she said my mother was working with her on a case, which is impossible."

"Why's that?"

"Because my mother is a front to back, top to bottom, through and through con artist. She'd never do anything to help even an ordinary person, forget the FBI."

"You work scams with your mother?"

That gave me a jolt. "Absolutely not." I paused a beat, because it wasn't totally true. "I mean—I did, but not anymore. I haven't seen her in nine years."

"So she could be helping the FBI. You wouldn't have any way of knowing. Unless you keep in touch?"

"I just told you—I haven't seen or heard from her in nine years. Look, what's going on? Why aren't I down at the police station looking at mug shots? I can give you a complete description of the guy who beat me up and the woman who said she was with the FBI. I mean, you found the body, right? They hadn't moved it before you got here?"

Officer Newman got out of the squad car and leaned his forearms on the roof. Lopez turned toward him. "There's nothing in the system for that name," he said. "Want me to try it with her social?"

Lopez shifted his gaze to me. "How about it? Give us a social security number. Let's see if your story checks out about not having a sheet."

I took a step back and bumped against the car. "You're unbelievable. Don't you know there's a dead man upstairs? Don't you want to find who killed him?"

"I will find who killed him." Lopez took a step toward me. "One way I'll do that is by finding out who didn't kill him. If I'm going to rule you out, I need to know who you really are. So what's your real name?"

I pushed away from the car. The movement snagged at my broken rib, but I was too angry to pay any attention to pain. "You're questioning what's real, Inspector? That's actually a philosophical question, you know. Or maybe you don't, if you haven't spent as many hours in libraries as I have. Take this quarter, for instance." I held up a quarter between thumb and forefinger. "You see it. It's real, isn't it? You know what a quarter looks like. Or do you? Because it's not a quarter at all." I took it with the thumb and forefinger of the other hand and displayed it with a flourish. "It's a half dollar. Now how could you make that mistake?"

I held out the half dollar to him still pinched between thumb and forefinger. He looked at it, but didn't move. I released the half dollar, let it fall into the palm of my hand and clenched my fingers over it. "But, look, you weren't mistaken after all." I uncurled my fingers and showed the quarter lying in my palm. "It really is a quarter."

I took in my audience. Officer Newman looked gratifyingly startled, but Lopez was definitely not amused. He looked from the coin to my face. "I'm not interested in tricks. I want facts."

"But that was my point exactly. What you think is a fact, may actually be an illusion. And vice versa. And that's me. The vice versa. As far as the official world is concerned, I don't exist. But, as you can see, I do exist. And, what's more, I'm exactly who I say I am."

Lopez clenched his jaw. "Stop with the riddles and give me a straight story or I'm taking you in and holding you as a material witness."

"I don't have a social security number."

"What?"

"Elizabeth says that she walked out of the hospital with me, but without paying the bill. So no birth certificate. You can't get a social security card without a birth certificate or some proof that you were born in the United States."

"The hospital still has a record of your birth."

"I'm sure they do, if I knew what hospital, in what city and the day and year I was born."

"You don't know when you were born?"

"I've been looking for Elizabeth so I could find out. I finally track her down and this happens. By now she's a thousand miles away."

"No, she isn't. The feebs have her."

"The who?"

He didn't answer. I heard a whirr and then a clunk from the elevator. He must've heard it, too, because he swung around in time to see the doors open and Eugenia "Call Me Phil" Philips step out. Watching her stride toward us gave me a really bad feeling. The "feebs" must be the FBI, and that meant that Phil was who she'd said she was. Or else she was running a con beyond anything I'd ever seen.

She slid her gaze over to me. Lopez kept his expression blank, but Phil's was steel. My bad feeling mutated into a rotten, stinking feeling. I was in a lot of trouble. "Everything all right, Inspector?"

Lopez regarded her impassively a few seconds before responding. "I'm interviewing the witness."

I had the distinct impression that he wasn't exactly happy to see Phil, which was exactly how I felt.

"We need to verify her identity and her home address," Phil said.

"What she has for identification isn't much use. No driver's license. No picture ID. But that's not a problem, right? You said she looks like the mother. And I suppose the mother can ID her."

"Yes. But we've run the name she gave me, and she's not in the system as far as I can tell," Phil said to Lopez while eyeing me.

"She's got a couple dozen library cards from cities all over the country. You could check with the local PDs."

"I don't have a sheet. I've never been arrested, and since I've been away from Elizabeth, I haven't done anything to be arrested for."

"Except for today," Phil said. "Leaving the scene of a crime against the specific orders of an officer of the law."

"I thought you were scamming me."

"I showed you my ID and informed you of the situation."

I turned to Lopez. "I called the police, and I'm here, aren't I?"

Lopez looked at Phil. "I've got no reason to believe she isn't who she says she is. Plus she's as close to an eyewitness we'll get. I'm not going to bust her chops about her ID at this point in time. I need to finish asking some questions here, then, like I already told you, we have to talk to this Beth Hull that you've stowed someplace."

"Beth Hull's an alias," I said. "Her name's Elizabeth Hill, and she's the one with a record."

I would've added more, but Lopez made an impatient gesture and kept his gaze on Phil. I clamped my mouth shut and watched. Silence hung between Lopez and Phil like a physical weight. These two might both be on the side of the law, but they weren't playing on the same team. Lopez hadn't mentioned what I'd told him about no birth certificate. Just told her she could chase down my library cards. And it sounded like Phil hadn't agreed to let Lopez talk to Elizabeth.

Neither Lopez or Phil said anything, just looked at each other. A classic standoff, and a giant waste of time as far as I was concerned. I'd bet that the poor dead guy upstairs would agree with me. I leaned against the fender of the police car. "Do you think we could sit down somewhere? My side is killing me."

They both turned and looked at me as if they'd forgotten I was even there.

Phil blinked twice. "My apartment?"

"Okay." Before Lopez could say anything, I pushed away from the car and headed for the door next to the elevator marked Stairs.

Lopez fell in step next to me. "Don't you want to take the elevator?"

I shook my head and opened the door.

"I thought you said your side hurt."

"It does. My head, too." I gingerly patted the lump on the side of my head. Touching it, even gently, did nothing to make it feel better. I dropped my hand and walked slowly up the stairs, Phil and Lopez single file behind me.

A few minutes later I sank down into the many patterned pillows on Phil's sofa. Or the sofa she claimed was hers. I knew it wasn't, but would keep my mouth shut for now. Phil could take me to Elizabeth. No point in antagonizing her.

Phil disappeared into the kitchen, but Lopez planted himself in one of the upholstered chairs on the other side of the coffee table facing me. He took out a small notebook and pen. "How about you tell me what happened here today?"

So I took him through it, from the lady in the mauve suit letting me into the building to my trip down the fire escape. He let me tell it without interrupting, jotting notes as I talked.

Phil returned to the room, carrying a plate of crackers and cheese in one hand and a couple of cans of soda in the other

She put them down on the coffee table with a gesture for me to help myself and settled into the other chair. Maybe she wanted to show me she had no hard feelings, or maybe she just wanted to soften me up.

Lopez ignored her and the refreshments. I ate some cheese and opened a soda.

Lopez leaned forward and rested his forearms on his thighs. "Did you know the man who was killed?"

"No." I glanced at Phil. Her face was unreadable. Hadn't she told them she knew the guy?

"He was shot and killed," Lopez said. "It's a very serious crime we're looking at here. We haven't been given access to the scene yet." He paused and gave Phil a hard look. "When we do, we hope to find the gun used in the crime. What I need to ask you now, is that when we do find it, is there any way at all that we're going to find your prints on that gun?"

I opened my mouth to reply. Lopez held up a warning hand. "Wait and think before you say anything. If you tell me now, I might be able to help you. You hold back, and I find out later, then there'll be no way in hell I or anyone else will be able to do anything for you."

I straightened. "My Aunt June taught me three rules. Never lie. Never swear—and I'll thank you not to swear in front of me. And never hit, unless someone hits you first. I promised her I'd live by them, and I have. I never even saw a gun, much less touched it, but I have some idea of what must have happened."

"You mean, what happened while you were unconscious?" Lopez asked.

"I think the first thing Dwayne did was lock the door," I said. "Then he dumped everything out of my duffle bag and started to go through it. Then, the other guy," I glanced at Phil briefly, "kicked in the door. He must've heard me screaming. I think Dwayne had the gun under his jumpsuit. You know how they're made with a slit instead of a pocket so you can reach into your pants underneath?" I looked at Phil again. "I'm sorry he's dead. He was just trying to help me."

Phil didn't say anything.

"You say you were unconscious during all this?" Lopez asked. I nodded.

"Then you can't really know what went down. Unless, maybe you were semiconscious? Sort of aware?"

"I was completely out cold. But, when I came to I noticed that my bag had been emptied, everything dumped out. The door frame was splintered, the lock just hanging, broken. But the door wasn't locked before, just closed."

"I'm sure you can see, Valentine," Lopez said, "that it's a little hard to believe that someone who's been knocked unconscious, the way you say you were, and who wakes up next to a dead body, could have the presence of mind to notice all these little details you're telling me about."

"Noticing—it's what I do, every minute. You, Inspector Lopez are wearing unmatched socks. One's black and one's black-brown. You've lost weight recently. Look at your belt. The leather's worn and stretched out at the notch where you used to wear it. Why do you think I didn't buy Agent Philip's story? Check out the apartment." I gestured toward the chintz curtains and the shelves of figurines. "Does she look like someone who'd decorate her place in pink and purple flowers? Or someone who'd collect Lladrós? She didn't even know they were Lladrós."

Phil gave me a level look. "You're a lot like your mother."

I slammed the soda can down on the coffee table. "I'm nothing like my mother."

"Whoa, there," Lopez said. "Take it easy."

I wrapped my arms around my middle and sank back into the sofa. The gesture with the soda can felt good emotionally, but had wreaked havoc with the broken rib.

Lopez turned to Phil. "Let me remind you, Agent Philips, that you're supposed to be helping us with our investigation. Upsetting a witness isn't helping. Just like keeping our crime scene unit from doing their jobs isn't helping."

"As I already told you, Inspector Lopez," Phil said "Clarifications will be made shortly about who is helping whom."

I stood up—slowly because my side required it. They both swiveled their gazes in my direction. "I've told you everything I know. I have something really important to do, and I can't wait around for you to settle your internecine conflict."

"Our what?" Lopez asked.

"Turf war," Phil said. She cocked her head on one side and looked at me as she said it, as though she only now realized I might have a brain.

A tall man with a buzz cut appeared in the doorway. He carried himself as if his suit had epaulets and gold stars. Phil jumped to her feet. "Sir."

He nodded in acknowledgement. His gaze paused briefly on Lopez before settling on me. He gave the impression that he was as good at noticing as I was. Only not in a friendly way. This had to be Phil's boss.

Phil approached him. "This is Inspector Lopez, SFPD, and Valentine Hill." She turned to us. "Special Agent in Charge Williams."

Lopez stood up and shook Williams' hand. I settled for waggling my fingers at him. "Hi."

"A word, Inspector Lopez?" Lopez crossed to join Williams. He probably figured he was finally going to get some cooperation from the FBI. Phil followed on his heels. Williams turned. "Philips, you stay with the witness. We'll speak in a moment."

Phil froze. Williams waited until Lopez was in the hall before closing the door. She rejoined me, her expression shuttered. "Why don't you sit down? We should talk."

Instead of sitting back down on the sofa, I perched on the arm. "So that's your boss. Guess you were right. This is a big investigation if he's taking a hand in it."

Phil sighed and ran her hands through her short hair. "Bigger than you know. The man who was killed, Eric Staller, was also an agent. That's why I needed you to stay here. I had orders not to alert the SFPD that Eric was an agent until SAC Williams got here. They couldn't think they'd be primary in the investigation. Plus without orders from higher-ups, they'd send all communications out on unsecured channels. Which, naturally, they did."

"That's why you're mad at me. I called the police. But honestly I simply couldn't believe Elizabeth was working with you."

"I get that. And I apologize if I offended you just now. I only meant that your mother…"

"Call her Elizabeth, please."

"Okay. I only meant that Elizabeth has the same ability to notice details and recognize their meaning. That's all."

"I know the difference between right and wrong and always try to do what's right. The only right thing, as far as Elizabeth is concerned, is to get what she wants. Two completely different people."

"I can see that. Believe it or not, she really is helping us. Right now she's crucial to our ability to proceed. And I believe that there's a connection between Dwayne and our investigation. So please tell me—this Aunt June you mentioned. Is she your mother's or your father's sister?"

I narrowed my eyes at her. Why would she want to know about Aunt June? "She was my maternal grandmother's stepdaughter, although she was a lot older than my grandmother."

"Your mother's half sister?"

"Stepsister. Elizabeth was ten when my grandmother married Aunt June's father. So Aunt June wasn't really related to me. But she was a good, kind person and took me in when Elizabeth went to prison."

"She's deceased?"

"Five years ago."

"And your grandmother?"

"I never knew her. Elizabeth told me she'd died." Then it hit me. "You don't know where Elizabeth is, do you?"

Phil made no pretense she didn't know what I was talking about. "We had a procedure in place for emergency exits like the one she had to make today. But we hadn't planned on there being a bystander."

"You mean me?"

She nodded. "We came back to get you out, too."

"And Elizabeth?"

"She didn't stay where I left her and hasn't made contact yet."

"You can't be expecting her to call you?"

"There's a lot riding on this operation for her, too. I thought—I still think she'll make contact."

"She's a thousand miles away by now."

"We have a watch in place at the airlines, at train and bus terminals."

"Car rental agencies?"

"She doesn't have a valid driver's license."

"You think she doesn't."

Phil shrugged. "If you know of anyone she might contact who'd help her out of a jam, would you give me a name?"

Before I could answer, Lopez and Williams came through the door followed by a half dozen more FBI types. "Special Agent Philips will show you the relevant portion of the recording," Williams said.

I looked at Phil. "What recording?"

"You understand, of course," Williams went on, "that you're not to repeat to anyone else the name that's mentioned by Beth Hull and by the perpetrator. The agency will pursue that line of inquiry."

Lopez nodded. "Understood."

I looked at Williams. "What recording?"

Williams gave me his flat gaze and ignored me. He nodded to Phil, who crossed to the media center.

I stood in front of Lopez and blocked his line of sight. "What recording?"

"The one you starred in with this scuzz, Dwayne. They had a hidden camera running the whole time."

Chapter Four

The picture was in high-resolution color, not the grainy black and white I'd expected. Elizabeth looked just the same as I remembered, which made for a weird time-machine effect, since it'd been nine years since I'd seen her. The haircut was different, but she always changed her hairstyle to suit the role. Never the color, though. She believed that being a "true" blonde gave her an edge.

I watched the scene unfold on the television that wasn't a television, just a monitor for watching the action in Elizabeth's apartment. On screen, Elizabeth crossed her living room and spoke into the intercom by the front door. The voice on the intercom was indistinct. The hidden camera's sound quality didn't match that of the image.

"You're delivering what from Mr. Kroy?" Elizabeth said into the intercom. She turned and lifted her face toward the camera, her eyebrows raised.

An indistinct answer came over the intercom. "A car? You mean, he's in the car?" Another muffled answer. "I don't quite understand what you're saying. Why don't you come up?" Elizabeth pressed the button to open the downstairs door, turned to the camera again and gave a palms-up shrug.

"She knew you were watching?" Lopez asked, not taking his eyes from the screen.

"The bell to her apartment rings in here, too," Phil said.

"And the phone?"

Phil nodded.

Lopez looked like he wanted to ask some more questions, but didn't because on the television screen we saw Elizabeth open the door for Dwayne and let him into her apartment. She left the door ajar and stood with her back to the camera so that we could get a clear look at Dwayne.

"I couldn't hear you very clearly over the intercom," Elizabeth said. "Something about Mr. Kroy and a car?"

Dwayne held up a key ring. "I'm delivering your new car. It's a present from Mr. Kroy." He looked like the same Dwayne I'd encountered, but sounded different.

"A new car? For me?" Overdoing it a bit, but Dwayne seemed to buy it.

"It's a Mercedes." He jiggled the keys.

"That's a Mercedes emblem on the key ring," Lopez said. "Did he really have one?"

"I don't know," Phil said.

Back on the screen, Elizabeth was nearly jumping up and down. "I just can't believe it! Bobby's been wonderful to me, but I never in my life imagined he'd give me a car."

"I'm supposed to give you a rundown of all the features before I hand over the keys. Can you come down now?" Dwayne still didn't sound like the Dwayne I'd met.

"It's a script," I said.

Phil reached over and paused the picture. "What do you mean?"

"He's giving a memorized speech. That's why he sounds so wooden. He's been coached, but he's a bad actor."

Phil gave me a thoughtful look and pressed the play button.

"Can I come down? Try and stop me!" Elizabeth doing a bit of bad acting, too. Not usual for her. Was she scared? "I'll just grab my coat and be right with you." We watched her turn and flick a sideways glance at the camera as she headed for the bedroom.

Phil paused the picture a second time. "The word 'coat' was our panic button. She came straight through the closet. We had disguises here for her, but she didn't want to wait. We took our emergency exit route. It's a back way that gets us to the cross street without being seen from the front. We always have a car there." She turned to face me. "We saw you coming up the stairs."

"I didn't see you."

Phil punched a button and the scene changed to the hallway where a couple of cops were talking. "We have cameras on the stairs, in the elevator, and the halls."

"Did she say anything?"

Phil's gazed skittered away for a brief moment. "She was panicky. She knew Kroy would never give her a car and figured that Dwayne wanted to kidnap her or worse. All she wanted was to get away. We just headed down the back way. You missed us by about fifteen seconds. As soon as we were in the car, I called Agent Staller to come get you. I left her in a safe place and came right back, but too late."

"Can we see the rest of it now?" Lopez asked.

Phil pushed play again and we watched a nervous Dwayne waiting for Elizabeth. He shifted from one foot to the other, patted his hip, and shifted his feet again.

"Checking his piece," Lopez commented. "He's not used to packing, has to touch it, reassure himself it's still there. Like, where else would it be?"

I watched Dwayne visibly jump when he heard the knock on the door, and then I heard my voice, faint but audible calling him Dwayne and asking for Elizabeth. From then on, it played out as I remembered it, only different and, in its own way, freakier, because I was watching it instead of living it. When the replay reached the point of Dwayne kicking me, I felt the others glancing at me, but I kept my gaze on the screen. I wanted to know what had happened after I blacked out.

It was worse than I'd imagined, though I'd come close in my guess. Once I was out cold, Dwayne stopped kicking me, but the rage was still evident in his body. He walked stiff-legged over to my duffle bag, grabbed it up and dumped everything out on the floor. He didn't have time to pick through my things, because the pounding on the door and muffled shouts of Phil's partner had him spinning around and reaching into his pocket for his gun. He crossed to where I lay and knelt down next to me, his back to the door and his body shielding the gun from view.

The door exploded open and Staller appeared in the doorway. "Move away from her."

Dwayne didn't move. "I hit her. I'm sorry. But, she was crazy, man. I didn't know what to do. She was just nuts, hitting me and screaming." Dwayne sounded frantic and worried. A much better actor when he was ad-libbing. "Can you help me? I'm afraid she's hurt."

Staller came into the room slowly. "I said, move away from her. Now."

Dwayne swiveled his head around and gazed at Staller, then still kneeling, he twisted around and fired his gun. Staller fell to the floor. Dwayne rose to his feet, smiling.

The room closed in around me.

"You okay?" Lopez said and took my elbow. He led me to the nearest chair and waited until I sat down. "Can I get you something? Some water?"

I looked around the room. It was a capacity crowd, only this was one time I didn't want an audience. "Do they have to be here?"

Lopez looked at Williams, who with a jerk of his head toward the door indicated the half dozen suits should leave.

"Did you see the look on his face? That smile?" I whispered.

Lopez crouched down next to me and peered at my face. "It was tough to see that," he said. "I've seen a lot, but I have to tell you that one's going to stay with me. It took a lot of guts to take him on and fight back."

"I shouldn't have screamed. He really hated that."

"Don't say that. You did right to fight him. And, hey, you looked pretty good there with the old one-two. You take lessons or something?"

"My Uncle Rocky taught me."

"Uncle Rocky? You didn't mention an uncle before." This from Phil, still looking for a way to find Elizabeth.

"I had to call all of Elizabeth's husbands 'uncle,'" I said before she could ask. "So he wasn't a real uncle, and they weren't real husbands, either. Just marks."

"Why didn't Staller identify himself and draw his weapon?" Lopez asked Phil.

"Our orders were to protect the operation and the informant. We didn't know who this Dwayne was. If he came from the person Elizabeth's gotten close to, then she'd have been blown and endangered her life."

She turned to me. "I'm sorry you got caught in the middle. It looks like you took a real beating. I can get the paramedics in here to see you, or have you taken to the emergency room, whichever you prefer."

"Don't bother. Please." All I needed was another encounter with official-type people asking for my identification. "I'm all right. I just want to go now. You don't need me. You never did. You can't keep me any longer, can you?"

Williams stepped in. "You can go, but don't leave the city. We'll need an address and phone number."

"Is Inspector Lopez going to work with you?"

"Of course. The chief has assured me the SFPD will participate in a joint task force to track down the killer."

"Okay, then I nominate him as my go-to guy." I held out a hand to Lopez. "Give me your number, and I'll call you with my info."

Williams looked like he wanted to object.

"I've already said I don't lie. You have to believe me now."

Lopez pulled a business card from an inside pocket and handed it to me.

I shoved the card in my back pocket. "What about my things? Can you give them to me or do I have to go back in there and get them?"

Lopez looked at Williams, who shook his head and said, "Our ERT Unit isn't finished yet. If you'll write up a list of your belongings, we'll see they're returned to you."

I stuck out my chin. "Write a list? You saw Dwayne dump everything out. How hard would it be to figure out what was in my duffel bag and what was already in the apartment? It's not rocket science. It's not even third-grade science. The toothbrush belongs to me. The bloody bullet belongs to you."

"I understand you're upset," Williams said.

"Do you understand that that's everything I own in there?"

"Look, if you need money, I can get you some from the victim's fund," Lopez said.

"I don't want charity, but I need my props."

"Your props?"

"For my magic act. It's all in my duffle bag. Or it was."

"We'll get your things to you as soon as possible. Wait here, and I'll get a patrolman to give you a ride to wherever you're going," he said.

"No offense, but I'd rather take a cab," I said the way people do when they really do intend to give offense. I didn't usually act that way, but I'd had it with all of them. Besides, I could just see Jeff's reaction if I showed up at his place in a police car. He'd be out the back before I could knock on the front door.

I started to stand up, but Phil put a hand on my shoulder. "Wait," she said. "You've been through a lot today. At least let me call a cab for you. I have a couple of cab company's numbers by the phone in the kitchen. I can get one that'll be here right away. Okay?"

I sank back into the chair. "Okay. Thanks." No point in being stupidly surly at this point. I would've had to have asked to use her phone anyway, since Jeff had walked off with mine along with my money.

Phil ducked into the kitchen to make the call. I leaned my head against the back of the chair and closed my eyes. I'd missed my chance with Elizabeth. How many more years before I'd track her down again? She didn't leave forwarding addresses. Now I had to start all over. Only this time she knew I was looking for her. Even steely-eyed Phil had avoided my gaze when she told me that Elizabeth had run out and left me to Dwayne's uncertain mercies. No surprise there. It wasn't the first time.

I opened my eyes. No point in thinking about that now. I'd missed Elizabeth, but I absolutely had to find Jeff. Once he'd handed over my money, I'd be able to rent a room for the night and buy a meal. Hey, I could even spring for a new toothbrush.

Phil came over to me and held out a small envelope.

"What is it?" I asked.

"Some pain pills."

"I'm okay," I said.

"You're managing now, but later it's going to catch up with you. It's just insurance in case you feel rotten later. You don't have to take them unless you need to."

I took the envelope. "Thanks."

She shook her head. "Don't thank me. You got hurt because I misjudged the situation."

Lopez's cell phone chirped. He answered with a curt, "Yes." Then, "That was fast. She'll be right down." He hung up and looked at me. "Taxi's here."

"Here," Phil said. "Let me walk you out."

When I reached the door, Lopez said, "Call me when you get where you're going. We'll get your things to you tonight or tomorrow morning."

Phil and I descended the stairs in silence. When we were outside, she said, "If you think of anyplace that Elizabeth might go or anyone she'd contact, will you let us know?"

"Which us?"

She gave me a brief glimpse of the lopsided grin I'd seen when she'd told me to call her Phil. It made her look more approachable and trustworthy. "The FBI us—specifically me. Let me see the card Inspector Lopez gave you."

"You don't have your own card?"

"I do, but not on me. I'm still undercover until I get new orders."

I handed it to her and she scrawled two numbers on the back. "The first number's my cell. If I don't answer and it's urgent, call the second number and explain who you are. Day or night.

Someone will answer." She gestured to a red taxi with white writing on the side that had pulled up behind a double-parked police car. "There's your ride. You take care."

"You too," I said and walked toward the waiting taxi. I glanced at the gawkers across the street. There were about the same number as before, but of the original five who'd been there all along, only Green Sneakers and Lies-About-Her-Age remained.

I opened the back door of the taxi and slid inside. The interior was filled with cigarette smoke. The cab driver sat slouched behind the wheel, one arm resting along the top of the seats. All I could see was the back of his head. He needed a haircut.

"Hi," I said and glanced at the large No Smoking sign that decorated the sliding plastic panels between the front from the back. Did the sign mean that only passengers couldn't smoke?

He turned his head. I caught a bit of profile. Hawkish nose and an unambiguous chin that could've used a shave three days ago. "Where to?"

"I have the address right here." I dug Jeff's letter out of my jeans pocket and glanced at it. "It's on Alvin Street. 145 Alvin."

"Alvin? It's in the city?"

"Yes."

"Never heard of it. Let me look it up." He punched the address into a GPS on the dash. "Okay. I got it. Off South Van Ness?"

"I don't know."

"No problem. I'll get you there."

That was encouraging. I leaned back and tried to concentrate on the streets we were taking. I always tried to learn my way around any new city as soon as possible. I'd been to San Francisco before with Aunt June. We'd take the bus down from Petaluma and visit the library or the museums. None of the streets the taxi took looked familiar. It had been some years, though. I might've forgotten.

We rapidly descended steep streets with upscale houses to less steep ones with apartment buildings that still looked upscale to my eye. Then we were in the stop-and-go of a wide busy street. I checked the street sign—Van Ness. Not far then.

I was wrong. We traveled quite a way on Van Ness and came across some familiar sights.

"That's City Hall," I said. "And the Opera House and Davies Hall." I peered at them through the smeared window as we whipped by. A stab of nostalgia and loss had me pressing my fist against my chest.

"You from out of town?"

"Yes, but I used to live in Petaluma. I'd come here with my aunt. Once we saw the ballet at the Opera House. Prokofiev's *Romeo and Juliet.* It was fantastic."

The cabbie glanced at me briefly in the rearview mirror. He nodded but didn't say anything. I didn't usually offer up bits of trivia about my past to strangers, but I hadn't been so poignantly reminded of Aunt June in a long time.

I blanked out the next few blocks and missed how far we'd gone. We'd crossed some invisible boundary, though, because the buildings that lined the street were noticeably shoddy. Spare-changers and homeless people stood in traffic with signs handwritten on cardboard that pleaded their particular case.

At a red light, one of them shuffled up to the cabbie's open window and mumbled something. The cabbie waved him away with a curt gesture. The man noticed me in the backseat and tapped on my window. He said something, but I couldn't make out what. I rubbed my toe over the money I'd stashed in my shoe.

"Don't give him anything," the cabbie said. "It doesn't help. It just makes it worse."

I met his eyes in the mirror. "Okay." I dropped my gaze. He'd misjudged me. It hadn't occurred to me to give the man some money. All I could think of was my own situation and how I'd always kept a cushion so I'd never end up like that man. Until now. Jeff had my cushion and I had to get it back.

The light changed and we moved away. I couldn't keep track of the streets or the route. We turned into a narrower street lined with houses. A few looked slightly gentrified with fresh paint, but most ranged from rundown to nearly derelict. All had wrought-iron gratings over their street level windows. We stopped in front of one of the more dilapidated houses.

"Here you go," the driver said.

"Would you please wait? It shouldn't take long."

He shrugged. "Okay, but I have to keep the meter running."

"Yes, I know. I'll be right back. Just wait, please." I got out of the car and mounted the steps to the front door. The roof over the front porch was supported by columns topped by carved wooden millwork. The house could've been nice with a little paint and attention. I rang the bell but didn't hear any sound inside the house.

I heard a car door slam and turned around. The cabbie stood next to his taxi, his hands cupped around the flame he held to a fresh cigarette. Maybe he welcomed a chance to stretch his legs, especially since he was doing it on my dime. I turned back to the house and pounded on the door.

The door was opened by a woman wearing jeans, a sweatshirt, and a black eye. She didn't say anything, just looked at me.

"Hi. I'm looking for Jeff."

"He's not here."

"When are you expecting him?"

"I'm not. He's gone."

"Are you his sister? He said this was his sister's address and he'd be here. He promised he'd be here today." Some of my desperation must have leaked into my voice, because she looked at me more intently.

"He's gone," she repeated.

"Where?"

"I don't know. Los Angeles?" She tossed out the city as if we were playing a guessing game.

"Look, this is very important."

"What's going on?" A man's voice came from the room behind Jeff's sister. He appeared in the flesh a second later. A lot of flesh. About three hundred pounds of it. A good fifty of them bulged out in a potbelly that draped over his belt. He shoved Jeff's sister aside and let his bulk fill the doorway. "Whaddya want?"

"Jeff. He has something of mine, and he promised that he'd give it back when I came here."

"He's not here, and we don't know nothing about any money," he said.

I stared at him. First Dwayne the Dumb, then this bozo. Maybe there was something in the water around here. "I didn't say anything about money."

His reply was to take a step back and try to shut the door in my face. My foot beat him by a half second. My side might hurt, but my reflexes were still good.

"Jeff stole my money. I have his confession in his own handwriting. He swore he'd give it back when I got here. I don't want to have to call the cops."

At the mention of the police, Bozo opened the door wide. "You fuckin' bitch. Get outta here." He moved toward me, and before I could back out of his way, he body-checked me. I slammed back against the porch pillar. The pain in my chest shot off fireworks in my head. My knees gave out and I slid down the pillar. All I could see were bright shooting lights. I heard the door slam.

Someone helped me to my feet and supported me by gripping my upper arm. I forced my eyes to focus. The cabbie. He wore a Hawaiian shirt that featured oversized monkeys swinging from undersized coconut trees. I stared at the shirt for several seconds and worked on getting air. "Hey," he said. "You okay?"

I pulled away and leaned instead against the porch railing. "Bozo?"

"No, I'm not Bozo."

"I mean." I paused for a breath. "The fat bozo. He gone?" I couldn't seem to find enough air to make whole sentences.

"Locked himself in the house. Want me to call the cops?"

"No." I turned and faced the street. "Car."

The cabbie stood back, and I edged down the front steps, clinging to the railing. It was just a couple of yards from the bottom step to the cab. The cabbie went ahead and opened the door for me. I sank down onto the backseat and pulled my legs inside. Once he'd closed the door, I slipped off my left shoe.

When the cabbie got into the driver's seat, I said, "Just around the corner. Anywhere Bozo can't see us."

While he drove, I fished the money out of my shoe. A twenty, two tens and three ones. They looked worn and wrinkled after all the time they'd spent rolled up in my shoe. Pathetic really.

The cabbie pulled over and turned his head in my direction. He glanced at the money in my hand, turned forward and flipped off the meter.

I edged forward in my seat so I could see his face better. I had a plan—of sorts. My version of standing in traffic with a handwritten sign. "The brother of the woman who answered the door took my money. When I find him, he'll give it back to me. Meanwhile, all I have is forty-three dollars and some change. I can pay you now. And I will, if that's what you want. But, if you could lend me enough money for a hotel for one night, I'll pay you back tomorrow."

"You think you're going to find him tomorrow?" Skeptical, but he hadn't flat out refused.

"No, I don't. But, I'll be able to earn money busking tomorrow. Maybe even tonight."

"Busking? What's that? A new word for hooking?" He ran an eye over me as if assessing my possibilities.

"No!" I paused. Had to be calm about this. Calm and convincing. "I'm a street performer—a magician. I can make money with my street act."

"You have an act? You don't even have a suitcase."

"I'm getting my suitcase back tonight or tomorrow at the latest."

"Who's got your suitcase? The guy who took your money?"

"No." My promise to Phil made it hard to explain my situation convincingly, but it had been worth a try anyway. I held out thirteen dollars, which covered the fare with a small tip.

He looked at the money, but didn't move to take it.

"I'd give you a much bigger tip, if I could. I really appreciate your helping me back there." When he didn't take the money, I dropped it on the seat next to him.

"Oh hell," he said. "Hold it. Just hold it." He pulled out a cigarette and lit it. "You don't want to get out in this neighborhood. What if I take you back to where I picked you up? You were talking to some people there. Maybe they could help you."

"No, they can't." I reached for the door handle.

"Wait a minute. I'll take you anywhere in the city. How's that? Anywhere you want. Off the meter. And you can keep your money." He grabbed up the bills I'd given him and stuffed them into my hand. "So, where do you want to go?"

I shook my head. "You don't understand. I don't take charity." I dropped the bills back into the front seat.

"What do you mean? You just asked me for money."

"A loan. I'll pay you back."

"How do I know that?"

"Because I don't lie."

He laughed. He didn't believe me. Not that I could blame him. I was probably the only person who'd believe me, and that was only because I could always tell if someone was lying. He tossed his still lit cigarette out the window, put the car in gear and pulled away from the curb.

"Stop. I'm getting out here."

"I don't think so," he said and took a corner at speed. "This isn't a good neighborhood."

"I'll be fine."

"Yeah, right," he scoffed.

"Just stop the car, okay?"

"Be quiet. I'm trying to think." A light turned yellow, and he accelerated through it as it turned red.

"There's nothing to think about. It's okay. You don't have to loan me money. I'll be fine."

"Just shut the hell up, okay?"

"There's no need to swear."

He turned a corner without slowing down, and I slid against the door. "Ow," I said. I straightened and pressed my hand to my side.

"Shit," he said. He pulled over and stopped.

"There's really no need to…"

He looked at me in his rearview mirror. "I know. No need to swear. Like you never swear."

"I don't."

"You don't lie. You don't swear. Anything else?"

"I don't hit, unless someone hits me first."

"That must've been what the fat guy was counting on, otherwise he would've been shaking in his shoes."

"Go ahead and laugh. It's the right way to live, so I'm going to stick with it." I tried to pulled on the door handle, but the door wouldn't open. "Hey, unlock the door. Isn't that illegal or something in a taxi?"

"Just hang on," he said. "I want to help you, but I'm not going to give you money."

"What then?"

"First, can we clear up this thing about the guy owing you money? I heard you tell the fat guy..."

"Bozo," I put in.

"Yeah. You told Mr. Bozo that the guy wrote a confession?"

"Yes. He did."

"Why didn't you take it to the police?"

"It's complicated. I had to come to San Francisco today, and Jeff knew it. If I'd gone to the police, it would've delayed me. Also, since Jeff was here, it wouldn't have helped me to go to the police in Las Vegas."

"You were in Vegas? Doing what? Gambling?"

"Working. I was Eddie the Wizard's assistant. He's a magician."

"And you're a magician."

"Right. Only I'm not to the point where I can do a whole Vegas show yet." I didn't mention there was also the problem of no social security number and no formal identification.

"Okay, here's the deal. I know a guy who lets me use this place whenever I want. No one's staying there. I got my own place. You could stay there, no charge. One night only."

Things might work out after all, but first I had to check this guy out. "Unlock the door," I said.

Without hesitation, he flipped the lock toggle. Okay, first test passed. I slid out of the backseat, closed the door, opened the passenger side of the front seat and got in. I didn't try to rush it. If I moved slowly and deliberately, then my side didn't hurt. As much.

I took a good look at his face. "You're unusual. Most American-born taxi drivers are older. The young guys are almost always foreigners. I'd guess you come from New York or New Jersey."

"For some people, Jersey is a foreign country."

I peered at the driver's ID clipped to the sun visor. The plastic covering it had yellowed and cracked, practically obscuring both the photo and the writing. "Okay, you have black hair, but even if you grew a mustache, you couldn't pass for Ali Muhammad."

"Name's Rico,"

"I'm Valentine. You have a cabbie's license?"

"I drive for Ali. It's his cab. You saw it said 'owner operated' on the side? He takes nights. I do days sometimes. And what's the deal with the third degree? I'm getting you a place to stay—for free."

"That's what I need to make sure about. The free part."

"Free and no strings. Wait, I take that back. There's one thing. No drugs. And that's a deal-breaker. So if you're using, I can't help you."

"I'm not and never have."

"And you don't lie."

"That's right."

"You look like hell."

My hand went automatically to my hair. As if patting the tangled curls could ever improve the overall ragtag effect. "It's been a rough day. All I need is a good night's sleep."

"If you say so." He put the car in gear and pulled into traffic. "It's not far."

Chapter Five

"Not far" is relative when you're the passenger and you don't know where you're going. I pretty much zoned out during the ride. Rico didn't have much to say either. At least, not to me. He lit another cigarette, told me to put my seat belt on, and took on the city streets like a kid playing Indy 500 in a video game arcade. He produced a cell phone from his shirt pocket, drove and held the phone with one hand and punched in a number with the other.

"Hi, Mom," he said into the phone. "Yeah, it's me, Rico. You know that loft apartment that Fred lets me use sometimes? Yeah, that one. Would you do me a favor and call him for me? The number's on the fridge. Just let him know I'm coming. No, not me. A girl I picked up needs a place for one night. Not in a bar. Picked up in my cab. Right. Love you, too."

"Does your mother live with you?" I asked.

"No. I have my own place."

"But you leave phone numbers on her refrigerator?"

"Yeah. What of it?" An edge to his voice. The New Jersey creeping in.

"Nothing."

We rode in silence for a bit. "Valentine your real name?" he asked.

Here we went with the reality versus illusion thing again. I opted for the short version this time. "Yes."

"Thought maybe it was your stage name."

"I haven't decided on that one yet. Right now I go by The Great Valentina, but I'm not sure it's quite right."

He turned into an alley. People had parked on both sides, which left just enough room for one car and a couple of inches to spare. I caught myself holding my breath as we rocketed along between two blocks of tall new buildings that were mostly under construction interspersed with small old buildings that were under deconstruction. Rico drove up over a curb onto a patch of gravel behind one of the old buildings, a three-story brick affair that looked like it had barely survived the 1906 earthquake.

I got out of the cab and looked around. "Is this the place?"

"Don't let the exterior fool you. It's nicer on the inside."

A homeless person appeared around the corner of the building and shambled at an angle toward us. When he came near, I got a whiff of rank stench. "Spare change?"

Rico pulled a bill out of his pocket and handed it to him.

"God bless you." The man shambled away.

"I thought you said not to give them anything."

"It's okay. I know that guy." He headed toward the building. I followed slowly. "Look," he said over his shoulder, "if you don't want to stay here, it's okay by me. My other offer still stands—I'll take you wherever you say."

The problem was that I didn't have anywhere else to go. My day so far ranked up there with my top-ten worst ever. I'd always been pretty good at blocking out physical pain, but the run-in with Mr. Bozo had pushed things too far even for me. I really needed to lie down somewhere safe.

Before we reached the battered back door, it opened and a sturdy woman with gray hair in a Dutch boy haircut stepped out. She had an unlit cigarette in her mouth and the lighter in her hands already fired up and halfway to her cigarette when she saw us. "Hey, Rico." The cigarette bobbed in synch with the words. She finished lighting up and took a long drag. She wore black jeans and a black knit polo shirt. When we came near, I saw that the shirt had an embroidered logo in bright blue that said "i-systems."

"Hey, Nancy," Rico said. "How's business?"

"Business is too good. I'm pulling down overtime and can't even get out of the office for a smoke break. Who's this?" She squinted at me through the cigarette smoke.

"This is Valentine. She's going to use the loft tonight."

"If you're going to smoke," a man's voice came through the open door behind Nancy, "then close the goddamned door." This order was followed by a screeching sound of some kind of machinery.

Nancy waved us toward the door. "Go on. I'll catch you later. Nice to meet you, Valentine."

We passed through the back door and immediately into a large high-ceilinged room that housed a whole carpenter's shop. I counted five different machines. A redheaded man stood next to one of them, using a notched stick to push a flat board lengthwise toward a spinning saw blade. The machine screamed its way along until the board fell neatly in two pieces. The man picked up the pieces of wood and added them to a stack he'd apparently already cut. He wore the same black pants and black shirt as Nancy. He looked up and saw us.

"How's it going, Mike?" Rico said.

"This oak's a real bitch to rip. It's so old it's like iron." Mike's gaze landed on me. "Hi."

"I think it'd be impossible to rip any kind of wood," I said, but I immediately pictured a magic act featuring the illusion of ripping wood like a piece of paper. It would make a great trick.

Mike blinked and smiled. "What have we here, Rico? A real blonde? Honey, a ripcut means you saw the wood with the grain."

I'd heard more blonde jokes in my life than almost any other kind of humor. Usually I let it go, but pain and fatigue made me grouchy. "And manners mean you don't speak condescendingly to people even if they don't understand something you think is basic knowledge."

"Ouch." Mike grinned. "She's pretty, but she bites. You should've warned me, Rico."

"We're going upstairs, so you have to turn off the machinery for now," Rico said.

"Sure. No problem. Have to get back to work anyway." He brushed at his clothes with his hands. "This damn sawdust. It's hell on the computers."

"Computers? This isn't a carpentry business?"

"No," Rico said. "The former owner left that machinery behind. I think they used it for the remodel they were doing. Mike's hobby is woodworking, so he spends all his free time in there." Rico led the way across the workshop to another door.

The doorway we passed through was the back entrance to the building's foyer. The low lighting dimly illuminated tarnished brass fixtures, a marble floor, and wood wainscoting.

"I see what you mean about it being nicer inside. It's amazing. It's like walking into another time."

"Yes. It's a damn shame that they're going to tear it down. Here we go." He stopped next to an old-fashioned elevator. He grabbed the handle of the folding metal gate and slid it open. The light inside the wood paneled elevator came on.

I shook my head. "I don't do elevators," I said. "I'll take the stairs."

"Not possible," Mike said, as he came up behind me. "No stairs anymore."

"What do you mean 'no stairs?' They're right there." I pointed to the oak banister supported by fancy wrought iron at the front end of the foyer.

"That's the staircase to nowhere," Mike said. "The treads and risers to the upper floors are in the process of becoming a beautiful set of oak dining room chairs. For my dining room."

I stared at Rico, who nodded and said, "The building's going to come down anyway, eventually."

"And the owner doesn't care?"

Mike gave a short laugh. "Ownership is—shall we say— unclear, at this point. Which is the only reason they haven't done the old wrecking ball thing on her already. Too bad for the building, but you can't beat the rent. Hey, Rico, you going to make a food run for us?"

"Sure. I'll be down in a couple of minutes. Decide what you

want, though. I can't stand around waiting for you guys to make up your minds. Come on, Valentine." Rico gestured toward the elevator. "It's just one floor. And the elevator's perfectly safe."

It wasn't that I couldn't ride in an elevator. I'd done it many times when the stairs weren't an option. But never when I was in such bad physical shape and so uncertain of what lay ahead. Why couldn't Rico's friend have had an apartment on the first floor?

"Go on," Mike urged. "You're going to love the loft. It's really nice. Not like downstairs at all."

I stepped into the elevator. Rico pulled the folding metal gate across the opening with a clang. He pushed a button and the elevator gave a jerk and began to rise slowly. Very slowly. In fact, the motion was barely perceptible. I felt the familiar cold sweat begin to form on my forehead and forced myself to breathe slowly while staring at the metal grill opposite. The doorway opening gradually disappeared as the car began to rise. The between-floors wall passed in slow motion. Someone had scrawled graffiti. Why bother with a just brief obscenity? You'd have enough time to write a whole novel by the time you reached the second floor.

At last the car jolted to a stop. Rico pulled the metal gate open, and I nearly fell in my rush to get out. It was dark in the hallway. The only light came from the elevator car. "Just open the door there. It's unlocked."

I crossed the few steps to the door and opened it. The early evening light came through tall windows at one end of the room.

"Light switch to your right."

I found it, flipped it on and instantly illuminated a large modern loft. Unadorned brick walls. Everything open in one huge space. Kitchen in the middle like a small island, but with a view to the surrounding room. The bedroom area to the far right, and living space to the left, with a wall of tall windows. All of it minimalist modern.

"It's wonderful. I thought it was going to be old-fashioned like downstairs. Thank you for letting me stay here. I appreciate it."

"No problem." He waved off my thanks and moved into the kitchen area. "Help yourself to anything here." He opened the doors of the empty refrigerator and a couple of equally bare cupboards. "Which, I guess, would be nothing."

"That's okay." I crossed into the kitchen and pulled a glass from one of the open shelves. "Water's all I want." I filled the glass at the sink and took a long drink.

"I'm going to get some takeout for the guys downstairs. I could get some for you, too."

I wasn't hungry, but I should eat something. It would help me deal with the profound fatigue I felt seeping through me. "Sure, that would be great." I reached into my pocket and pulled out a ten. "Here."

"No, that's okay." He waved a hand at me and backed toward the doorway.

"Take it, or I don't share the food."

He took the money with a shrug. "You'll get change, though. I know a place that's real cheap, if Chinese is okay with you."

"It's great. Thanks." I leaned against the kitchen counter.

"You okay?"

"Just tired."

"Okay. Be right back." He walked out the door with a wave of his hand.

When I'd reached for my money in my pocket, my hand had briefly touched the small manila envelope of pain pills Phil had given me in case I felt rotten later. She must've had ESP or something, because I felt really rotten now. I pulled out the envelope and extracted two pills. I'd just lifted my hand to put the pills in my mouth when the door opened and Rico reappeared leaning inward on the door handle. "You have a thing about MSG? Because this place..." He stopped in midsentence. "What the hell?"

"What's the problem?" I popped the pills into my mouth and downed them with the rest of the water in the glass.

He strode over to me, grabbed me by the shoulders and gave me a hard shake.

"Ow!" I cried out. "Stop it." He dropped his hands, and I backed away from him.

"Didn't I tell you no drugs? What've you got there?" He snatched up the envelope I'd put down on the counter.

"They're just pain pills. That's all."

He tilted the envelope and spilled one of the pills into the palm of his hand. "Shit. Just pain pills. There's no 'just' about it. This is oxy. Good for pain, sure. What've you got? Junkie pain?"

"What's oxy?"

"Don't try to play me, okay? Those blue eyes aren't going to cut it now. I said no drugs, and I meant it."

I shook my head. "You're making a mistake."

"My mistake was falling for your sob story. A guy stole your money, but was going to give it back. I must be getting old."

It was humiliating to be accused of using drugs. If he only knew me, he'd know I'd never do it. No matter what. "Just listen to me. I'm telling the truth. I don't know what oxy is. I thought the pills were like aspirin."

"You expect me to believe that you've never heard of oxycontin? No one's that naïve."

I turned and headed for the door.

"Hey, where're you going?"

"I'm leaving, because you are so full of it. You know what? Not knowing the current slang for some drug isn't naïve. Naïve is a thirty-something man thinking he's an adult living on his own when he doesn't even have to keep track of his own phone numbers or make his own phone calls, for that matter, because he can have his mother do it for him." I stopped to catch my breath.

Rico stared at me. "What?"

"And if she picks out your clothes, too, you're really in trouble, because that has to be the ugliest shirt I've ever seen."

He looked down at his monkey-coconut tree-patterned shirt, as if noticing for the first time what he was wearing. He lifted his head and frowned. "How did this get to be about me?"

"It was always about you. That's the problem. You had a good impulse, to help me when I asked for help. But that's all it was—an impulse."

"Look, I told you the rules. No drugs."

"Rules are good. I have my own rules, and I live by them. But you don't. You don't even have good rules. You say not to give one man any money, then you turn around and give money to this other man. Because you know him. If you took a minute to talk to that man who stood in traffic asking for money, you'd know him, too. Your rule is flawed, because you have to make exceptions. And that makes you fall back on your impulses to guide you. That's why it's all about you."

He gave me the sidelong stare people use when they're not sure whether you're sane or not. That was okay. I'd said what I had to say. Maybe he'd think about it later and realize I was right. I turned to leave.

"Wait. You can stay. Just no more oxy."

I turned back. "Agreed. No more oxy. But I'm going anyway." I turned again to leave and a funny thing happened to my feet. They staggered and threw me off balance. I tried to right myself, and instead ended up crashing backwards against the refrigerator. The broken rib really hated that. "Ahhh!" I cried out before I could stop myself.

"What the hell?" Rico said.

I stood with my eyes closed until the lights stopped flashing in my brain. When I opened them, Rico stood in front of me, frowning. "What's the matter?"

"I don't know. My feet wouldn't work right somehow, and I stumbled." I pressed my hand against my side.

"What's wrong with your side. Are you hurt?"

"Of course I'm hurt. Why else would I take pain pills?"

"I know that fat guy got rough, but I didn't realize…"

"No, it was before the bozo." I stayed with my back leaning against the refrigerator. Somehow, it seemed easier than trying to stand upright on my own. My eyes wanted to rest a minute, too. I let my eyelids fall. Just for a few moments, what would that hurt?

I heard Rico calling my name over and over again, and saying, "Stay with me now." Why would he say that when I'd broken his rule?

Chapter Six

Daylight forced my eyes open, even though all I really wanted was to keep them closed and stay in the soft darkness of sleep. It took a few seconds to focus. I lay on my side, and I wasn't alone.

Rico.

Asleep next to me.

With his hand between my breasts.

"Argh!" I tried to scream, but my vocal cords didn't work very well. I tried to roll away, but got tangled up in the blankets and ended up sliding slowly to the floor in a blanket cocoon.

"What the hell?" Rico was off the bed and on his feet before I could get upright. "You okay?" he asked and started to come around the bed.

I managed to get on my feet. I was wearing some awful Hawaiian shirt. Where were my clothes? "Stay away from me, perv."

"Perv? If babysitting a dopehead all night makes me a perv, then okay."

"I'm not a dopehead. And you had your hand on my breasts."

"Don't flatter yourself. I was asleep on the couch when you freaked out, yelling, carrying on. I came over here to wake you up, and you grab my hand. The only way you'd stay quiet was if I let you hold onto my hand." He held out his hand and flexed it. "It's been completely asleep for hours. I may never get all the feeling back into it."

"Yes, and I suppose I also undressed myself in my sleep." I looked around the room for my clothes. "No wonder I was having nightmares if I was wearing this awful thing." I pulled at the oversized red Hawaiian shirt that sported green and yellow parrots.

"I didn't take your clothes off, if that's what you're thinking. I had Nancy come up and do it."

"Oh, you had a complete stranger undress me. That makes me feel much better." I strode into the living room end of the loft, but couldn't see my clothes anywhere.

He followed me. "Look, what was I supposed to do? You'd said that you'd been hurt, then you pass out. I didn't know if I should call 911 or not, so I asked for a second opinion. Hey, you're moving pretty good for someone who obviously took a hell of a beating. But, I have some bad news—you're not going to be wearing a bikini for a while. Not with those bruises."

I stopped rummaging among the sofa cushions. "You had someone else take my clothes off and then you looked at me? I got it right the first time—perv." I pointed my finger at him. "If you messed with me in any way, I have a friend in the San Francisco Police Department who'll fix your wagon for you."

"Fix my wagon? What's that supposed to mean? If your friend is Hector Lopez, I've got news for you. He's in homicide, and you're not dead. And you can probably thank me for that. Though it doesn't look like you will."

I stared at him. "You went through my pockets?"

"Think about it. Girl who goes by the unlikely name of Valentine, pops some oxy, complains of severe pain and passes out on me. What else could I do? Not that I learned very much. No ID, just a wallet with fifty library cards from all over the country."

"Twenty-seven library cards," I corrected him. "And they're actually very good ID. They tell you a lot about me."

"Sure, whatever. But not as much as the so-called confession from Jeff. *True Confessions* is more like it. He's just holding your money hostage, the way you're holding his heart hostage. You like to put all your boyfriends through the wringer, or just this one?"

"Jeff is not my boyfriend. He's a person who imagines things and thinks they're real. He admits he took my money. That's a confession. Now it's your turn to confess. Where are my clothes? And you'd better hand them over right now, because there's no way I'm appearing in public in this hideous shirt."

"Don't start in on my wardrobe again. Your clothes are in the bathroom. We left them in there with a clean towel, so you could take a shower in the morning."

"Oh. Where's the bathroom?"

Rico pointed in the direction of the sleeping area. I turned and headed that way.

"You're welcome," he called after me. "And just so you know, I'm leaving now."

"Good," I said, continuing toward the bathroom. I heard the door close and a second later, the clang of metal. I stopped in my tracks. The elevator. I'd forgotten all about it. "That's okay," I said aloud to myself. "I'll deal with it when the time comes." That's what my Aunt June had always said, and she was mostly right.

In the shower with hot water washing away the kinks, I could see that Rico had had it right about the bruises. Definitely not for public display. But if they hadn't faded by the time I returned to Vegas, I could always apply the body makeup I used for my scars when I had to put on the skimpy outfit Eddie the Wiz had his assistants wear. That is, if he still had a job for me when I returned to Vegas.

I couldn't worry about that, because I'd never get back to Vegas if I didn't make some money. To do that, I needed to call Lopez and get my things back. So, freshly showered, and not so freshly dressed in yesterday's clothes, I walked around, finger-combing my damp hair, and looked for a phone. No phone.

Okay, time to face the elevator. I had to leave the apartment door open to see, because it was completely dark in the hall. I pushed the call button, then waited for the elevator car to make its snail-like progress to the second floor. The folding metal gate needed some force to make it close all the way, and I discovered that the car wouldn't budge if it wasn't closed. On the way down, I breathed in and out slowly, the way I'd trained myself to do. No rapid heartbeat, no clenching stomach and no sweat, literally and figuratively. The car stopped at the ground floor with a little bounce. I pushed open the gate and stepped out with a little bounce myself. I'd never had such an easy time of it. Maybe I'd finally conquered my fear?

"Hey, Blondie. How's it going?" This from flame-haired Mike, who lounged against the wall, looking as if he'd been waiting for the elevator to come down.

Time to nip this "blondie" bit in the bud. "Hello, Carrot Top. My name is Valentine."

He grinned and nodded. "Okay, not too subtle, but I get it. Valentine."

"Were you waiting for the elevator?" I stepped away from open car.

"Nope. For you. Heard the machinery going and knew you were on the way down. Rico asked us to keep an eye out for you. Make sure you were okay."

"Why wouldn't I be?"

"Gee, let me see." He scratched his head in a parody of puzzlement. "Could it be because someone used you as a punching bag? Or, was it your overdosing on a level four prescription drug—for which you had no prescription? Or maybe, it was your obvious elevator phobia. Wait, I know. The answer is—all of the above."

"Rico exaggerated."

"I got it from Nancy, not Rico. And, believe me, no one accuses Nancy of exaggeration. You can ask her yourself. Come on." He gestured for me to follow him and walked toward a wide doorway near the front end of the building.

I hurried after him. "I don't want to interrupt. I know you're busy." And I didn't need to hang around explaining myself to people I didn't know. But what I did need was to call Lopez. "I really have to make a phone call. Do you think I could use your phone?"

"Sure, but let's let Nancy take a look at you first." He proceeded through a doorway flanked by tall double wooden doors that bore a tastefully small brass plate. It said simply, i-systems, with no further explanation. We entered a large room with a high curved ceiling with plaster curlicues around the edges. The modern office cubicles and computers that filled the room made a jarring contrast.

"Hey, Nancy," Mike yelled out. "Someone here to see you."

Nancy's head appeared above one of the dividers. "There you are," she said to me and came out to join us. "How are you feeling?"

"I feel great, thanks. I'm embarrassed that I was so dumb about taking those pills. It was nice of you to look after me in my passed out condition. I'm really grateful."

"Rico was pretty worried about you."

"That was nice of him, too," I said with less sincerity. "Do you mind if I use your phone?"

"Sure, go ahead." She waved me toward an unoccupied cubicle. "When you're done, come on back this way." She pointed to the opposite side of the room.

"Okay." I sat down in the desk chair. The surface of the desk was bare except for a computer and a telephone. The computer was on and had an "i-systems" screen saver slowly flowing back and forth across the monitor. I pulled out Lopez's card and punched in the number. It rang four times and Lopez's voicemail message came on. I hung up the phone. Stupid voicemail. Why couldn't they have a person answer? What if it was an emergency, like a person needed to get her things back so she could put on some clean clothes and earn some money.

"You get through okay?" Mike asked behind me.

I stood up and slipped the card back into my pocket, but I had a feeling that Mike had seen it. "No. I'll have to try again in a few minutes. If that's okay."

"No problem. Come on back to our employee lounge." He led the way to a far corner of the room that housed a kitchen sink, a counter with a microwave on top and a small refrigerator underneath. Nancy sat at a round table just large enough for three chairs.

"It's not very spacious, or even lounge-like," Mike said. "But it doesn't matter because we never use it. On break, Nancy goes outside to smoke, and I go into the shop. We eat at our desks."

"We're using it today, though." Nancy stood up and opened the microwave. "Thought you'd be hungry since you didn't get dinner last night." She checked her watch. "Or breakfast or lunch today." She put a plate with a large burrito on it in front of me. "Would you like a soda?" She opened the refrigerator and peeked in. "Or juice?"

I took a step back. "Look, I appreciate your helping me last night, but I don't expect you to feed me."

"Protest duly noted," Nancy said. "Now sit down and tell me, do you want soda or juice?"

I sat down. "Juice would be very nice." I picked up a fork and took a bite. I hadn't realized I was hungry until I smelled the food. But then I hadn't realized that I'd slept half of the day, either. "This is great. Thanks."

"We do very good takeout in this establishment," Mike said.

"So it's just the two of you?"

"For now there're three of us," Nancy said. "Becky's on nights."

"What exactly do you do?"

Mike and Nancy glanced at each other. I had the distinct feeling I'd overstepped some boundary. What had I been thinking? This whole setup in a condemned building couldn't be a conventional business. More like something barely on the edge of legitimate, if that. "I'm sorry," I apologized. "Forget I asked. It's none of my business."

"We provide private businesses the service of monitoring and managing their products from point of manufacture to customer delivery," Mike said.

"Huh?"

"He means that private businesses hire us to pick up goods they offer for sale and get them delivered to customers. These businesses usually don't manufacture the goods themselves so we spare them the hassle of maintaining a storage and shipping facility," Nancy explained.

"It's called drop-shipping only with the extra benefit of complete confidentiality and protection against theft," Mike added. "We keep an eye on everything. That's why we're called 'i-systems.' Clever, huh?"

"So you're the middle-men for middle-men?"

"Something like that," Mike said.

It all sounded a bit sketchy to me, but I didn't say it out loud. I just ate my food and listened.

"Okay, enough about work," Nancy said. "It's bad enough that I spend so many hours doing it, do I have to talk about it, too? You know, Valentine, I was wondering if you might want to see a doctor."

My mouth was full so I settled for shaking my head no.

"You sure? That was some beating you took. Rico said your side hurt a lot. It's possible you broke a rib."

"I think I did, but I'm fine. The last time I broke a rib was when Eddie the Wiz got drunk before the late show and messed up the wires for the levitation illusion. I did two shows the next day, no problem. They don't do anything for a broken rib, you know. It's not like breaking an arm where you get a cast."

"Who's Eddie the Wiz?" Mike asked.

"The magician I've been working for in Vegas. He calls himself Edward the Wizard, but he's the only one who does."

"Rico said something about you being a magician," Nancy said. "What kind of things do you do?"

"When I'm working for Eddie, I just assist, which means I smile like an idiot and try to make sure he doesn't mess up. Especially when I'm the one he's levitating. But when I'm doing my own street gig, I do lots of different things."

"Yeah? Like what?" Mike asked.

"Well, I always start by juggling, because that draws a crowd quicker."

"You juggle? I've always wanted to learn how to juggle."

It was an obvious opening for me to offer to teach him, but I needed to make contact with Lopez. "I don't have my gear with me, or I could show you."

"So you need special equipment to juggle?"

"I use balls. They're the easiest to learn with, but you can juggle just about anything." I stood up, carried my empty plate to the sink, and turned on the water.

"How about plates?" Mike asked, pointing to the plate in my hand.

"Yes, I've done plates, but I wouldn't want to practice with yours." I washed my dirty plate, put it in the dish drainer, and turned to Nancy. "Thanks for the meal. Okay if I use the phone again? I didn't get through last time."

"Sure." She indicated the closest cubicle.

I dialed and this time Lopez picked up.

"Hello, Inspector. This is Valentine Hill. You said I could pick up my gear today."

"Valentine. I was beginning to wonder if we'd hear from you. Sure, you can pick it up. I have it right here."

"Where's here?"

"Well, where are you? I can send a car to pick you up."

"No," I said quickly. "I can find my way there. Just give me the address."

"It's the central station at Sixth and Bryant."

"And you'll be there? Or someone who'll know to give it to me?"

"I'll be here as long as you're coming right now."

"I am. Thanks. Bye." I leaned back in the chair. What a relief.

"Everything okay?" Nancy asked.

I got up and stepped around the corner of the cubicle. "Everything's great. Thanks for everything. I'm going to be taking off now."

"Well, you'll be back later, won't you?"

"I don't think so. Rico and I didn't part on very good terms. I'd feel funny staying in his friend's loft."

"We have more say over the loft space than Rico does," Nancy said. "You should stay there. Unless you have other plans."

"Well...," I hesitated.

"It's settled," Mike said. "You're coming back to teach me how to juggle."

"I might not get back until late."

"Just push the buzzer," Nancy said. "You'll see it when you go out. Becky's doing the night shift tonight. I'll tell her to expect you."

"I'll probably be here late myself," Mike said. "There are some bugs in the program I need to fix."

"Thank you. I appreciate it. I'm pretty sure that after tonight, I'll be able to pay you rent."

"Rent?" Mike said with a laugh. "We don't pay rent, why should you?"

"You're both really nice." I headed toward the door, stopped and turned. "Can you tell me, where's the nearest bus line that'll take me to Sixth and Bryant?"

"Just go out the front door. Your ride's waiting," Nancy said.

I stared at her. "You mean Rico?"

"Sorry. He made me promise I'd call him if you came downstairs. You don't have to let him drive you if you don't want to, but I can vouch for him. He's harmless," Nancy said.

Mike laughed mirthlessly. "That's not the first adjective that comes to my mind. But don't worry, you're safe with him."

Not a very reassuring endorsement. "So long." I exited through the front door. I scanned the façade of the building and the neighboring ones on either side. One on the left was under construction. The one on the right looked just finished. The building I stood in front of seemed like a once-handsome but now elderly and very poor relation.

Rico, freshly shaved and wearing another truly awful shirt, watched me look the building over. He leaned against the taxi's front fender, his legs stretched out and crossed at the ankle. Even without the pose that drew attention to his feet, I would have noticed the shoes. Pale tan leather that looked glove-soft and fit his feet like a glove, too. I'd seen high rollers in Vegas, Atlantic City, and Miami who wore shoes like that. Italian, very expensive and probably handmade. Not the old sneakers he'd worn yesterday. Not a taxi driver's shoes.

He opened the front seat passenger door and gestured for me to get in.

I spoke to him across the width of the sidewalk. "I don't need a ride. Thanks anyway."

"Okay, but could you get in for just a minute? I have something of yours, but I can't give it to you out here in the street."

"What is it?"

"Just get in, will you? You know I'm not going to try anything."

Did I know that? "Give me your keys."

"What?"

"You heard me. Your car keys."

He pulled his keys out of his pocket and tossed them at me. His throw went wide, but I snagged them one-handed keeping my gaze on his face all the while. He raised his eyebrows in surprise. But then he hadn't seen me juggle. Or throw a punch. I shoved the keys all the way to the bottom of my pocket, crossed to the taxi and got in. Rico circled the taxi and slid in behind the wheel.

I shifted and leaned against the door so I could see him easily. "Okay, give it to me."

"Is it that you just don't do the small-talk thing, or you're still holding a grudge?"

"I don't hold grudges. I'm just careful. You said you had something that belonged to me."

"It's under your seat."

I reached under the seat and pulled out a small brown paper bag, the top folded over several times. I unfolded the bag and gazed inside. It was filled with money. A lot of money.

Chapter Seven

"What's this?" I asked, holding the bag toward him.

"Your money."

"No, it isn't." I tried to hand the bag to him. "Look, I appreciate the gesture. I really do, but I don't take charity."

Rico pushed my hand away. "It's not charity. It's your money. Remember Mr. Bozo? There's a note in there from him."

How bizarre was this? I looked in the bag and saw a torn piece of paper. I pulled it out and read the uneven handwriting.

"To Valentine Hill, Here is your money. I'm sorry I pushed you. Jerry Scott"

I looked up from the note. "I don't understand. How did you get this?"

Rico shrugged. "I heard what he said to you and the way he said it. It was pretty clear that either he knew Jeff had your money or that this guy had it himself. Turns out he'd sniffed out the money the second little Jeffie landed on his doorstep. He relieved the poor chump of it and tossed him out."

"So you went and asked him nicely to give it to you?"

"Not me. I know a couple of guys who owe me a favor. They had a little talk with him for me."

"What guys?"

"Just some guys."

"You mean goons, don't you?"

"No. If I meant goons, I would've said goons."

"No way would what's-his-name Jerry hand the money over just because someone asked him nicely. He's a bully. Didn't you see Jeff's sister?"

"I'm telling you the truth. They talked to him. He'd already spent some of it, but they convinced him he should replace what he'd taken. Had him write a little note, because I knew you'd make a fuss getting your money back if it wasn't all on the up and up."

"What's your definition of 'talking to him'?"

Rico held up his right hand. "I swear, no bozos were harmed in the taking of this money." He grinned, pleased with his joke.

I stared. The grin transformed him. He was already plenty good-looking, but didn't need to be, because he was a natural charmer, his grin an irresistible invitation to join in and be included in the fun. How had I missed it? I put my hand up to my forehead, like you do when the sun's too bright. Or when you have a headache.

"What's the matter?"

"Nancy said you were harmless. Mike disagreed with her. I'm with Mike."

"Hey, if this is about last night, I swear I never laid a hand on you. Well, okay there was hand at one point, but only one hand, and like I told you, it was your idea."

I lowered my own hand and met his gaze straight on. "Who are you?"

"What do you mean? I'm Rico. Your taxi driver from yesterday."

"Taxi cab drivers don't wear handmade Italian shoes."

Without missing a beat, he said, "You noticed those? Aren't they something? Check them out." He tried to lift his foot to show it to me, frowning with the effort. The steering wheel blocked him from fully displaying his shoe. He gave up trying to show it off. "I got these from a guy I know. He deals in clothing and stuff. Big discounts. You know what these will cost you if you buy them retail?"

He was so plausible. "You know a lot of guys," I said dryly.

"I guess I do."

"It's a lot of connections." I leaned on the last word.

"You implying something?"

I ignored his question. "So what's the deal with the money? I pay you a finder's fee?"

"No!" he exploded. He jerked his head away and stared out his side window. After a few moments, he turned back to face me. "Okay, it's good that you're suspicious. Except I have to say, I don't know why you're suspicious of me, but you'll take drugs when you don't even know what they are."

"I had good reason to trust the person who gave those pills to me."

"And I haven't given you good enough reason to trust me? I found you a place to stay. I took care of you when you were drugged up and freaking out. I got your money…"

"Hold it. Back up a minute. What do you mean I was freaking out?"

"I told you before. You were crying—well, not crying exactly, but like crying. You'd say, 'No, no, I'll be good.' Or you'd call 'Aunt June,' over and over again. So I came in and tried to wake you up, but you just grabbed my hand and held on. That was the only thing that'd keep you quiet."

So that accounted for my dream. It was so vivid. I'd felt like Aunt June was really right there with me. Holding my hand the way she did in those first months after I came to stay with her. But it was Rico all along. "How embarrassing." I said the words out loud without meaning to.

"Don't be embarrassed. Drugs affect people all kinds of ways. Besides the drugs, someone'd worked you over pretty good. Right?"

"I'm not going to tell you about that, so quit hinting."

"Okay, okay. I don't want to know. So there's your money. No strings. I swear. So where do you want to go? Airport? Bus station?"

"Police station."

It was his turn to stare at me. "You sure? You have your money. You have no reason to stay around here, do you? Maybe get beat up again?"

"I have a reason. Besides, the police have my gear."

"Your gear?"

"My duffle bag and all my worldly possessions."

"How'd the cops…?" At a look from me, he stopped mid-question. "I know. None of my business. What if I drive you there?"

"Only if you take me as a regular fare this time. You know I'm good for it." I shook my bag of money.

"I'll need my keys back."

"Right," I said. I dug them out of my pocket and handed them over.

He started the engine, but instead of putting the car in gear, he looked over at me. "Does your gear include a cell phone?"

"Jeff had my cell phone, too. That's okay. I'll get one once I'm busking again."

"Maybe you'll need it before then. Like, if someone put you in a situation where you needed to call 911. Or a cab. Whatever. Anyway, look in the glove compartment."

I opened the glove compartment. A cell phone and a pack of cigarettes fell out. I caught them both before they hit the floor. I moved to put the cigarettes back in, but Rico reached for them. "You shouldn't smoke so much. Or at all, for that matter." I handed the pack to him.

"I know. I'm going to stop pretty soon." He pocketed the pack. "There's a charger in there, too."

I pulled out a black wire with an electric plug at the end. I held the phone in one hand, the wire in the other and sighed audibly.

"What's the matter?" he asked.

"I'm going to ask where this came from, and you're going to say, 'I know this guy.'"

"Are you psychic or something? That's just what I was going to say. I know this guy has a store and sells these pre-paid phones. That one was a demo and the model's discontinued. He can't give it away. Everyone wants phones with games, video, email, music, television, and a kitchen sink. This one's more phone than entertainment center. I thought you could use it, you know, in case."

"Is it your phone? Like will people call me on it and order a cab?"

"Didn't you hear what I said? It's new, except that it was a demo in the store. Sometimes I pick up guys from out of the country. They need a phone that works here. I'll take them to this guy's store, and they'll pick up a pre-paid phone at a good price. So the guy that owns the store gives me this phone with about hundred minutes already paid for."

"Does he also give you a percentage of what he sells to your fares?"

Rico shrugged. "We're all businessmen, you know?"

"Okay, businessman." I reached into my money bag. I pulled out a twenty and handed it to him. "I'll rent this phone from you while I'm in town."

"You don't have to do that." He tried to push the money away, so I leaned forward and tucked it into his shirt pocket behind his pack of cigarettes.

"Yes, I do." No point in explaining my moral outlook. Someone like Rico would never really understand. With his lazy grin and his many connections, he was trouble, pure and simple. I'd learned to walk away from trouble. I'd take another cab or a city bus to get back to the loft tonight. And when I was ready to leave town, I'd have Nancy return the phone to Rico for me. But I didn't have to announce it. With men like Rico, you just played along, then when you had the chance, made your exit.

He drove me to the police station. I paid him, thanked him, and got out of the taxi. "See you later," he said. I just smiled and waved. There wouldn't be any later, if I could help it.

〉〉〉

He sat at a metal table in an interview room. I gazed at him through one-way glass. The last man in the world I wanted to see again. Or one of the last. Lopez had brought me directly to this vantage spot without explanation. I just wanted my duffle bag, but here I was on a trip down memory lane.

"You know this guy?" Lopez asked me.

"Uncle George," I said. "I don't remember his last name."

"Your uncle?" Lopez asked, eyebrows raised.

"One of Elizabeth's marks. She made me call them uncle." I hadn't seen him for many years, but he looked just as I remembered. Short, fat, and graying. Elizabeth had made a point of describing him as "portly." Pudgy and unprepossessing were more like it. Elizabeth's ideal mark. A wealthy widower with no children, until the stunning Elizabeth appeared on the scene with her golden-curled girl. He'd adored Elizabeth and been nice to me.

"What's he doing here?"

"Looking for your mother—he says. We picked him up when her neighbors complained that he was ringing their doorbells and asking questions."

"You arrested him?"

"Nothing like that. He's just answering some questions for us. Only he's asking more than he's answering. I put him off, waiting till you got here. Only you took your time getting here, and he's about to walk."

"What do you want from me?"

"See if you could tell us something about him."

"I don't know anything. Not his last name or where he's from. I couldn't keep track of cities very well when I was little, we moved around too much."

"He's from Cleveland. Flew in this morning. He says. We're checking on it. Says he hasn't seen your mother in fifteen years."

"That sounds about right. How'd he find her?"

"That's what I want to know," Lopez said.

"Weird coincidence—his showing up today."

"Yeah, weird. What say you go in there with me and help us figure out what his story is?"

I took a step away from him. "Me? I don't think that's a good idea."

"Why not?"

"Elizabeth stole from him. She might have ruined him, for all I know."

"Sure, but you were just a kid. He can't hold it against you."

I shook my head. "You don't understand. I was part of the con, and he knows it."

"Look, this guy isn't telling me anything, and I can't make him. I want to know why he's here, how he knew your mother lived here. There's a chance he'll tell you."

What was it with Lopez? He'd done this yesterday—appealed to my better nature. It'd worked then, too. "Okay."

"Great. Thanks." He led me to the door to the interview room and held it open for me.

Uncle George's mouth fell open as I entered the room. He rose to his feet, his mouth working, but no words came out. Finally he croaked out, "Valerie? Is that you?"

"Hello, Uncle George." I would've stayed right in the door-way, but Lopez propelled me forward into the room.

"Good Lord," Uncle George said. "For a moment there, I thought you were Betty. You look so much like her, but younger, of course."

"Betty?" Lopez asked.

"Elizabeth's alias at that time was Betty," I said to him over my shoulder. "Mine was Valerie." I turned to Uncle George. "My real name is Valentine. Valentine Hill."

"Yes, yes. I know that. I discovered it after…But I still think of you as I knew you then."

"Look," Lopez said. "I'm going to get some coffee. Would either of you like some? It's actually not bad stuff."

Something cued me that Lopez wanted me to say yes. "Sure. Black is fine."

"Nothing for me," Uncle George said.

Lopez left, closing the door behind him. I moved to the interview table and sank into a chair. Uncle George sat, too.

"It's pretty awkward for me, seeing you again," I said. "I don't even remember your last name. I always thought of you just as Uncle George."

"The name's Hunsinger, but I don't mind your calling me Uncle George. You were a very nice little girl. Although, when you and Betty first came to live with me, you were a handful. I don't know if you remember, but one time, you punched me in the face. Tried to knock me down."

I winced. Actually, I had knocked him out, but what would be the point of challenging his version? "I remember getting into a lot of fights at school. The kids teased me for being behind in math. You taught me fractions, and I got A's on all my math tests because of you. No one teased me after that."

"You caught on quickly. You could have achieved a lot academically if...." His voice trailed off.

"If Elizabeth hadn't stolen your money and run off," I finished for him. "I didn't really understand that what she did was wrong until later. I'm sorry."

"You were as much a pawn as I."

"Actually, I was more than a pawn, but I simply didn't know right from wrong at that point. Now, it's different." He didn't have anything to say to that and silence fell between us. Where was Lopez with the coffee? He'd left me to do his work. I'd have to just dive in. "I'm really curious, so I have to ask—what are you doing here?"

"I admit to the same curiosity about you. I'm looking for Betty, of course. And you?"

"Same thing."

"Do you know where she is?"

This must've been what Lopez meant about Uncle George asking more than he was answering. "No, sorry. I got here yesterday, but I just missed her."

"Do you know anything about what happened? The people in her apartment building said that someone was murdered, but they wouldn't tell me anything else. It wasn't Betty, was it?"

"No," I said briefly and let it go. If Lopez wanted him to know anything else about it, he'd have to tell him.

He sighed and sank back in his chair. "That's a relief. I was afraid..." He left what he feared unspoken.

"You said you were looking for her, but how did you find her?"

"Through this." He reached into an inner pocket, pulled out a folded page and handed it to me.

I unfolded it and spread it out on the table. It was glossy like a magazine, but larger. A photograph at the top of the page caught my eye right away. It featured four smiling people in formal dress. Two I didn't know. The other two were Bobby Kroy and Elizabeth. The caption identified them by name. I bent over the page to study it.

Lopez came in with the coffee. A woman came in with him. Thirty-something and black-haired, her badge clipped to her belt. "This is Inspector Springer," Lopez said. Springer nodded in our direction and took a chair at the end of the table.

Lopez handed me a steaming cardboard cup and leaned across the table to get a better view of the clipping. "What's this?"

Uncle George lifted his hand as if he wanted to snatch the page out of sight, but Lopez had already slid it over so he could study it.

"It's how Uncle…, I mean, Mr. Hunsinger found Elizabeth. I guess it's from some magazine?"

Lopez's eye drifted to the print at top of the page. "Nob Hill Express. It's an upscale shopper. Along with the ads it has a lot of society news and photos." He slid into a chair and pulled his coffee cup toward him. "My mother-in-law always reads it so she can tell my wife how well so-and-so is doing. So-and-so being someone my wife supposedly could've married instead of a cop. What I get for marrying into an old San Francisco family. Great-great granddaddy made his money the old-fashioned way. By stealing it. I try not to bring that fact up too often." He took a sip of coffee.

Inspector Springer chuckled softly at Lopez's joke. I drank some of my coffee and watched Uncle George. He remained stiffly upright in his chair, but under the barrage of personal details from Lopez, some of the tension left his face.

"You don't live in San Francisco, Mr. Hunsinger, so how'd you come by this?" Lopez asked, gesturing to the page on the table.

He didn't reply right away. His answer, when it came, seemed wrung out of him against his will. "I subscribe to a clipping service. Over the years I've uncovered all of the pseudonyms

Betty uses. She's careful, though, and has never before allowed her picture to be published."

"What are you after, Mr. Hunsinger? Restitution? You know the crime she committed against you has passed the statute of limitations."

Uncle George reached across the table and retrieved the newspaper clipping. "My reasons for being here are completely legitimate. I'm a respected businessman. I simply wish to see Betty, if that's possible."

"It's not possible at this time," Lopez said.

"Is she being held by the police? Has she been charged with a crime?"

"No."

"And Valerie?"

Lopez raised his eyebrows. "Ms. Hill is a concerned citizen who's given us a lot of help with a homicide investigation."

Uncle George turned to me, eyes wide. "Help? How? Betty's a suspect, isn't she?"

"No," Lopez said.

"Then why won't you put me in touch with her?"

"What if you give us a way to contact you, and we'll pass the information on to her?"

Uncle George pursed his lips. "Very well. I'm staying at the Four Seasons. And, is there a number where I can reach you?"

"Sure." Lopez pulled a business card out of his inner coat pocket.

Uncle George pocketed the card and stood up. "I'm glad I had a chance to see you again, Valerie, even though the circumstances are regrettable." He held out his hand and I shook it. His grip was surprisingly firm. He didn't offer to shake hands with Lopez, just gave him the briefest nod and headed out the door.

I started to stand up, too, but Lopez put his hand up, palm out until the door closed on Uncle George's departing back. "Wait a sec, would you?"

I sank back into my chair. "I'm going to get my stuff back today, aren't I? My belongings?"

"Sure. Just give me another minute, okay?" He turned to Inspector Springer. "What did you turn up?"

She pulled out a notebook and opened it. "He was on the passenger list for United flight 662 which arrived at eight this morning. Booked into the Four Seasons. We have a query in to the Cleveland PD. Haven't heard back yet."

Lopez turned to me. "You know him. What's your take on the guy? What does he want?"

I shrugged. "I know what you know. I assume you were watching and listening after you left me in here to do your work for you," I gestured toward the two-way mirror. "If you'd waited a few more minutes, he might've told me why he's been trying to find her."

"You're right. I jumped the gun there. I just wanted to see what he was going to show you. Afraid he'd put it away before I'd get a look at it. But you know the guy from when you were a kid. So, what's he like? What's your best guess about what he's up to?"

"He's just what he looks like. Elizabeth always targeted men like him. Older. Not overly attractive. A little socially challenged but wealthy. Widowed and no children. His wife arranged all their social life, and he just had to show up. When she died, there went his social circle, until Elizabeth managed an accidental meeting, and suddenly he'd found the cure for loneliness and the fountain of youth all in one easy-to-swallow pill."

"Okay. That was then. What about now?"

I shrugged. "I already told you—I have no idea. Can I have my things now?"

"Sure, sure," Lopez said without making a move to stand up. "Just one more thing. Hunsinger said something about your trying to knock him down. You had to be pretty young. What was that about?"

"One of Elizabeth's 'husbands' coached kids in boxing at a local gym. Everyone called him Rocky. When some kids at school beat me up, he taught me how to fight. He said I was a natural. He was a really great guy." My voice got husky. I stood up abruptly. I often thought about Uncle Rocky, the only one of my many uncles who really deserved the title, but I hadn't talked to anyone about him since Aunt June had died. "Where do I go to get my gear?"

"Inspector Springer will take you there."

"Sure, I'll help you with that," she said. "But could you finish the story first? Why did you try to knock this Hunsinger down? What did he do?"

"Nothing. I was just demonstrating my boxing prowess, because I was proud of it. I expected him to spar with me, the way Uncle Rocky did."

"You were a little kid and hit him with your fists? I thought he meant that you brained him with something," Springer said.

"He didn't want to admit it, but I actually flattened him with one punch. He has a glass jaw. Went down like a felled tree."

Springer stared at me in disbelief.

Lopez spoke up. "She could slow down guys who don't have glass jaws. She's a helluva fighter. Wait till you see the recording."

Chapter Eight

Luckily for me, Lopez didn't show Springer the ghastly rerun of Dwayne killing the FBI agent. He had her take me to another floor to reclaim my gear, which of course couldn't just involve the simple act of the property officer handing me my duffle. First we had to go through the drill of verifying I was who I said I was, which involved a call to Lopez, my identification being what it was—or, in their eyes, what it wasn't. Then I endured the protracted process of going through each item and agreeing that they were giving me everything, and nothing was missing or damaged. In the end, my relief at finally regaining my worldly goods was attenuated by the embarrassment of having everything I owned, right down to my underwear, scrutinized by a stranger.

Even once I'd hoisted my duffle over my shoulder, I still couldn't simply slip away—although I nearly did. I'd just exited the building when Inspector Springer came hurrying after me, calling my name. I stopped and turned around.

"I forgot to ask you where you're staying," she said.

"Why don't I give you my cell phone number? Then you can reach me whenever, wherever. Especially if you locate Elizabeth."

She agreed that a phone number would be a good idea, jotted it down in her notebook and promised to pass it along to Lopez.

I walked to the side of the building to get out of the way of the constant flow of people going in and out. Lopez hadn't had any information about Elizabeth, but maybe Phil did by now.

And I hadn't had a chance yesterday to ask Phil about what she had on Elizabeth to coerce her into cooperating with the FBI. Or pretend she was cooperating, anyway. I had to put my duffle between my feet while I pulled out my cell phone with one hand and fished Phil's number out of my pocket with the other. She answered on the first ring with a curt "Philips here," but warmed up when she heard my voice.

"Any news of Elizabeth?" I asked.

"Sorry, no. Where are you?"

"In front of the police station. I picked up my stuff. And guess who came to town this morning? One of Elizabeth's marks from fifteen years ago. Lopez tried to grill him, but no luck. Funny coincidence, huh?"

"What? I need more details about this. Look, I'll come pick you up. There's something I want to ask you."

"Okay, what is it?"

A seconds-long pause on her side, then "I'd rather wait till I get there. I'm just a few minutes away."

I pocketed my phone. A gray-haired woman in a stained raincoat walked by swearing viciously. I pressed back against the wall, but she wasn't interested in speaking to me. Some unseen entity had invoked her wrath. Two men in suits passed in front of me, both talking at once. It took me a second to realize that they weren't talking to each other but into their cell phones.

I felt a prickling feeling on the back of my neck. I swiveled my head from left to right, scanning the immediate area. A woman across the street wearing a coat with the hood up, turned away when I looked her way. I was pretty sure she'd been staring at me. I got the barest glance at her face, but thought I'd seen her somewhere before. I closed my eyes for a second to try to picture her more clearly.

"Valerie?" Uncle George's tentative voice at my elbow.

I snapped my eyes open and turned to face him. He'd startled me, but I hoped it didn't show. "Hi again."

"I've been waiting to speak to you, but I didn't want to interrupt you while you were on the phone. I was hoping for a chance to speak to you privately." He paused, as if waiting for my reaction.

I glanced briefly across the street, but the woman in the hooded coat was gone. I returned my gaze to Uncle George's earnest face. Might as well get right to the point. "What do you want to talk about?"

"Actually, I was wondering if we could go somewhere quiet. Maybe a nice restaurant? As my guest, of course."

"Thanks, but I'm meeting someone in a few minutes. Could we talk while I'm waiting?"

"Certainly. I appreciate your sparing me some time. I've been looking for Betty for so long, and this is the closest I've ever come to finding her. I don't know if you can understand that just seeing you is a significant occurrence for me. I'd like to know more about you. What your life's like. What you're doing."

"Why do you want to find Elizabeth? I'm pretty sure that Inspector Lopez is right. She can't be prosecuted, and I doubt that there's any hope of getting your money back."

"I know that. Not that they'd provide any more assistance in recovering it now than they did in the first place. Such hopeless incompetence."

"Then why are you here?"

He gazed off into the distance for a moment. "It's difficult to explain. I loved her so much, and of course I was very angry when I found out what she'd done. I tried to track her down. Not an easy task, I'll tell you. I followed her trail and ended up locating a number of the other men she'd deceived. She's quite a chameleon. She becomes a different person with every husband."

I bit my lip but had to ask. "Did you meet Uncle Rocky?" I couldn't keep the eagerness out of my voice.

He frowned and considered. "No one by that name."

"It's not his real name, just the only one I knew him by. He used to coach kids in boxing."

"Ah, yes." Uncle George nodded his head several times. "Mr. Costello, Harold Costello. A very angry man. Extremely bitter. He particularly resented the fact that he'd been taken in by a child."

"I see," I whispered before I could stop myself. Embarrassing to sound so dismayed.

"I'm sorry, my dear. I tried to tell him that you had to have been too young to know what you were doing, but he was adamant in his feelings."

"It's only natural."

He tilted his head to one side. "Do you think so?"

I nodded. I didn't really want to pursue this line of conversation. Where was Phil, anyway?

When I didn't say anything, he went on, "For my part, I think that forgiveness is a better path. That's why I need to locate Betty."

I stared at him. "To tell her you forgive her?"

"Yes. It's an important step in the process. Do you know that there are parents who have forgiven the men who murdered their children? Seems impossible, doesn't it? But it can happen. And it's very healing. For everyone."

"Amazing." I tried to put some conviction into my voice.

"I can tell that you're skeptical. That's all right." He waved his hand as if he could manually brush away my doubt. "Many people feel that way at first. That's why I was hoping we could sit down together, perhaps over a meal, and have a quiet conversation. It would do us both good."

"You know, Mr. Hunsinger…"

"I meant it when I said that you can call me Uncle George."

"The timing isn't good right now."

"There's always time for forgiveness, Valerie. You're here. I'm here. And, Betty's here, too, isn't she? Somewhere nearby?"

"She was here, but she's probably gone now."

He did the head tilt thing again. "You wouldn't lie to me about that, would you?"

I stuck out my jaw. "I don't lie," I said slowly, giving equal stress to each word.

"Please don't take offense. It's just that it's been a long journey for me, spiritually, as well as physically. And I need to complete my journey."

Had he been this weird fifteen years ago? I probably had no basis for judging back then. I shifted my gaze to the curb. Phil had just parked in a space reserved for police cars. Uncle George turned his head and followed my gaze. "The person you're meeting?"

I backed away a step. "Yes. I have to go now. It's pretty amazing to see you again after all these years." I couldn't bring myself to say I was glad to have seen him.

He moved forward and closed the distance I'd tried to put between us. "If we can't get together now, how about later on? Where are you staying? I have a car and could pick you up."

"I'm not sure what I'm doing later on. Maybe I could call you at your hotel?"

"Certainly, that's a possibility. Although, like you, I'm not there most of the time. I know, give me your cell phone number. That way, I can call you later and see if you're free." He produced a pen and a little address book from his jacket pocket.

I hesitated. There was no way he was going to let me off the hook. How could I outright refuse? I gave him the number, while I watched Phil approach. For some reason, she'd taken her time getting out of her car. She looked different—haggard.

"Hi, Valentine." Phil flashed me her crooked grin, but let her gaze slip over to Uncle George. The way her eyes moved gave me the feeling that she was as good at noticing things as I was. "Hello," she said to Uncle George. "I'm Eugenia Philips." She held out her hand. He hesitated for a split second before shaking hands.

"This is George Hunsinger," I said by way of introduction.

"I didn't think you knew anyone in San Francisco," Phil said.

"I seem to be making friends pretty fast. But, actually Mr. Hunsinger's from Cleveland. He's here looking for Elizabeth, just like me." I turned to Uncle George. "We have to get going now." I backed away again, and this time Uncle George didn't try to keep me there.

"I'll call you later. We really have to talk. It's important," he said to me, and, ignoring Phil altogether, turned and walked away.

Phil watched him leave. He didn't look back. She looked at me and lifted an eyebrow. "You're going to tell me all about him, aren't you?"

"Sure, not that I know much. He's weird, for one thing." I followed Phil to her car. She opened the trunk, took my duffle bag from me, and dropped it inside. We moved in tandem to the two sides of the car and climbed inside.

"Weird, maybe," Phil said. "But more interesting was his reaction when he made me."

"He made you do what?" I fastened my seat belt.

She laughed. "Sorry. It's cop talk. I forget that you're not a cop or a criminal. It means he recognized that I was in law enforcement."

"Were you trying to hide it? You're parked in a cops-only parking space."

She looked at the sign. "Oh, right." She rubbed her forehead with the tips of her fingers. "I guess it doesn't matter. I'm no longer primary on the Kroy investigation, and they have a separate team tracking Eric's killer."

"You've been demoted? That's not fair. It's all Elizabeth's fault. You shouldn't have to take the blame."

"No, not demoted. Just pulled back from the front lines, because…"

I waited for her to go on.

She drew a deep breath and let it out. "I was involved—romantically involved—with Eric."

"The agent who was killed?" No wonder she looked so haggard. She was grieving. "And it's against the rules to get involved with another agent?"

"No. There's no policy against fraternization. But my boss thinks I should do research and desk work for now. He's trying to be considerate. He didn't say it specifically, but he thinks I wouldn't be as effective in the field."

"I'm really sorry."

"Thanks. I appreciate that." She started the engine.

"You said you wanted to ask me something?"

"I will in a minute. Why don't you tell me about George Hunsinger first?"

She drove, and I told her the whole story of Uncle George—from what I remembered of him in my childhood to his strange reasons for tracking down Elizabeth in the present. I'd just finished my story when Phil made a sharp left turn without signaling. Horns honked behind us. Before I could brace myself, she turned left again, drove two blocks and turned right.

"Phil? What's going on?"

"I think we're being followed." She continued straight at faster than the speed limit and rolled through a stop sign.

"Really?" I twisted around in my seat and looked out the back window. "Who is it?"

"I don't know. Two people. I couldn't see their faces."

"Why don't you let them follow and call your office? They could send some agents to follow them while they're following us, right?"

"I can't. They…" she paused. I waited her out. "Might've been my own people."

I stared at her. "Why would they follow you?"

"I think they have a hunch that I might not take myself out of the field, even though I've been ordered to."

"Are they right?"

She didn't answer me, just looked stone-faced and drove on in silence, checking her mirrors frequently. We passed through one commercial street and then it was all residential, mostly uphill. As we ascended, the houses we passed were grander and larger. The road narrowed and curved into a park-like area lined with pine trees. We ended up at the top of a hill with a view of the ocean and the Golden Gate Bridge. She parked by the side of the road and turned off the engine.

"Where are we?" I turned in my seat to get a better look at the view.

"We're at the point of my disobeying orders, but only if you agree."

"It doesn't involve lying, swearing, or fighting, does it?"

"Nope."

"Then it's fine by me. Will you get in trouble?"

"That's totally irrelevant to me at this point."

"Okay. So what are we going to do?"

"Come on, I'll show you." We got out of the car. Phil opened the trunk and took out a pair of binoculars and handed them to me. "Let's go up this way." She headed up a trail that wound among pine trees. I'd expected the sharp tang of pine, but the air smelled musty and loamy. Where the path curved, the wind had blown leaves and needles against the base of the trees. We shuffled through these drifts, and a moldy odor drifted on the breeze. We stopped at a vista point and she gestured to the houses below us that lined the cliff above the ocean. "See that big modern house?"

It was easy to spot—all glass and wood and sharp angles. It looked radically different from its staid palazzo-style neighbors. "Yes."

"That's where Bobby Kroy lives."

I lifted the binoculars to my eyes and adjusted the focus. I could see one corner of the house that jutted out at an angle. Trees and foliage blocked my view of the rest of the house. I lowered the binoculars, but kept my eyes on the house. "You're disobeying orders by showing it to me?"

"Since my cover's been blown, just being in the vicinity puts the operation at risk. But we're shielded here and I won't take you any closer. At least not on foot."

"I met Kroy, you know."

Phil grabbed me by the arm and turned me toward her. "You what? When?"

"In Las Vegas. It's how I found out where Elizabeth was. He saw me perform. You know how much I look like her. So he wanted to know who I was."

"What did you think? Or what did you notice?"

I thought for a moment. "He has a manner, a style that makes people want to be around him. Like it gives them some special cachet to be part of his entourage. He likes that. He likes that it gives him power over people."

"Anything else?"

"He's bad news—just like so many guys Elizabeth got involved with, except he has big money and social standing."

"What do you mean 'bad news?'"

I thought for a few seconds. "Criminal by nature."

"Do you think she never intended to help us with our investigation?"

"I think she used you to get access to Kroy."

"What's your best guess—has she told Kroy that we're investigating him?"

"Probably not. That's her edge. Unless telling him would give her a better edge." I lifted the binoculars and gazed at Kroy's house again. Light reflected against the broad expanse of glass. I couldn't see any part of the interior. "What's it like inside? All modern steel and glass?"

"Want to go in and see?"

I lowered the glasses and turned to look at her. "You mean we just walk up and ring the doorbell? Is that a good idea?"

Phil looked out at the ocean. "Not we, you."

I stared at her. "Why would I do that?"

"Because we need someone on the inside, someone with your particular experience and talents."

"You mean take Elizabeth's place? Cozy up to Kroy?"

"No. You'd just be looking for your mom."

"Elizabeth," I corrected her. "And when he says 'she's not here,' and closes the door in my face, then what?"

"It sounds better to call her mom. Ask him to help you find her. If that doesn't work, you'll think of something to get yourself in the door."

"You mean lie."

"You'd be playing a role. It's different."

"No, it's not."

"Look, you're a magician, right? How's that not like what I'm asking you to do?"

"Magic is not real life. It's for fun. And no one gets hurt." How could Phil think for even one minute that I'd follow in Elizabeth's footsteps?

"You wouldn't have to do anything dangerous. Just notice things. You're good at that. When does he go out? Where does he go? He might talk about it, want to brag. He's the type. Who comes to see him? He uses social occasions as a cover to do his deals. We'd put in lots of backups and fail-safes for you. You'd be completely protected, I promise."

"Don't make promises you can't deliver on."

Phil winced and lowered her gaze.

I bit my lip. That had been a low blow. "I know you'd do your best," I said, "but I'm not the person for this job."

"Don't you care that an FBI agent was killed trying to help you? Don't you want to see Dwayne brought to justice?"

"If you think Kroy had a hand in it, then what makes it so safe for me to go marching in there?"

"Actually, from the information we have, we think someone else hired Dwayne as a way of getting to Kroy. But we won't know who until we find out who he's dealing with. And who he's cutting out of deals." She looked away for a moment and turned back to face me. "Kroy is into some really bad stuff that I can't tell you about, and it's better anyway that you don't know. You have to take my word for it that lives are at stake, innocent lives. I'm just asking you to use your eyes and ears, that's all."

It seemed like an unanswerable argument. But I couldn't be the only person who could do this for them. They had to have lots of trained agents who worked undercover who'd be much better at it than I'd be. Besides, if I did this, it meant Elizabeth's trail would be completely cold by the time I was free to try to find her again.

"I can't help you."

"Can't or won't?"

"They're the same in this case. I don't run cons anymore."

"Don't be so naïve. It's not a con. It's a way of tracking down Dwayne."

There was no way I could do it, but what else could I say to convince her?

Phil must have taken my silence as partial agreement. "Look, I'll set it up that when the job's done the agency will secure a Social Security card for you, all up-and-up and legal. That's what you want isn't it?"

"No, it isn't. I want to know who I am, where I was born, what day, what year. My father's name. That's what I want. The truth about me. Can you give me that? No, you can't. And your Social Security card would be a complete lie. Maybe in your world I am naïve, but do you know that I didn't even know what a lie was until I went to live with Aunt June? In Elizabeth's world you just say whatever you want to be true for the moment, whatever serves your own interest best. I promised Aunt June that I wouldn't lie, ever. If I break that promise, I'll be just like Elizabeth. I'm sorry, I can't do it."

Phil gazed at me for a long minute, then shrugged her shoulders. "Okay." She turned and headed back toward the car. I followed her slowly. We drove back downtown in silence. I felt rotten. I liked Phil, and I was sorry that her boyfriend had been killed, but it was completely unfair of her to expect me to act against everything I believed in. I tried saying this to myself over and over again, but it didn't help. I still felt horrible. We drove back downtown in silence. I tried to apologize again, but she just brushed it off.

I had her drop me off near the loft, but not right at the front door. Probably better if she and the rest of the FBI didn't know exactly where I was staying. When I rang the bell below the small brass plate that said "i-systems," a scratchy voice came out of the intercom asking what I wanted.

"Nancy?" I said. "It's Valentine."

The door buzzed and I pushed it open. I paused by the doorway to the i-systems' office and a woman who wasn't Nancy popped her head over the top of a cubicle. "Hi, I'm Becky. Nancy told me you'd be coming in."

"Great. Thanks," I said and headed for the elevator. I could hear the screech and buzz of Mike's woodworking equipment. Good, I wouldn't have to talk to anyone. I really needed to be by myself and think. I pushed the folding metal gate open, stepped inside, closed the gate hard, the way I learned to do that morning, and pushed the button for the second floor.

The elevator began its slow progression upwards, but only briefly before it jerked to a sudden halt and the light went out. I froze and felt the dark close in on me like a living thing intent on smothering me. Dizzy and gasping for breath, I leaned on the paneled wall for support, but had to slide to the floor because my legs couldn't hold me up. Then the pain hit—a sharp and crushing pain in my chest, and I knew I was going to die.

Chapter Nine

I must have passed out. When I came to, nothing had changed. Total darkness still pressed on me with a suffocating weight. I was on the floor, slumped against the back wall of the elevator. The pain in my chest had lessened to just barely tolerable pressure. I pulled my knees tight against my chest and buried my face against them, eyes squeezed shut so I couldn't see the darkness. If I yelled and banged on the wall, would anyone hear me? No point in even thinking about it. I couldn't get enough air in my lungs to whimper, forget yelling. As soon as the thought of calling for help popped into my head, the pressure in my chest ratcheted up several notches. *Don't think. Don't think about yelling. Don't think about the dark. About being stuck here forever. Don't think about anything*—I told myself over and over and squeezed my eyes even more tightly shut.

A loud thump reverberated around me. The entire elevator car shuddered. My breath turned off altogether, and blood roared in my ears. The cable was breaking, and the car would fall any second. With me in it.

"Valentine?" Rico's voice, but faint and far away. "You okay? Valentine, answer me."

Another thump and the same vibration in the floor and wall of the car. One more minute and I'd plummet to my death.

"Valentine, it's all right." Rico, right next to me now. How had he gotten in? "Hey, come on, look at me." He tried to lift my face from my knees, but I held rigid and didn't move.

"Just look at me, please?"

I gasped for a bit of air. "Can't," I whispered. "Dark."

"No, it's not. The light's on again, and I have a flashlight. Look."

I kept my eyes squeezed shut. Didn't he know he was risking his life? "Get. Out." The pressure in my chest made it impossible to talk in anything but gasps.

"That's why I'm here—to get you out."

"You. Stupid. Cable. Break."

"The cable's fine. Dirty, but solid. A circuit blew. That's why the car stalled. I just have to reset the call button now and get us out of here."

I felt him move from my side. The elevator jolted. I hunched into a tighter ball and a sound like a whimper came out of my throat.

"Everything's going to be okay," Rico said. He sat down and wrapped his arms around me. The car jerked, but instead of plunging into freefall, it rose.

Without lifting my head, I opened my eyes a fraction. He'd told the truth. The light was on. Relief swept over me. I sagged against him, and he pulled me closer as the elevator made its sluggish progress upward. When the elevator lurched to a halt, Rico stood up and helped me to my feet. My legs felt as if they could barely hold my weight. He opened the folding gate, and I staggered past him. "Thanks. I can make it from here."

I kept my eyes averted as I headed into the loft.

"That's it? Thanks and see you?" He followed me in.

"Yes, that's it." The tremors began, as they always did, in my head and shoulders. I clenched my teeth against them. Why couldn't he just go away? I'd made enough of a spectacle of myself already.

"That's gratitude for you. I risk my life climbing up a rickety fire escape so I could get on the roof and climb down the elevator shaft. Look, I even ruined my favorite shirt."

I crossed to the sofa and sat. My legs weren't going to hold me up any longer. I wrapped my arms around my middle to force my body to keep still and gazed up at him. His face and hands were streaked with dirt. His hideous monkey and coconuts shirt was filthy and ripped along one side. "You're a m-m-mess."

"I think it's a toss-up which one of us is the bigger mess." He turned and headed toward the bedroom end of the loft. He came back with a blanket, knelt in front of me and wrapped it around my shoulders. "You've got the shakes. Better get you warm. Don't want you going into shock."

"I'll b-be okay. It g-goes away."

He gazed at me for a second, then glanced at his hands. "I'm going to wash up." He got to his feet. "Be right back." He disappeared into the bathroom.

I pulled the blanket closer. The warmth helped slow the shaking. Rico reappeared in a few minutes, face and hands scrubbed, wearing a clean shirt—purple hibiscus on a red background. He sat down next to me on the sofa.

"Good thing I keep extra shirts here. Since you showed up, I've gone through them pretty fast."

"I'm really s-s-sorry. I am g-grateful...." I wanted to say more, but couldn't get the words past my chattering teeth. I felt the pressure of tears behind my eyes. I gritted my teeth and covered my face with my hands. I wouldn't descend into self-pity now.

"Hey," Rico said softly. "I wasn't being serious." He put his arm around my shoulders and pulled me toward him. I let my head rest against the warm comfort of his chest. "There, that's better. I'm the one who should be sorry that I didn't permanently shut down that freaking machinery a long time ago. Mike just gets into his own little world back there."

"Mike? What does he have to do with the elevator?"

"The building's not wired for the machines in the back. When they're on, they suck up so much juice that running the elevator trips the circuit breakers."

"Then the computers went down too. That's not good. Are Nancy and Mike mad at me?"

"Nothing happened to the computers. They're on a separate circuit. And nobody's mad. We were just worried as hell because you didn't answer us."

"I didn't hear you."

"You didn't hear us? We were yelling our heads off."

I straightened and lifted my head. It was nice to lean on his shoulder. Too nice.

"Valentine?" He lifted a hand and stroked my cheek. "What happened in there?"

"I don't want to talk about it," I mumbled, but couldn't stop myself from tilting my face against his hand.

"Okay. You don't have to." He cradled my chin in the palm of his hand and leaned toward me.

I could have pulled away. I didn't want Rico to kiss me. Really I didn't. But right then in that breath of a moment when he paused, his lips an inch from mine, all I wanted, all I could ever want was for him to kiss me. I waited, nearly holding my breath, as his lips touched mine. Soft, caressing, giving. The prelude, the overture to something longer, deeper and fulfilling.

"What the hell is going on?" Mike demanded.

I jerked away and Rico took his hands from my face.

Mike stood in the doorway. "Becky and I have been waiting downstairs to hear if you survived being trapped in the elevator, but do you come down and tell us you're okay? No, you're up here getting ready to dive into the sack. Thanks a lot."

Rico stood up. "Watch it, Mike. It's your fault she got trapped in the first place."

"My fault?" Mike said nearly yelling. "She's the moron who got in the elevator while I was running the lathe."

"She didn't know about the circuit problem, because you didn't tell her. So who's the moron now?" Rico said, raising his voice and taking two steps closer to Mike.

"Stop yelling. Please," I said. "It was all my fault, and I'm sorry. I caused you both a lot of trouble."

Mike had drawn in a breath to continue his tirade. He let it out and gazed at me. "It's okay. I should have told you about the tricky circuits."

"You assumed I knew, that's all."

"Sorry, man, didn't mean to get into it with you," Mike said.

Rico shrugged. "No problem, we were both pretty quick to lay blame. So, hey, what do you have there?" He pointed to a Styrofoam box Mike held in one hand.

Mike looked at the box as if he'd forgotten he was carrying it. "This? It's just some takeout for Valentine. In case you're hungry?" He held it out to me.

"Thanks, I am," I lied. "Could you leave it on the counter for me?" I wasn't ready to get up from the sofa. Everything was out of balance.

"Sure, sure," Mike said and put the box on the counter that divided the kitchen from the living room. "Glad you're okay. I'm going home now before my wife forgets what I look like." He crossed to the door, turned, and said, "You coming, Rico?"

Rico gazed at me for a long moment. "You going to be all right?"

"Yes, of course. I'm perfectly fine now. Thanks again for all your help." The words came out stilted and formal, but how else could I reestablish the necessary distance between us? That kiss had to be a one-off thing, not to be repeated.

"It was my pleasure, I assure you." His words matching mine in formality, but said with a smile that gave the word "pleasure" a special emphasis.

"Rico?" Mike prompted from the doorway.

Rico didn't move. "One of us will come and get you tomorrow morning, so you don't have to ride down by yourself. Or you can call me. You have my number on speed-dial, remember?"

"Oh, right. Thanks, but I'll be fine now. Honest."

"Good," he said with a brief nod, turned and headed out the door, Mike on his heels. No sooner had the door closed than it opened again and Rico, minus Mike, strode across the room and sat down next to me. "One more thing. I don't regret kissing you. I'm not going to apologize for it, but it's not going to happen again." His eyes lingered on my mouth for a beat, then he was on his feet and out the door again.

The loft echoed emptily with the sound of the door closing behind them. I pulled the blanket tighter around my shoulders. "Good," I whispered. The last thing I needed was an entanglement with someone like Rico. Even if he took the trouble to climb down an elevator shaft to rescue me. Even if he did have incredibly soft lips and was an amazing kisser. He was trouble. Handsome, sexy-smiling, good-kissing trouble.

I spent some time sitting on the sofa lecturing myself about Rico. I finally put my head down, too tired to find my way into the bedroom. I might have dozed, or maybe just floated in twilight sleep, but my phone rang and pulled me back to full awake. What did Rico want now?

I sat up, dug the phone out of my back pocket and answered it before I could give myself the lecture about Rico being trouble. "Hello?"

"Hello, Valentine?" Not Rico. A woman. "This is Inspector O'Hara. Sorry to be calling so late, but we got a tip on your mother."

I sat upright. "You found her?"

"We think she's still in the city, staying in a motel. We're on our way now. Inspector Lopez would like you to come down here to make the identification. We don't want to pull in the wrong person."

"Sure, of course. Where is it?"

"It's the Sand Dune Motel out on the Great Highway, room sixteen. We'd send a squad car for you, but everyone's busy right now. It's one of those nights."

"That's okay. I'll take a cab."

"Can you come right away?"

"Yes. I'll leave now."

"Excellent." She hung up without saying good-bye.

I sat staring at the phone and let the news sink in. I'd found Elizabeth after all. And finally I'd know who I really was—or try to find out, anyway. I'd find some way or another to convince her to tell me. I had to.

And then it hit me. I could make it up to Phil that I hadn't gone along with her plan.

She answered on the first ring. "Philips here."

"Guess what? Lopez has found Elizabeth. He wants me to meet him and make an identification."

"Where?" she asked.

"The Sand Dune Motel, room sixteen. Thought you might like to have a chance to talk to Elizabeth yourself. I'm on my way right now."

"Lopez has probably already alerted the Bureau, since the SFPD is working jointly with them."

"If you're worried that your boss won't like you being there without an invite, just tell the truth—that I asked you to come as my friend."

"Gotcha." I could hear the grin in her voice. "I'll meet you there. Thanks for the heads-up. I appreciate it."

"Sure. No problem." I wanted to say something about being sorry for our disagreement earlier in the day, but I couldn't quite get the words out. Phil said good-bye and hung up.

I got up from the sofa and crossed to the door. My heart rate notched up. I opened the door and looked at the elevator gate across the corridor. Sweat broke out over my entire body. I stepped back into the loft and let the door swing shut. I stood still, waiting for the reaction to fade. All I had to do was open the door and get in the elevator. Nothing was going to happen to me this time. I put my hand on the doorknob, but couldn't make myself turn it.

I turned around and my eye fell on the Styrofoam box. Food—that was it. I needed to eat. I just had low blood sugar. The box held a huge Mexican dinner of enchilada, tamale, chili relleno, rice, and beans. I ate slowly and deliberately. I thought about going into the hallway and getting into the elevator, and my stomach roiled. I put the remaining food aside.

Who needed an elevator anyway? If Rico had climbed up the fire escape, I could climb down. I crossed to the tall windows at the front of the loft and gazed out. No fire escape. I hurried into the bathroom, which had the only other window—dingy safety glass with chicken wire embedded in it. It was dark on this side of the building with no street light illumination. I could just see the rusty fire escape outside, but the window frame was covered by at least eight coats of paint. I pounded the frame with my fists, then kicked it with my feet until my leg and hip ached and my ribs yelled at me to stop. It didn't budge. I kicked the glass itself. Nothing. Even if I cracked it, how would I get the wires out?

I turned around and paced the loft several times. I ended up in front of the door. This time I couldn't even make myself put my hand on the knob. I paced some more. I could do this. I had to do this.

Asking for help ranked among my least favorite things to do, but I couldn't see another choice. I picked up my phone and pushed the button that automatically dialed Rico's number and let it ring until it went to voicemail. I hung up and called Phil again. I should have asked her to come get me when I'd called her. No answer there either. Maybe that woman, what was her name, Becky? Maybe she was still downstairs. I called information and asked for i-systems, but there was nothing listed in the directory. If it had been a regular phone, I would've slammed it down. Just touching the end call icon on the screen provided no satisfaction at all. I went back into the bathroom and kicked the window again and again. A few small cracks radiated out from the point of impact, but the window itself didn't give.

Okay. I had no choice but the elevator, and when I got out of here, there was no way I'd come back, so I needed to get ready. I went through the contents of my duffle, took everything out, refolded and repacked it.

Stop wasting time!

I took a shower and changed my clothes. Then I had to pack my duffle again.

You're a useless coward.

I sat and rehearsed what I planned say to Elizabeth.

Now get up and go, I told myself. *Go now.* I picked up my duffle, opened the door and felt so light-headed I had to hang onto the door frame. The faintness passed once I was inside the loft again with the door closed.

I'd wasted so much time, they'd all probably left and taken Elizabeth with them.

I can't do it.

Pull up your socks, Sister, Aunt June said—as if she were right by me and spoken the words out loud.

And she had said it out loud, standing in the chicken coop after the coyote had slaughtered five of our seven hens. I stood next to her, staring at the carnage of bloody feathers and crying. By lantern light, I'd helped her shovel out the remains, bury them, and wash down the roosts. I sobbed over the white-and-black speckled feathers of my favorite hen, but I'd done what had to be done.

Pull up your socks, Sister. Her words for facing something awful that had to be faced. She said it only when she knew I could deal with a situation, no matter how I felt. Like the savaged chickens. Like Aunt June herself, pale and shrunken and about to slip off to her forever sleep. I'd held her hand and sat with her until the end. And what could be worse than that?

Shaking and sweating, I exited the apartment and pulled the metal gate open. I moved slowly into the elevator, but didn't let myself stop, even when vertigo nearly felled me. I pulled the gate closed and pushed the button for the first floor. Eyes tightly shut, I pressed against the wall of the elevator car. When the car jolted to a halt I hurried too fast to open the gate and the handle slipped from my sweaty grasp. I wiped my hands on my jeans and tried again. This time the gate opened and I staggered out. I slipped by the open door of the i-systems office and out the glass front doors. I had to walk two blocks before I could flag down a taxi. I gave him the motel name and address and sat in the back of the taxi, hugging my duffle to my chest and staring into space until the driver pulled to the curb.

"This okay?" the driver asked. "I can't get any closer."

I looked out the window. Two police cars, lights flashing, blocked the motel's driveway. "This is fine." I handed him his money and got out of the cab.

I didn't see Lopez. He was probably in the room talking to Elizabeth. I glanced up at the buzzing neon sign above the motel office. The first and last letters were out, so it read "_and Dune Mote_." Elizabeth would stay in a place like this only if she needed to hide out and couldn't leave town. She must be pretty desperate.

I started to walk past the cop cars, but a uniformed officer stopped me. "It's okay," I said. "Inspector Lopez asked me to come."

"I don't think so. We just put in the call to the squad. Plainclothes aren't even here yet."

"Yes, they are. Inspector O'Hara said they would wait until I got here so I could identify Elizabeth."

"Well, no one told me," he said. He turned and waved to another uniformed officer who crossed toward us. "Would you escort her to the scene? She's here to make the identification." The cop nodded and asked me to follow him.

Something wasn't right. "What scene?" I asked, hurrying after him around the back of the motel office. That's when I saw the yellow crime scene tape. I ducked under the tape and ran toward the door of room sixteen. A third cop put out an arm and barred my way.

"We're not supposed to let anyone in until the ME gets here."

"Yeah," my escort said, "but homicide asked her to ID the body."

"What body?" I almost asked. But of course I knew. I was too late. Someone had gotten to Elizabeth after all. Regret tugged at the edges of my mind. For the mother who'd never been a mother. For the lost chance to know who I was.

"Okay," the cop at the door said. "Sure you're up for this? It's not pretty."

"Yes," I said. It couldn't be any worse than the poor FBI agent who'd been killed the day before.

He stood aside to let me move forward. "You can look from the doorway, but don't step inside."

I moved to the spot he indicated, gazed at the horror in the room and screamed.

Phil lay sprawled on the carpet, her head in a pool of blood, the fingers of both hands grotesquely twisted, and rows of cigarette burns marched up both arms.

Chapter Ten

A uniformed cop drove me to the police station and handed me over to an officer who put me in the same interview room I'd been in the day before. He had me take the seat Uncle George had sat in—the one facing the two-way mirror. He brought me coffee without asking whether I wanted any. Or maybe he'd asked and I hadn't heard him. I had trouble hearing anything but my own screams echoing in my head. I wrapped my hands around the paper cup just to feel some warmth and tried to make my mind a blank. My hands liked the heat but my head kept replaying images of Phil's tortured body.

The coffee grew cold, and I shoved my hands into my pockets and huddled down into my coat. The room was warm enough, but a chill had formed at the core of my body. If only I hadn't called Phil. If only I'd gone to the motel right away. If only I'd called Lopez back to see if the call was legit. If only…I could go on for hours with the if onlys, but it all came back to one thing—everything was my fault. My own stupid fault, because I couldn't get in an elevator like a normal person.

Lopez came into the room and sat down across from me at the table. "How you doing?"

I opened my mouth to speak, but my throat closed up and I felt tears burning my eyes, so I settled for just nodding.

He reached over the table and took my coffee cup. "You're not drinking this, are you?"

I shook my head.

"I'll be right back." He left carrying my cup with him.

I straightened in my chair and rubbed my eyes until the tears retreated. No point in losing it and embarrassing myself in front of Lopez.

Lopez came back and put a steaming cup of tea and a plate of doughnuts in front of me. "You don't look so good. Sugar and caffeine will help." He pulled some sugar packets out his pocket and tossed them on the table. "Put that in the tea."

I wrinkled my nose.

"Or I could take you to the ER and have the docs check you out for shock."

I tore open a packet of sugar and dumped it in the tea. Lopez nodded approvingly and nudged the plate of doughnuts closer to me. He waited for me to stir my tea, take a sip and bite into a glazed doughnut. "Helluva thing you saw."

I nodded and continued to chew the doughnut.

He pulled a notepad and pen from his coat pocket and flipped open the pad to a clean page. "So you told the officer at the scene that I'd called you and told you to meet me there?"

"Inspector O'Hara. Someone who said she was Inspector O'Hara gave me a message that you'd found Elizabeth and wanted me to identify her because you weren't absolutely sure it was Elizabeth."

"Did this O'Hara sound familiar to you?"

"You mean, did she sound like Elizabeth? I don't think so."

"We have two O'Hara's. Neither one's female or an inspector."

"No kidding," I said, leaning on the sarcasm. "Look, I know I was set up."

"So you think they called because they wanted you to be the one to find Agent Philips' body?"

"No." I dropped the half-eaten doughnut back onto the plate. "I was the one they wanted to hurt, to kill. I called Phil and told her, then I...was delayed, so she got there before me."

"Any idea who'd want to kill you?"

"Dwayne, of course. I'm an eyewitness, right? And he didn't know that they'd recorded him at Elizabeth's."

"So who's the woman?"

"How should I know?" I said, my voice rising. "All I know is that it was supposed to be me, not Phil. They called me, and she's the one who ended up all…" My throat closed up and I broke off.

Lopez nudged the tea closer to me. "Take a couple of breaths and drink some more tea."

I did as he said. In a few moments I was able to talk again. "You saw what they did to her? Her fingers? And those burns? Elizabeth might have had something to do with it."

"What makes you think that?"

"The cigarette burns." I paused. "That's something she used to do to me when I was….uncooperative."

"Jesus," Lopez muttered.

"What I'm trying to work out is who called me. I just got that cell phone today. Or I guess now it's yesterday. I gave my number to Inspector Springer, to Phil, and to Uncle George."

"Uncle George who was in here yesterday asking more questions than he answered?"

I nodded.

"We had him checked out. He came into town yesterday like he said. Checked in to his hotel alone, but we don't know what he did after he left here. I'll get someone to check his alibi for tonight." He made a note on his pad. "So they're the only ones who had your number?"

I hesitated. "Except for the guy who gave me the phone. His name's Rico. I don't know his last name, but I have his cell phone number. It's on speed-dial." My hand shook as I pulled out my phone and handed it over to Lopez. I didn't realize how much I didn't want to think that Rico might be involved until I'd said his name.

Lopez took the phone, checked the number and jotted it down in his notebook. "So this guy's local? Not from Vegas?"

"He's the taxi driver who picked me up from Elizabeth's apartment. Only I'm pretty sure taxi driving's not his regular job. He's kind of an entrepreneur. I think he might be…connected."

Lopez gave me a steady look. "Connected," he echoed. "You mean like organized crime-connected? And how do you know anything about that?"

"When Elizabeth wasn't conning nice men out of their life savings, she tended to hook up with that kind of guy. Since then I've worked in casinos in Miami, Atlantic City, and Vegas, and I've seen the type, overheard some of their talk."

"Anything more than overheard talk? Did you do something to make someone mad? Get on their wrong side?"

"No. Nothing."

Three loud raps on the mirrored wall made me jump. "Who's that?"

"That would be the FBI."

I lifted my gaze to the mirrored wall, staring at it as if I could see the faces behind it staring back at me.

Lopez pushed back from the table and stood up. "Drink your tea and eat another doughnut."

I made a face.

"Just do it. It'll help you keep it together. I'll get you some real food as soon as I can." And he was out the door.

I did as Lopez ordered, and he was right. The caffeine and sugar helped me feel less shaky—until he came back into the room with Special Agent in Charge Williams and two other agents. Lopez and Williams sat across from me but the two agents remained standing behind them. If Williams had intended to intimidate me, he'd succeeded. It wasn't just the feeling of being in front of a military tribunal that made me want to shrink back into my chair, it was also Williams' demeanor. Even before he asked his first question, he conveyed profound skepticism, as if no matter what I told him, he wouldn't believe me.

Williams folded his hands on the table. "Now, Valentine, you met mobsters in various casinos. Give me names, dates, and places."

"I didn't meet them. I just saw them and overheard bits of conversation."

Williams leaned forward. "Two highly decorated federal agents have been killed. So, don't waste my time. Names, dates, places, and what you overheard."

I closed my eyes and retraced my steps over the years since Aunt June died. I didn't need to close my eyes so I could remember, I just needed to shut out the somber, skeptical gazes of the four men in front of me. I gave them a detailed account of my travels, where I worked, who I worked for, and descriptions of everyone I'd guessed had mob connections. When I opened my eyes, no one had moved or changed. "Aren't you going to write any of this down?"

Without taking his eyes from my face, Williams pointed to a wall-mounted camera behind him. I hadn't noticed it—testament, if I needed it, to how upset and distracted I was.

Williams wasn't done. He made me repeat everything I'd already told Lopez. When I reached the end of my narrative, he narrowed his eyes at me. "The part that puzzles me, Valentine, is that you called Special Agent Philips and agreed to meet her at the motel, but you didn't, because in your words, you were delayed. So you didn't get to the motel until nearly two hours later. Can you elaborate on this *delay?*"

I tried to give the short version—trapped in the elevator when the circuits overloaded, panic attack, inability to get back into the elevator for over an hour because of my phobia. I kept my tone neutral, nearly clinical. I didn't want to involve Rico, Mike, and Nancy. Most of all, I didn't want anyone to see how embarrassed and ashamed I was. But Williams wouldn't have it. He hammered away at me, picking apart my story, making me recount every stupid second I'd spent not getting into the elevator. I gave him every detail. I even told him I'd heard my Aunt June telling me to pull up my socks and that, in the end, was how I managed to take the elevator to the ground floor. Once I'd said Aunt June's name aloud, the tears began and I couldn't blink them away. I lowered my head onto my folded arms on the table and hid my face.

The questions stopped. I heard feet shuffling out of the room, the door closing behind them. Good. I was sick of all of them. Lopez being nice with the tea and doughnuts. Williams being mean, acting as if I knew Phil was going to be murdered.

I stayed with my head down for a long time, too exhausted to sit upright. Finally, the door opened and I lifted my head. Lopez entered, bearing a sandwich and a bottle of juice, which he placed in front of me. I eyed the food. "Softening me up again? Is Williams having too much fun being mean cop to let you have a turn?"

"There's a schedule. I get every other Thursday," Lopez deadpanned.

"I'll make a note on my calendar." We exchanged wry smiles, and I pulled the sandwich closer. "You're giving me food. Does that mean I have to stay here?"

"Nope. We're not going to keep you here. We just need to get you some place where you'll be safe."

"I'll be okay."

"That's the plan—for you to be okay staying in a hotel on the city's dime."

I could tell that he wouldn't listen to any objections I might have. "Okay, I'll stay in a hotel."

"And you'll have to keep a low profile."

I nodded, which Lopez took as my agreement as I'd intended.

A woman officer drove me to the Pacific Arms and checked me in. It wasn't the Hilton, but the room was clean. It was morning, but I needed some rest. So I set the alarm, stripped off my clothes, and slipped between the covers. I fell straight to sleep. When the alarm went off it took me a bit to remember where I was. I washed my face and hands and dressed. With my duffle on my shoulder, I took the stairs to the lobby and went into the hotel's coffee shop. Lopez or Williams might've left someone to watch me, so I went through the kitchen and exited through the back door. I flagged a taxi and gave him the address of the place I knew I'd have to go from the moment I saw Phil's broken body.

>>>

Ashley Kroy didn't answer the door as I'd hoped, but neither did Bobby Kroy, as I'd dreaded. A heavily built Asian man in a white shirt with black pants and tie opened the door and stood silently waiting for me to state my business.

"Hi, I'm Valentine Hill. I'm a friend of Ashley's. Is she home?"

His gaze drifted from my face to the duffle slung on my shoulder. "Wait one moment," he said and closed the door in my face.

I shifted from one foot to the other while I waited. I'd ask Ashley to intercede with her dad to help me find Elizabeth. I was pretty sure I could get Ashley to ask me to stay with her. If Ashley wasn't there, I'd have to ask Kroy directly for help. It wouldn't be quite as easy to get an invitation to stay, but I'd wangle it. And if Kroy wasn't there, I'd improvise as needed. I'd do anything necessary to get in the door. Phil had wanted me inside, so that's where I was going to be.

Bobby Kroy opened the door and did an exaggerated double take. "By God, it's the Great Valentina materialized as if by magic on my very doorstep. Connie said that you're looking for Ash? Come in. Come in." He stood aside, and I crossed into the marble-floored foyer. "Ash," Kroy yelled in the general direction of the stairs. "Show your face. You have company."

The house's interior matched the exterior—modern and impressive. The two-story-high circular foyer was bigger than some apartments I'd lived in. The staircase's treads jutted out from the curved wall and gave the illusion of floating in space.

Kroy turned to face me. "She'll be right down. Come into the living room." He strode ahead of me through a wide door-way to an expansive room. My feet sank into the thick white carpet. I'd expected the glass and chrome tables, but not the cushy white sofas and chairs clustered in different sections of the room. Except for the blue ocean and sky that dominated the view from the ceiling-high windows, the only color in the entire room came from large abstract paintings that covered all available wall space. I crossed to the nearest and gazed at it.

"Diebenkorn," Kroy said as if I'd asked.

"Wow," I breathed. I didn't have a clue who Diebenkorn was, but I knew how to play on vanity.

Kroy chuckled and looked pleased with himself.

"Don't you worry about burglars?"

"State of the art system throughout the entire house and property." He spread his arms in an expansive gesture. "No one comes near without my people knowing."

The security system was something I wanted to know more about, but I heard the click-click of high heels on the foyer marble. I turned, expecting to see Ashley.

Elizabeth came through the open doorway. She looked good, almost better than she had when I'd seen her nine years ago. Still slim, blond with a face unmarked by lines or sag. She stopped, frozen, her hands to her cheeks, her eyes wide. "Valentine!" she breathed. Her eyes rolled back in her head and she collapsed onto the carpet.

"Beth, what the hell?" Kroy crossed the room and knelt by Elizabeth's unconscious form.

What was I going to do now? Just when I didn't want to find Elizabeth, she shows up. Could I convincingly fake a sentimental reunion with Elizabeth? Never. I'd have to play it the other way. Sticking close to the truth was always the best way to lie anyway. "Hi, Elizabeth. Nice to see you, too."

Kroy lifted his head and gave me an assessing look.

I kept my gaze neutral.

Ashley appeared in the doorway and stared wide-eyed at the scene of her father kneeling by Elizabeth's body. "Dad, what happened?"

"Damned if I know. She took one look at Valentine and passed out."

"Hey, Ashley," I said. "How's it going?" I crossed the room and stepped over Elizabeth's unconscious form to reach Ashley. Kroy and Ashley stared at me. "Oh, don't worry about Elizabeth. She can faint any time she wants. It buys her time when she's in a tricky situation."

"For real?"

"Fake for real." I grinned. She grinned back. She still wore her full anime getup, but her sticking-out hair was brown not purple, and her makeup was subdued. "What happened to your hair?"

"I got tired of it." She darted a look in Kroy's direction.

"Looks good."

"Thanks, I guess."

Elizabeth opened her eyes. "What happened?" she said weakly. She gazed at Kroy who helped her to her feet.

"That's what I'd like to know," he said.

"Valentine, it's really you," she said. Clearly she didn't want to deal with Kroy's implied question.

"Surprise." I said. "It's been awhile, hasn't it?"

"Well, don't I get a hug?" She opened her arms.

"If you want," I said with as little enthusiasm as possible and didn't move. She crossed to me and I submitted to her embrace. She squeezed too tightly around my broken rib. "Ouch." I pulled away. She kept her hands on my shoulders and looked me up and down. "I can't believe it. My little girl is all grown up."

I rolled my eyes. "Staying a little girl wasn't an option. Just like being 'all grown up' wasn't an option when I was a little girl. Remember we had that discussion the last time I saw you—nine years ago?"

Elizabeth dropped her hands from my shoulders. Tears swelled up in her eyes and spilled down her cheeks. She turned to Kroy. "She still blames me for so many things. I tried to be a good mother, but I was young and on my own, and I made mistakes." she said, her voice breaking.

"Kids," Kroy said. "What are you going to do? You can't live with them, and you can't kill them."

"Bobby!" Elizabeth gave him a playful push. "You just love to shock everyone, don't you?"

"What I want to know is why are we all standing around? Let's have a drink. What sounds good to you?" he asked me. "White wine? Or mixed drink? What's that drink the young crowd likes now?" He turned and yelled, "Connie!"

The Asian man appeared immediately. Had he been standing just out of sight the whole time?

"Connie, what's that drink the kids like? Has mint in it?"

"A mojito."

"That's right. Mojitos all around. Not for Ash, of course. What would you like, Ash?"

"I'd like to show Valentine my room. I mean, you said you came to see me, didn't you?"

"Yes, I did," I said. "But the funny thing is that I came to ask for help in finding Elizabeth."

"The funny thing," Kroy said, "is that she's right here and you don't seem all that happy to see her."

I shrugged. "There's a difference between being glad I found her and happy to see her. Right, Elizabeth?"

"I don't know what you mean. I'm certainly happy to see you. But how in the world did you know to come here to see Ashley and Bobby?"

I stopped myself from glancing at Kroy. He hadn't told Elizabeth that they'd seen me in Vegas. Interesting. "Ashley saw me doing my street gig," I said before Ashley could chime in, "and asked me if I was related to you, because we look so much alike. I went to your apartment, but you weren't there. I found a dead guy instead."

Elizabeth's hand went to her throat. "See, Bobby, I told you. Someone is after me."

Kroy put his arm around Elizabeth's shoulder. "Come on, Beth. Don't worry. No one's going to hurt you now. Where are our drinks? Connie, what's the hold up?" he yelled and guided Elizabeth to a seat in the living room. "Come on, girls. Sit down." Ashley and I followed them into the living room. I sat near Elizabeth and Kroy, but Ashley slid into a chair off to one side.

Connie appeared bearing a huge tray laden with the requested mojitos, and also ice, soft drinks, bottles of imported water and three kinds of appetizers. He unloaded the tray onto the coffee table in front of Elizabeth, and handed drinks around. "No, thanks," I said when he offered me the mojito. "Just water, please."

"Cheers," Kroy said, took a sip of his drink and made a face. "You like this crap?" he asked Elizabeth.

"I do," she said.

"You women will drink anything. Connie, get me a real drink." He handed the glass to Connie with one hand and picked up a large shrimp from the appetizer platter with another. I sipped my water and watched him chew. "Have one of these." He gestured to the tray. "Ash, you too. Eat something."

"No, thanks. I had a big lunch."

He looked at her straight on. "Eat something," he ordered and snagged another shrimp for himself.

"I'm really not hungry," she said.

"Goddamn it, Ash!" His face turned red and veins popped out on his forehead.

"Dad, please, take the blue pill," Ashley said, but got up and crossed to the coffee table. She picked up a large napkin and put one of each kind of appetizer on it while Kroy watched.

He watched until she sat down again and took a bite. "That's my girl. None of that anorexic crap for us, right?"

I focused on a point midway between Kroy and Ashley so I could see them both in my peripheral vision. Ashley stopped eating after Kroy switched his attention back to the platters in front of him and popped another shrimp in his mouth. Some kind of suppressed tension emanated from Ashley, but Kroy seemed oblivious to it.

So, Miss Magic," Kroy said fixing me with his gaze, "tell me, how did you know where I live? Are you a psychic as well as a magician? I'm not listed in the phone book."

"Come on, Mr. Kroy. You're a public figure. Everyone knows you live in the huge modern house in Seacliff."

"Who's everyone?"

"The concierge at that big hotel next to the cable car tracks for one."

"The Saint Francis?"

"I don't know the name of it."

"But you were staying there?"

"He thought I was."

Connie returned with Kroy's "real" drink—a martini with two olives. Kroy took a sip and smacked his lips. "That's more like it. Okay, you've found your mother. So what now?"

I leaned forward and put my glass on the coffee table. "Now we have a little chat. In private," I added. "Then I'm on my way."

"Where to? Leaving town?"

"No, I like San Francisco. I think I'll stick around for awhile."

"Where will you stay?"

"Hotel."

"You have money?" he asked in tone that implied he didn't think I did.

"Thank you for the refreshments, Mr. Kroy." I stood up and addressed Elizabeth. "Can I talk to you for a minute?"

"So you're going to ask your mother for money? Is that it?"

"No," I said without looking at him. "Elizabeth?"

"You can talk in front of Bobby and Ashley," Elizabeth said.

"It's personal."

"We think it's best not to have secrets from each other." She reached over to squeeze Kroy's hand.

"If you say so," I said and crossed to the doorway. I turned briefly and waved to Ashley. "See you sometime, maybe?"

She looked surprised and slid her gaze to Kroy, as if expecting him to react. Good. I expected it, too. Or hoped, anyway. Gambling for sure on the fact that he always had to be in control. Or believe he was.

I crossed into the foyer. My duffle had disappeared. I returned to the doorway. "I think your," I paused, "um, butler put my bag somewhere."

"Connie," he yelled.

Connie appeared. He must never go very far away to show up so quickly. Didn't Kroy know that he didn't have to shout to get Connie's attention?

"What did you do with Miss Magic's bag?"

"Put it in the room next to Ashley's."

Kroy barked a laugh. "There you go. Connie's not my butler. He's my oracle, and Connie has spoken. He's decided you're going to stay with us."

"Yes!" Ashley said, jumping to her feet. "Thanks, Dad."

Kroy waved her away. "Don't thank me. Thank Connie."

"It's very nice of you to offer," I said, "but…"

Ashley crossed the room and grabbed me by the arm. "Stay, please, Valentine," she pleaded.

"Elizabeth?" I asked, looking at her.

"Of course, you'll stay," she said in her I'm-so-sincere voice. "You and I have to catch up on everything, and this is our chance. Thank you, Bobby. It means so much to me to see my little girl again."

"See?" Ashley said. "Come on, I'll show you your room." She led the way upstairs.

I let out a slow breath as I followed her. My bluff had worked. *I did it, Phil. I'm in.*

Chapter Eleven

I followed Ashley upstairs. I had no idea how I was going play this, but if I wanted information on the household, it wouldn't be a bad thing to have Ashley on my side. Knowing Kroy had a short fuse when it came to Ashley might help.

At the top of the stairs Ashley turned right and led me down a wide hall. She pointed without pausing to a closed door. "This is my room. Yours is the next one down." She continued to the next room. The door stood open and she walked in ahead of me.

"Wow." I took in the large bed, chaise lounge and sliding doors that led to a balcony. Like the downstairs, walls, carpet, and furniture were all white. "It's very…white."

"Yeah. Boring." Ashley plopped down on the foot of the bed. "My room's just like this one. I wanted to paint the walls, but…." Her voice trailed off.

"But your dad's decorator has a thing for white. There's always the artworks." I nodded toward the large painting over the bed that featured wide bands of primary colors. "If you like that sort of thing."

Ashley made a face.

I heard a high-pitched sound. Ashley reached into her pocket, pulled out a cell phone, and checked the read out.

"That was your phone ringing?"

"Pretty cool, huh?" She kept her eyes on her phone.

"Well it's different anyway," I said, trying to be diplomatic.

She glanced up at me briefly. "We can hear it, but old people can't."

"You mean like your dad?"

"Yeah. Anyone over thirty."

"And you don't want your dad to know you're getting phone calls?"

She shrugged. "He gets kind of nosy about it. I like my privacy." She continued to stare at her phone.

"Aren't you going to answer it?"

She looked at me and frowned. "I am answering it. I'm texting. You know what that is, don't you?"

"Sure. Just never had much reason to do it."

"Not even in high school?'

"I didn't go to school. My aunt taught me at home."

"Why?"

"My mom's a major screw-up is why. Know what I mean?" It was a stab in the dark, but I wanted to find some common ground with her.

"Oh yeah, I know what you mean." She returned her gaze to her phone, tapping out a message.

"Maybe we could text each other?" I asked.

"Sure. Give me your number and I'll send you a message."

I gave Ashley my number, and pulled my phone out of my pocket waiting for the ring, but nothing happened. I pushed the on button, but the screen remained blank. "It's not working."

"When's the last time you charged it?"

"Oh, right. I have a charger right here." I dug through my duffle and came up with the wire with a plug on the end that Rico had given me along with the phone.

Ashley took it out of my hands, attached the phone to one end and plugged the other into an electrical outlet. The phone lit up and beeped. "See? That was it."

I heard two light taps on the open door and turned around. Elizabeth stood in the doorway. "Sorry to interrupt. Ashley, I'd love to have a few minutes alone with my daughter."

"Okay." She stood up. "Hit me back later, okay?"

"Sure," I said, assuming she meant come by her room.

She left the room and Elizabeth closed the door after her. "Just so we can have a little privacy."

"Whatever." I crossed to the chaise and sat down, leaving Elizabeth to sit on the bed or stand.

She remained standing. "What do you want?"

I took my time and inspected her top to bottom. "You're looking good. Kept your figure. And had a little work done around the jowls, the eyes?"

"I don't need plastic surgery. I take care of myself. Always have. It's paid off."

"Uh-huh." I let the disbelief seep into my voice.

She pressed her lips together. "I asked you a question."

"Yes, you did. Let's see, what do I want?" I tilted my head back and gazed at the ceiling. "What I wanted was for you to be long gone. Which I thought you were, since you left me, as usual, holding the bag. Your friend Dwayne beat the shit out of me and then killed the guy who came to help me."

"I don't believe you."

I stood, pulled my sweater up and turned around so she could get a good view of all my bruises, which were now turning into a rainbow of colors. I pulled my sweater down and took my seat on the chaise again. "I know you read about the murder in the papers or saw it on the news since you told Kroy your life was in danger."

"All right, I heard about the murder, but I never saw Dwayne before in my life. So stop playing games and answer my question." She folded her arms across her chest. "What do you want?"

"In a word? In. I want in."

"In? That's it? Well, you made it. You're in the house, in a guest bedroom."

"Now who's playing games? I want in on the con."

"Well, you've changed your tune haven't you? What happened to Miss Priss, who couldn't tell a lie? Did you finally get tired of living with that old hag, June? Last time I saw you—what is it now—nine years ago, you wouldn't come with me. Said you wanted to stay with her forever. I couldn't believe it. Thought you'd be fed up with living in the sticks."

I looked down at my hands as if inspecting my non-existent manicure. "She got tired of me, actually. The bitch threw me out."

That got a smile out of Elizabeth. "I can believe that. You could be a real brat."

"Let's not get into character attacks. You'll lose that competition. So, what about it? Are you going to tell me what you're planning, or…"

"Or what?"

"Or I might have to have a little conversation with Kroy."

"That would be pointless. He already knows all about me."

"All about you? Really? Even that you're in bed with the FBI?"

"That's a lie! You're just making things up to get back at me." She paced to the balcony window and back again.

I laughed. "Why should I lie when the truth is beyond anything I could make up? I have to admit I was pretty surprised. Elizabeth Hill a snitch? Unimaginable—well, almost anyway. But when my new best friend who's a homicide inspector tried to find out about you, he ran into a brick wall. Your sheet—all your arrests, convictions, even your fingerprints were blocked by the FBI. And do you know who that guy was—the one who tried to help me and got shot in the head for his trouble? An FBI agent. But what I want to know is why you let them kill Phil."

Elizabeth stopped her pacing and sank slowly down onto the bed. "Phil's dead? When?" She seemed truly shocked, but then I had to remember she was an excellent actress.

"Last night. They tortured her first. She had burns on her arms just like the ones you gave me."

"You can't think I had anything to do with it."

"It doesn't matter what I think. It's what the police and the FBI think that you should worry about. They know the killers lured her to a motel by telling her you were hiding out there. So you," I went on, "are in some really deep shit." That made the third time I'd sworn in the last few minutes. Funny that I could do it so naturally. Didn't pause or stammer. I'd already lied like I did it every day, and now swearing came off just as easily. All that was left for me to do was start a fight and I'd be three for three.

"Did you talk to the FBI?"

"I wouldn't describe it so much as talking to as being inter-rogated by the FBI. They want you, of course. Now that I know where you are, I may have to pass that information on, unless you decide to include me in your plans."

"It's not really up to me."

"Elizabeth, it's me, Valentine, remember? I know your MO. Whatever you're into with Kroy, I know you have your own scam in place, or at the very least a backup plan." She didn't say anything. I sat in silence for a minute, then said, "I don't expect to be let in for free. I can make a contribution. I'm good, you know, probably better than you ever were." I rose from the chaise and crossed to the door. "Why don't you think about it and give me your answer later on tonight?" I opened the door.

She stood up and gazed at me for a few moments as if she'd never seen me before. "Dinner's at seven," she said and walked out the door.

Ashley must have been listening for Elizabeth to leave because she appeared in my doorway seconds after Elizabeth left. "What happened? Beth didn't look too happy."

"We have some stuff to work out, that's all. Could you do me a favor? Would you mind showing me around? I've never been in such a big house."

"Sure," she said. "Come on." I followed her out into the hall. "There are four bedrooms at this end, but you and I are the only ones here for now. Sometimes Dad has company and people stay here. If you turn left instead of right at the top of the stairs that's the way to Dad's room and a couple more guest rooms."

"Is that where Elizabeth is staying, down the hall?" I asked.

"Yeah, but in her own room."

"So that's this floor. What about downstairs?"

"Follow me, I'll show you a secret staircase." She pressed a panel at the end of the hall. It swung open and revealed stairs.

"Not really secret, I guess, except that I didn't know it was there at first and was really surprised when Connie or Miss Carmel Candy would show up all of the sudden."

"Okay, I have to ask—why is his name Connie and who is Miss Carmel Candy? Is that something like Miss America?"

Ashley giggled. "Dad gives people names. Connie is short for Confucius, which isn't really his name either. But Dad says he's really wise like Confucius was."

"Is he?"

"Dunno. He doesn't talk much." She led the way down the stairs.

"He looks more like a wrestler than a butler," I said.

"He doesn't do butler-type stuff for anyone but Dad. If I ask him for something, he just ignores me." She paused a moment before going on. "He's like a bodyguard."

"Excuse me for being nosy, but why does your dad need a bodyguard?"

Ashley paused on the stairs and looked back at me. "He told me he's had death threats, but don't know who or why. I just came to live with my dad a couple of months ago. I'm still figuring stuff out."

The door at the bottom of the stairs opened into a kitchen just as vast and modern as the rest of the house. A middle-aged Latina paused in dicing tomatoes and looked up at us.

"Carmela," Ashley said, "this is Beth's daughter, Valentine. She's going to be staying with us for awhile."

"Nice to meet you," I said.

She gave me a brief unsmiling glance and returned to chopping tomatoes.

I looked at Ashley and raised my eyebrows. She gave a little shake of her head as if to warn me not to pursue the conversation.

I crossed to a door. "Where does this go?" I opened the door without waiting for a reply and took in the garage that held three large shiny and expensive cars. Behind me, Carmela gave a disapproving sniff.

"Does the garage go to the back garden?" I needed to know all the escape routes.

"No, just the side yard," she said. "To get to the back you have to go this way." She crossed to another door and opened it. I followed her and pointedly ignored the sour look Carmela gave me.

We passed into a hallway. I closed the door to the kitchen behind me. "That's Miss Carmel Candy? She sure is sweet—not," I whispered conspiratorially.

Ashley giggled. "Isn't she awful? She won't let me get anything out of the kitchen if she's in there. Dad says she cooks like a dream and that's all that matters."

The doorway directly opposite led to the dining room. The long table could seat twelve easily and sixteen if everyone was friendly.

"If you go that way," she pointed to my right, "you'll end up in the front hall. The other way goes to my dad's study, but don't go in there," she warned me. "He gets upset if anyone goes into his study."

"Even Elizabeth?"

Ashley made a face. "No, sometimes she goes in there, but he yelled at me when I did."

"Sounds like he's not used to having you around yet."

She shrugged. "Yeah, right."

I heard anger and disappointment behind her words. Time to change the subject. "Can I see your room? It's this way to the main staircase, right?" I headed down the hall with Ashley right next to me.

At the end of the hall just before it opened up into the huge foyer were two doors opposite each other. I opened one and found a row of coats. "Oops, not this way." I crossed to the other door. Ashley put out a hand as if to stop me, but I was too fast for her and pulled the door open. Connie sat, newspaper in hand, in the cramped quarters of a small windowless room, in front of a bank of screens, each one displaying a different place inside or outside the house—the state of the art system Kroy had bragged about.

Connie heaved himself out of his chair. "What do you want?" he growled, fixing me with his hooded gaze.

"Hi," I said brightly. "Ashley's taking me on a tour of the house. Wow, this is amazing." I slipped past him into the small room and peered at one of the monitors. "It's like a TV department, only they're all tuned to different stations." Did I sound ditzy enough to be non-threatening?

A computerized voice interrupted my gushing commentary. "Side door open."

Connie reached over and tapped a button below a blinking light on the console in front of him. One of the screens switched images and we watched as Carmela exited through the laundry room. Connie tapped another button and on the adjacent screen we saw Carmela from the front view.

"That's really weird, isn't it?" I jabbered on. "We're seeing her from the front and the back at the same time. Kind of makes you dizzy, doesn't it?"

"Get out," Connie said. "You don't come in here."

I wanted to see more of the system and didn't move. "So you're like head of security for Mr. Kroy? That's awesome. He told me he has a Diebenkorn painting and lots of others that are really valuable, but he said he doesn't worry about burglars and now I know why. You're here taking care of it all."

I felt Connie right behind me, but kept scanning the security set up until he grabbed me around the back of my neck and lifted me in the air. I jabbed sideways with my elbow and clipped him on the cheekbone. He tossed me out through the door. I would have slammed into the wall but Ashley caught me.

I rubbed the back of my neck. "That's going to leave a mark," I complained.

"I said don't come in here."

"Okay. You made your point. I'm out."

He closed the door with a click. I turned to Ashley who stared at me wide-eyed.

"We're not supposed to go in there," she whispered.

"You know, I sort of got that impression," I whispered back straight-faced, then giggled.

She couldn't help smiling back and the tension left her face. "I guess I know more about Connie now. I mean, omigod, don't mess with him or he'll get you in a Vulcan neck pinch."

I gazed at her for a moment. "I thought I'd read them all, but I don't remember that myth. Whose neck did Vulcan pinch?"

Ashley stared at me. "What are you talking about?"

"Greek myths, right? Vulcan, or Hephaestus as the Greeks called him? Isn't that what you meant?"

"No, I was talking about *Star Trek*. Mr. Spock?"

I shook my head. "*Star Trek*? I haven't read very much science fiction."

"Where have you been? It was a TV show. An old one. There are movies, too."

"That explains it. My aunt didn't have a TV."

Ashley stared at me. "No TV? Omigod, you don't know anything, do you?"

This was my in for Ashley. Make her my mentor. "Maybe you can help me catch up?"

"Maybe," she said slowly, as if she thought I might be a hopeless case. "Let's go to my room."

We didn't meet anyone on the stairs or in the hallway. Ashley led the way into her bedroom and locked the door behind us.

"You have to lock your door?"

She leaned close to me. "Can you keep a secret?"

"My lips are sealed."

She waited a moment as if debating whether to trust me or not.

"I promise," I said.

Ashley crossed to her dresser, opened a drawer and pulled out a pack of cigarettes. "Want one?"

"No thanks. You have to hide them?"

She crossed to the balcony door and slid it open. "Dad doesn't want me to smoke, but I can't stop. I tried, but it made me way too antsy." She struck a match, held it to a cigarette and inhaled deeply. "He says I'm too old for that 'rebellious crap.'" She perfectly mimicked Kroy's tone. "But smoking's not rebellious. It's just something I really like to do."

"At least you have a dad, even if he is a pain. I never knew mine."

"Really? Not at all? Did he send you birthday presents, stuff like that?"

I shook my head. "I don't even know his name. All I know is that he's a magician."

"Really? And you're a magician, too. Do you think he might see you? Recognize you?"

"I doubt it. He probably doesn't even know I exist. I don't think Elizabeth told him."

"Why? Was he mean and she had to get away from him?"

"I don't think so. I think she didn't want the complication of having him in her life. She likes to be the one who calls all the shots."

"Just like my dad."

"Really?" I carefully kept a straight face, turned to the bookcase, and pulled out a book. It had a drawing on the cover of an androgynous figure flying through the air. The extreme foreshortening of the drawing gave a near three-dimensional effect of the figure's fist about to punch right out of the page. The most noticeable feature to me was the haircut, which was identical to Ashley's. It was actually a kind of comic book; every page held a series of drawings with very few words exchanged between the characters. "Is this your favorite anime character?"

"Actually, the graphic novels are called manga, but yes, that's Hideko."

"You know, I've never read these. Could I borrow one?"

"Sure." She dropped her cigarette on the balcony and stepped on it to put it out. "But start with the first one." She crossed the room and pulled another book from the shelf.

I took it from her. "Thanks. What do you like most about manga?"

"I like everything. The characters. The stories. In Japan they come out every month, but here we have to wait for enough of the series to come out, then they translate and publish them in a book, but I'm going to learn Japanese so I can read them right away."

"Really? That's terrific." This was the most enthusiasm I'd heard from Ashley. They might be comic books, but they mattered to her, so for the time being they'd matter to me, too. "Hey, can I ask you something? It's sort of gossipy."

"Sure," she said, interested.

"What's the deal with your dad and the public/private girlfriend thing? Your dad's rich and good looking. Seems like he could go out with anyone he wanted."

"Well, he really likes Marcie. But she doesn't fit the image he needs to keep up."

"Image for what?"

"He runs a really big foundation. He raises money for kids with AIDS."

"Really?" I couldn't keep the disbelief out of my voice.

"It's totally for real. He sold his business and everything and spends all of his time now on his charity. It's really important to him to help children all over the world."

"Wow. He's a big humanitarian. I had no idea. And this woman, Marcie, doesn't want him to do it?"

"It's not that. I guess she does. But the people he gets donations from didn't like her very much. I mean, she's really young and kind of...you know. Not from the same background as Dad."

I flashed for a moment on the image of the twenty-something triple D-cup blonde in Vegas who had hung on Kroy's arm while simultaneously nearly hanging out of her low-cut dress. "I get it." And suddenly I did. Elizabeth as Beth Hull could be the well-bred woman with impeccable manners if she had to. She could easily transition from stealing the life savings from susceptible men to conning people out of their money in the guise of helping sick kids.

"I kind of feel sorry for your mom," Ashley said.

"Really? Why?"

"Dad will never marry her."

I had to laugh. "I'm sure that's not a problem for her." I stood up. "Look, I'd like to have a bath, maybe take a little nap before dinner. Okay?"

"Sure. I'm going to check my email anyway."

I went down the hall to my room and on into the bathroom. It was as white and as luxurious as the rest of the house. There was a fluffy terrycloth bathrobe hanging on the door and the tub was as big as a small swimming pool. I filled the tub with hot water and sank into it. Waves of weariness swept over me. I'd had only a few hours sleep before coming over to Kroy's and sleep deprivation had the effect of making everything seem strangely unreal. My panic attack in the elevator, seeing Phil's body, talking to Lopez—it all felt as if it had happened to someone else. And maybe it had. The person I'd become lied and cursed and even said bad things about Aunt June.

I closed my eyes. I'd come to San Francisco to find out who I was, and instead I'd become someone no one who knew me would even recognize. I sank deeper into the steaming water.

When I opened my eyes the water was lukewarm. I must have drifted off to sleep. I added more hot water to the tub and scrubbed myself all over with a fancy sweet-smelling new bar of soap. I turned the water off, rinsed off the soap and sniffed. Another smell overcame the soap's perfume. I sniffed again. Cigarette smoke. Yuck. I'd have to make it clear to Ashley that I wasn't going to tell anyone about her smoking, but that I really didn't want the smell of stale cigarettes in my room. I stepped out of the tub, pulled on the thick toweling robe and threw open the bathroom door.

Rico, cigarette dangling from his lips, had my duffle bag open and half the contents strewn on the bed. He turned and squinted at me through the smoke rising from his cigarette. He held up my magician's cloak, the one that Aunt June had painstakingly sewn by hand for me the last Christmas we had together. "You actually wear this thing?"

Chapter Twelve

I stood, frozen, staring at Rico. He no longer sported jeans and a garish Hawaiian shirt. Now his clothes matched his handmade Italian shoes—slacks and a silk shirt unbuttoned far enough to show off a gold chain and lots of dark chest hair. I strode across the room and snatched my cape from his outstretched hand. "Leave my things alone." The movement loosened the belt of my bathrobe. Rico's gaze slid down over my body. I clutched at my cape to cover the gap and retied the robe's belt. "What are you doing here?" I demanded. "How did you get in?"

He removed the cigarette from his mouth. "I came in through the door. How about you?"

"You know Mr. Kroy?"

"Bobby and I are acquainted. How about you?"

I paced to the balcony window and gazed out, my back to Rico. My heart pounded from the shock of seeing Rico in my room and my face felt hot from feeling his eyes on my body. I needed to calm down and think. "Put out that stupid cigarette," I said without turning around.

"Yes ma'am," he said, laughing at me. I heard him go into the bathroom and flush the toilet.

I swung around to face him as he reappeared from the bathroom. "Who sent you to play taxi driver and pick me up the other day? Kroy?"

He shoved his hands in his pockets and rocked back on his heels. "I wasn't supposed to pick you up. I just went to do a little recon, but you got into my cab and there were cops all around, so what could I do?"

"So you work for Kroy?"

"No. Bobby and I are doing some business together. I just happened to be around when your mom made her 911 call to him and I offered, as a friend, to find out what I could."

"So you knew all along who I was?"

"I guessed. You look just like her. But I didn't tell her or Bobby that I'd picked you up."

"Why not?"

"I had my reasons."

"Like it gave you an edge in your business with Kroy to know something he didn't?"

He shrugged. "Something like that."

"And you search my belongings to get an edge on me?"

"I don't know anything about you, except that you claim you never lie, but that was a lie, and you say that you can make a living as a magician. That, I'm guessing, is another whopper."

I straightened and stuck out my chin. He'd given me an idea. "It's God's honest truth. I am, in fact, a superb magician. I have amazing skills." I put on my cape over the bathrobe, swung it around my shoulders with a flourish. "Want me to show you?"

"What, right now?"

"Why not? I'm going to prove to you that I was telling the truth. Let's go downstairs. There's not enough room in here." I strode to the door and held it open. "Come on."

Rico crossed to the doorway. I timed my movements in sync with his. As he took one step over the threshold I pushed him hard in the small of the back with one hand and lifted his wallet from his back pocket with the other. He staggered forward two steps and caught himself, but I slammed the door and locked it before he could turn around. He didn't pound on the door or try to break it in, so he mustn't have felt me taking his wallet. Amazing that I hadn't lost my touch after all these years. I flipped it open and checked the contents. Not much in there, but enough for what I had in mind.

I raced to the bed where most of my belongings lay in a pile. I dropped the cape and the robe, pulled on jeans and a long-sleeved sweater. No time for a bra, but that could work in my favor. Nothing like unfettered boobs to distract male attention. I stuffed everything into my duffle as rapidly as I could, shouldered it, and tucked Rico's wallet up my sleeve.

Rico wasn't waiting for me in the hallway when I opened my door. I hurried past Ashley's closed door, down the stairs and headed straight for Kroy's study. I knocked once and opened the door without waiting to be invited in. Kroy and Rico stood near Kroy's large desk. Both turned to face me.

I paused dramatically on the threshold, mainly so I could take in the room. French windows along one wall gave Kroy an easy exit to the front drive and also a view of anyone approaching. Floor to ceiling bookshelves along another wall were only half-filled with books. Like daughter, like father—not a reading family. And in the middle of it all, Kroy's expansive desk furnished with a computer and littered with papers.

"See?" I said to Rico. "I told you I was a superb magician. I made you disappear."

"Valentine," Kroy said eying my duffle, "Are you going somewhere?"

"That's up to you." I crossed the room and dropped my duffle on Kroy's desk. "If you wanted to know what I brought with me, all you had to do was ask." I unzipped my bag and started pulling out my belongings. "Sending your errand boy to paw through my bag while I'm in the bathtub isn't acceptable to me. And he did a terrible job, by the way. If you don't want someone to know you're there, you shouldn't smoke while you work."

I gestured to the pile I'd amassed on the desk. "So there it is. Go ahead, look all you want. If you don't like what you see, then I'm out of here. Inviting me into your home just so you can spy on me is pretty despicable, don't you think?"

"No, I don't think," Kroy said coldly. "And to clarify, Rico doesn't work for me. Now get your crap off my desk."

"Fine," I said and, head down, I began repacking my duffle more methodically and much more slowly than I'd emptied it. When I finished I looked up and addressed Kroy. "May I talk to you? Alone? There's something you should know."

"There's something *you* should know," Kroy said. "I don't care for all this drama. So just say what you have to say."

I stepped away from the desk. "But it's all about drama, because I'm a magician and dramatic things happen when you're around me. For example, your friend Rico's full name is..." I put my fingers to my temples as if concentrating very hard. "Rico DiSera. He has an out of state driver's license and carries just one credit card in his wallet." I did the concentrating thing again. "American Express, number 8881437273454200."

As I started rattling off the number, Rico patted his back pocket. "You lifted my wallet. Give it back. Now."

I held my ground. "You say you lost your wallet? Maybe I can help you find it." I made a flourish with my hand and produced his wallet as if out of thin air. "Is this your wallet?" I held it out to him and he took it.

"Wait a minute," Kroy said. "Is she right about your credit card?"

Rico shrugged. "I don't know the number by heart."

"Do me a favor and check, will you?"

Rico opened his wallet and handed his credit card to Kroy. "What's the number?" Kroy asked me. I repeated it. "She's right." Kroy handed the card back to Rico.

"So?" Rico said. "She didn't receive the number through her psychic powers. She stole my wallet."

Kroy gave me a considering look. "Would you mind waiting outside for a minute, Rico?"

"Sure, whatever," Rico said, and crossed to the door. He turned to face us his hand on the doorknob. "Just be careful, Bobby. My people won't want to hear that you're being careless about who you hang out with."

Silence hung in the air between them for a long moment, before Kroy burst out laughing. "Rico, ease up, will you? So she picked your pocket. She won't do it again, will you?" he asked me.

"No, sir." I held up my right hand with my fingers crossed. "Scout's honor."

Kroy laughed again. "She's got a sense of humor, too. I like that. Go on, Rico. Get yourself a drink. I'll just be a few minutes."

Rico went out and closed the door behind him. The smile immediately faded from Kroy's face. "Sit down." He gestured to a chair in front of his desk. I did as he said, resting my duffle at my feet. He perched with one hip on the side of his desk. "Okay, let's have it without the drama this time. What do you want? And don't give me that crap about your mother."

"What I want, is what I've been doing—interviewing for a job."

"A job picking pockets? Sorry, I don't have any openings for that currently."

"Maybe not literally, but what about metaphorically?"

He frowned. I might have gone too far. Maybe he didn't know what a metaphor was. I hurried on before he could reply. "You have five different kinds of documents on your desk. A letter about renting a hotel ballroom, a spreadsheet of planned expenses over the next three months, an electrician's bill, and a contract from a company called i-systems."

He narrowed his eyes at me. "How much was the electrician's bill?"

"Three thousand six hundred and eighty-two dollars."

"Which hotel's ballroom?"

"The Sheraton Palace."

"And the expenses on the spreadsheet?"

"I only caught the biggest one—for 'wine et cetera.' Fifteen thousand dollars. You must really like your wine."

He crossed his arms. "You named only four. You said there were five."

"I was being discreet, because the fifth is so personal. A letter in a woman's handwriting describing a very explicit sexual fantasy. I'm guessing it's Marcie and that she asked you for money on page two."

Kroy smiled at my comment. I hadn't embarrassed him. Just the opposite. "All right." He stood up.

"All right, what?" I got to my feet.

"I'm interested. You have some unusual skills. I'll let you know."

I picked up my duffle. "Okay." I crossed to his desk, picked up a pen and notepad. "Here's my number." I jotted my cell phone number on the pad and handed it to Kroy. "Call me when you make up your mind."

"Call you? Where are you going?"

"Someplace where I can have my privacy."

"How're you going to pay for it? Or did you pick my pocket just now?" He felt for his wallet.

"I told you I have money." I pulled my wad of cash out of my jeans pocket. Or some of it anyway. I had a lot of it stowed in a safer place than my pocket. I held the folded bills up for a moment. "See?" I stuffed it back into my pocket and crossed to the door.

"Wait a minute," Kroy said. "I invited you to stay in my home. The invitation still stands."

I was going to bet that playing hard to get was the best tactic for keeping Kroy interested in me. I opened the door and turned to face him. "So you could have Mr. Confucius train your cameras on me? If I wanted to be in the movies, I'd have gone to Hollywood." I left the room, closing the door behind me.

What a great exit line. I'd never have a chance to match it. I nearly laughed out loud.

"Not so fast, Valentine," Rico said.

I jumped. I hadn't expected him to lie in wait for me. "I don't have anything to say to you."

"Good, then maybe you'll listen." He took me by the elbow and propelled me down the hall away from Kroy's office. He spun me so my back was against the wall and trapped me there by putting his hands on the wall on either side of me and leaning in close. "Whatever you're thinking of doing here," he said quietly. "Think again."

I couldn't let him intimidate me. "Oh, take the blue pill, Rico," I said, imitating Ashley.

Rico sighed and shook his head. "You're not listening. You're in over your head here. You have your money. Go back to Vegas."

"I think you underestimate me," I said.

"No, I misjudged you. You underestimate me."

"Maybe, maybe not. We'll have to see which one of us is wrong, won't we?"

I moved to duck under his arm, but he caught me by the shoulders and pressed me against the wall. His gaze dropped to my mouth. I couldn't help but look at his. I couldn't let him kiss me again. Not now that I knew what he really was. Not even if he wasn't a mobster, a shark, I couldn't. I could punch him in the solar plexus and give myself a few seconds to get away. Who was I kidding? With him gazing at me with those brown eyes, with that wonderful mouth so close to mine, with the memory of the heat of the kiss we'd shared so fresh, I couldn't even breathe.

He leaned closer and I closed my eyes. But he didn't kiss me. He put his cheek on mine and his lips next to my ear. "You wouldn't have known I was in your room if I hadn't wanted you to. Next time will be different." He stepped back and dropped his hands to his sides.

I picked up my duffle and nearly ran down the hall to the foyer and out the front door. Let Rico think he'd chased me off. I had other plans. Granted, some of those plans included avoiding all private encounters with him in the future.

I made my way down the street and kept an eye out in case anyone followed me. Once I was sure no one had, I called a cab. My phone showed a list of missed calls, all from the same number. Someone had tried to reach me repeatedly when my phone had needed charging. Maybe Lopez had figured out that I wasn't at the hotel. I tucked my phone in my pocket. I'd call him later.

When the cab arrived I was relieved to find the driver was a fifty-something guy with a heavy Spanish accent. Clearly a regular cab driver and not a New Jersey mobster in a Hawaiian shirt. I kept looking out the rear window during the whole trip. I remembered my wild ride with Phil as she eluded our tail. At the time, I'd thought she was being a little paranoid. Now I knew better.

When we reached the busier streets of downtown, my phone rang. The phone's screen showed the same number as all the missed calls. "Hello." I nearly added "Inspector Lopez" but stopped myself.

"Valentine? It's George Hunsinger. I've been trying to reach you all day but your voicemail didn't pick up."

I sighed. Uncle George. I forgotten all about him and his quest to find Elizabeth so he could forgive her. "Hi," I said. "It's a new phone. I haven't set up the voicemail yet."

"Well, no matter. I have some news about Betty. Where can we meet?"

"Um…you know this isn't the best time for me." I could have bitten my tongue as soon as the words were out. I should have been more definite.

"Very well, when would be better for you? Name the time and place."

"I'm sorry. I should have been clearer. I really can't see you for the time being. Something has come up that I absolutely have to deal with."

"Does this have to do with Betty?"

"No, it doesn't."

"Won't you at least help me, then? I'd like to know your thoughts about the information that's just been relayed to me. It's very important for me to get closure with that time of my life and those events. I won't have any peace until I do. Please?"

"I'm very sorry, but I just can't. And I think I should warn you that there are some very bad people after Elizabeth. It's really not safe to try to find her, at least not now."

"Not safe?" his voice notched up to a higher pitch. "My dear child, whatever do you mean?"

"Just that. I wouldn't want you to get hurt."

"Nor would I. But what about you? Aren't you concerned for your own safety?"

"I'm not looking for her any longer, so I don't think they'll bother me." Just then the cab driver pulled up in front of my hotel. "I have to go, Uncle George," I said and hoped the "uncle" would soften my refusal. "Please, just go back to Cleveland. I have to hang up now. Bye."

I hung up the phone, paid the cab driver and made my way into the hotel. I took a look around the lobby on my way to the stairs in case Lopez had posted someone there. The lobby was deserted except for a redhead with big hair reading *Vogue*. She glanced up and as our gazes met, I felt little electric buzz zip over me. I knew her. Or, at least I'd seen her before. Outside Elizabeth's apartment, in the group of rubberneckers. It was Lies-About-Her-Age in a wig. She stood up and walked away from me, but not before I saw the flash of recognition in her eyes, too.

I hurried to the stairs. I had to call Lopez. Her being here was no coincidence. I punched in Lopez's number as I climbed the stairs, but there was no ring. I looked at my phone. Did it need charging again? No. The indicator said fully charged. I tried Lopez's number again with the same result. Stupid modern technology. I shoved the phone back into my pocket. I'd have to use the phone in my room.

I hurried out of the stairwell and down the hall to my room. I had to pause to extract my hotel room card from the hidden pocket in my jeans. Lucky thing that Aunt June had taught me how to sew with tiny, nearly invisible stitches. Rico could paw through my things all he wanted, he wouldn't find my secret stashes.

As soon as I entered the room I knew something wasn't right. I stopped just inside the door. Light filtered in from the balcony window, barely illuminating the place where I stood at the opposite end of the room. I pressed the light switch and that helped. One more step into the room and I'd be by the alcove with mirrors and washbasin. You had to pass through the alcove to get to the room with the toilet and shower. The shower room had a door for privacy and from where I stood I could see that door in the alcove mirror. It stood partly ajar, and Dwayne peered out, watching me in the mirror. And in his very Dwayne-like way, he didn't seem to realize that if he could see me, I could see him.

Chapter Thirteen

I had one bad second when it seemed that my legs weren't going to obey my brain's clear order to run, but after that brief moment the adrenaline hit. I dropped my duffle and ran down the hall. I slammed into the stairway door so hard it crashed against the cement wall with a metallic clang. I took the stairs at a top speed, trusting my feet not to miss a step. The banister supported me as I vaulted each turning downward. I had to outrun Dwayne, no matter what.

I nearly made it.

I thought Dwayne would chase me down the stairs. I hadn't counted on someone coming up and didn't even see him until I nearly crashed into him as I took a leap around the last turn downward.

"Whoa," he said, grabbing me before we collided. Not Dwayne. Rico.

A sick feeling swept over me. Stupid vicious Dwayne worked for Rico. Killed for Rico.

"You slime. You despicable evil slime." I tried to take a swing at him, but he tightened his grip on my arms.

"Wait a minute. What did I do?"

"Let go of me." I struggled but he held on.

"I'll let go. Just tell me what's going on."

"I get it. You're going to stall until Dwayne gets here. Does Dwayne do the torture for you too, or just the killing?"

Rico released his grip. "Valentine, I don't know what you're talking about, but no one's going to torture and kill you if I have anything to say about it. I swear."

I hesitated. "I don't believe you."

"Fine. Don't believe me. Just tell me what's going on. Where's this Dwayne?"

"If we stand here any longer, you'll find out. Now let me go." I pushed my way past him, down the last of the stairs, and out the door to the lobby, Rico on my heels.

"Valentine, wait a minute." He made a grab for my arm, but I pulled free and kept on running to the reception desk.

I scrambled over the counter and dropped down next to the reception clerk, who stared at me startled. "Call the police," I ordered.

"What is it?" she asked, but she reached for the phone before I answered her.

"There's a man in my room. Please hurry." I faced Rico over the counter.

"Is that him?" the desk clerk asked.

"No." I pawed through desk items under the counter and opened drawers. "Do you have a gun? Or some kind of weapon?"

"N-no." She began to talk to the 911 operator, her voice shaking.

I opened drawer after drawer, but couldn't find anything to protect myself, not even a pair of scissors. I grabbed a stapler, straightened and faced Rico on the other side of the counter. I had a pretty good arm. If he tried to come at me, I could pitch it at his head.

Rico glanced at the stapler in my hand. "What are you going to do, staple this Dwayne to the counter?"

"I'm going to do whatever it takes to stop you from coming after me."

"I'm not going to hurt you. Why can't you believe that?"

"Because you're here, and Dwayne's here and Lies-About-Her-Age was here, too, and that can't be a coincidence."

"Lies about her what? You're not making sense."

"Just stop, okay?" I turned back to the desk clerk. "Tell them the man is a killer. He's on the FBI's most wanted list."

Her eyes widened in fear, but she relayed the information.

I turned to face Rico again, but he'd disappeared. Like the rat he was. That just went to show that he was guilty, didn't it? But he'd sounded really puzzled about Dwayne. And if he'd wanted to kill me, he could have done it in the stairwell. I stared at the stapler in my hand and quickly put it down on the counter. I must have looked ridiculous, threatening him with a stapler.

I glanced around the empty lobby. Why couldn't Lopez have stashed me in a busy hotel instead of this deserted dump? What if Dwayne had followed me down the stairs? He could show up in the lobby any second. I could use some help from responsible citizens right about now. Assuming any of those still existed.

Actually, what I really needed was to get out of there. Who knew what crazy Dwayne would do? He could still be waiting for me in my room, or he could be hiding behind the door to the stairs—with his gun.

The desk clerk continued to hold the phone. I got her attention and asked, "Are they sending the cops, or what?"

"They're on their way. They want me to stay on the line until they get here."

"Okay," I said, "I'll go see if they're coming." I headed for the glass front doors. Astounding that I could lie so easily now. I hadn't even blinked.

Once outside, I headed up the street at a fast clip, checking right, left, ahead, and behind. No sign of Dwayne. Or of Lies-About-Her-Age. But what if they had a confederate? Someone I hadn't seen yet? I looked even more closely at the people around me. They seemed not to have the slightest interest in me. I slowed my pace. I needed to sit down somewhere safe and quiet so I could think. Maybe there was a branch library in the area. That would be perfect.

My phone beeped, and the comforting thought of sitting in a library evaporated. I pulled out my phone, afraid to answer it and equally afraid not to. I pushed "talk" and said "Yes?"

"Ms. Hill?" A man's deep voice. It tickled the edge of my memory, but I couldn't place it.

"Yes?"

"This is Special Agent Carter of the FBI. I understand you've had another encounter with the man known as Dwayne. We need to talk—now."

"Okay, if you're from the FBI, what's the name of the agent who was killed?"

"Which one? There were two."

That stopped me. He might just be who he said he was. "The second one."

"Her name was Philips."

"First name?"

"Eugenia, but everyone called her Phil."

I flashed on Phil's crooked smile when she'd said, "Call me Phil," and my throat closed up.

"Ms. Hill? Are you still there?"

I cleared my throat. "Where do you want to meet?"

"That's you walking up the street from the hotel, right? I'm in a Lincoln Towncar half a block away, heading toward you."

It was getting dark. I could see only headlights. How was I supposed to recognize his car? "The cops tell you that Dwayne showed up here?"

"Something like that."

"And they still haven't showed up." The words were barely out of my mouth when two cop cars, lights flashing, screeched around the corner and sped past me toward the hotel. "Or, I guess they're here now."

"Right. So let's get you out of sight." A car with tinted back windows pulled up at the curb. A tall black man dressed in FBI-standard suit, shirt, and tie emerged from the driver's side and approached me. "Before Dwayne or his cohorts spot you."

I could still hear him on my phone, but he wasn't holding a cell himself. Then he turned his head slightly, and I saw a small Bluetooth in his ear.

He opened the door to the backseat for me. I got in and waited until he was behind the wheel. "I'd like to see your identification."

He pulled his ID out of his jacket pocket and handed it to me. I flipped it open. It was just like Phil's. Special Agent Carter was who he said he was. I didn't have to jump out of the car and run away. All the tension that had been holding me together since I'd seen Dwayne, left my body, and I started shaking all over. I handed Carter's ID back to him, leaned back in my seat and closed my eyes.

"Are you all right?"

I opened my eyes. That voice. I knew I'd heard it before. "You came to help Phil, didn't you? When the other agent was killed."

"That's right. You saw me? When you were supposedly lying down?"

"No. I heard you talking to Phil in Elizabeth's apartment, right before I climbed down the fire escape. You have a distinctive voice."

"Are you going to run out on me again?"

"I ran because I didn't believe that you were FBI. Things are different now."

"That's good to hear. Now, if you're done vetting me, I'd like to get moving. Buckle up." We pulled away from the curb, and he muttered something I couldn't hear.

"What did you say?"

He turned his head slightly. "Sorry, I was on the phone to SAC Williams."

"Oh. Is that where we're going? To see him?" Just what I didn't need—another go round with the big boss.

Carter looked at me in his rearview mirror. "You don't want to talk to him?" My reluctance must have come through in my voice.

"In a word? No. You've heard of giving someone the third degree? He gave me at least the tenth degree after Phil was killed."

"He's going to leave the questions up to me this time. He's busy orchestrating the manhunt for Dwayne. And right now

I'm busy making sure no one's following us, because it looks like someone's been keeping tabs on you. Seems like Dwayne has had some help."

I opened my mouth to tell Carter about Rico, then closed it again without saying anything. Why was I hesitating? Rico was following me all right, but I wasn't sure he was helping Dwayne. Or maybe I just didn't want to believe it. I rubbed my temples. I must be losing it. Dwayne-helper or not, Rico was trouble. And, he was in on something with Kroy. I had to tell Carter what I knew. "Agent Carter?"

"Yes?"

"Where are we going?"

"North Beach. Get some Italian takeout. That okay with you?"

"Sure. But I have something to tell you. There's this guy, Rico DiSera? He's from New Jersey, and Kroy's doing some deal with him. I don't know what the deal is. Yet."

"That's okay. We know about it."

"That's good. But did you know he followed me to my hotel?"

"Yes."

I sank back against the seat. They knew about Rico. I'd been worrying for nothing. We rode in silence in slow traffic. Carter left the crowded street we'd been inching along and turned into an alley lit only by the light from an open doorway. We pulled to a stop outside the open door, and I could see a busy restaurant kitchen inside. A man stood outside in the shadows, smoking a cigarette. Carter rolled down the passenger side window and said, "Hey, DiSera, ditch that butt. This car is a no-smoking zone."

DiSera? I jerked around and peered through the tinted glass. The shadowy figure approached the car and opened the door to the backseat. "Hey, Valentine," Rico said, giving me his charm-the-shirt-off-your-back smile.

I tried to slide away from him, but couldn't because of the seat belt. "Agent Carter, what's he doing here?" I fumbled with the seat belt release.

"Damn it, Carl," Rico said. "You were supposed to tell her."

"Tell me what?"

"It's okay," Rico said. "Just hang on a minute, all right? Pop the trunk for me, will you Carl?" Rico closed the car door, disappeared through the open doorway and reappeared in a few moments carrying a large white plastic bag in one hand and a familiar-looking duffle bag in the other. He dropped the duffle in the trunk, circled to the other side of the car and climbed into the backseat. He carefully placed the plastic bag on the seat between us.

"Is that my duffle bag? What are you doing with it? What's going on?"

"I went up to your room looking for this Dwayne character. He was long gone, so I picked up your bag because I knew you'd need it. And I called Carl so he could pick you up and explain things to you." He lifted a white Styrofoam box from the plastic bag and tried to hand it to me.

I batted his hand away.

He jerked the box out of my reach. "Watch it. This is the best gnocchi Bolognese in San Francisco. You should treat it with more respect. Here, Carl." He held the box out to Carter.

"Forget the gnocchi and give me some answers," I said.

"I was just about to do that," Carter said from the front seat. "DiSera is helping us out. He's a CI."

"CI? What's that? Complete idiot? Criminally insane? All of the above?"

"He's a confidential informant. I'm telling you this only because he thinks you can be trusted not to give him up to Kroy."

"Tell her what you want from her," Rico said.

"You've been inside the Kroy house. Have you seen or heard anything at all about his business dealings, or contacts with people like Rico?"

"Not yet, but that's my plan."

"For real?"

"That's what Elizabeth said she would do for you, right? So she wouldn't get sent to jail? Only, you've guessed by now that she never intended to hold up her end of the deal."

"Forget it, Valentine," Rico said. "You should go home before you get me or yourself killed."

"You could have gotten killed without any help from me if Dwayne had still been in my hotel room."

"I bet you'd be a lot less crabby if you ate something. Here, take this." He pulled out a second Styrofoam box. "Let's see if I'm right."

"You arrogant…I just might kill you myself."

"Kids, don't make me come back there," Carter said. "I'm going to pull up behind this dumpster so I can eat dinner. And you two stop fighting so I can eat in peace. We have some important things to talk about."

"Like what?" I asked.

"Eat first." Carter pulled the car over and turned off the engine. The light from the restaurant kitchen cast a dim illumination into the interior of the car.

Rico handed around napkins and plastic forks. Carter started eating, and the warm smell of good food filled the car. I opened my own Styrofoam box and shoveled the gnocchi into my mouth. Even if it wasn't the best gnocchi in San Francisco, I'd have eaten like a starving animal. I couldn't remember my last meal.

"Okay, I'm done," I said eventually. "You were going to tell me about Kroy?"

Carter twisted around in his seat so he could see me. "Here's the deal. Kroy is into some seriously bad stuff. He raises money to buy drugs for kids with AIDS in different countries—Thailand, South Africa, all over."

"Ashley mentioned that to me. She says he's a big humanitarian. What does he do? Take the money for himself?"

"Worse than that. He buys the drugs okay, but he also buys phony drugs. He ships the fakes overseas and sells the real ones on the black market."

"Sounds like you already know enough to arrest him. What do you need me for?"

"He's slippery, and he has friends in high places. Our goal is to bring down the whole network. Kroy, the black marketers he deals with, and most of all the drug counterfeiters. We've never been able to get even a whiff of them."

"Tell me what I need to find out and where to look for it."

"Not so fast," Rico put in. "What he's not telling you is that the FBI already had one CI who was supposed to know something about the fake drug makers. They found him trussed up on his stomach, legs bent, rope knotted around his ankles and looped around his neck. So when he couldn't hold his legs up any longer he slowly strangled. They couldn't tell if that killed him or if he bled to death, because they also cut out his tongue. Since then, no one wants to help them."

I gulped. "So that's who Dwayne works for?"

"Wait a sec," Carter said. "I've got a call." He muttered at his earpiece.

I put my Styrofoam box on the seat and pulled a quarter out of my pocket. I did a basic routine of palm and pass, French slip, and thumb palm vanish. I started at half speed and slowly went faster. I made myself focus only on the coin to block the gruesome image Rico had drawn.

"Is that your magic act?" Rico asked.

"I hate waiting so I always use the time to practice. I'm getting rusty. I haven't been able to practice since I left Vegas."

"Bobby talked about seeing your act. He was pretty impressed. I can see why. You're good."

"I'm not interested in impressing creeps."

Rico leaned toward me and whispered. "Are you referring to Bobby or to me?"

The quarter slipped from my hand to the floor of the car. I bent over and felt around for it.

"Here," Rico said. "I see it. I'll get it for you." He reached over and his hand brushed against mine.

I jerked my hand away and straightened.

He held out the quarter and dropped it into my outstretched palm. "You didn't answer my question."

I didn't intend to answer it. I was already way too attracted to the man. He might be helping the FBI, but he was still a gangster—or worse. "Why did you follow me from Kroy's to the hotel?"

"I didn't exactly follow you. Carl located you through the GPS signal."

"What GPS signal?"

"The one in your phone."

"You mean the so-called demo phone that some guy who supposedly owns a phone store let you have?"

"As it turns out, that guy was Carl."

"And that's how you knew I went to Kroy's house?"

"Yeah."

"Talk about invasion of privacy."

"We were worried about you. Or at least, I was. Carl just wanted to know what you were up to. You really should think twice about getting involved in this, Valentine."

"Too late," I said. "I'm already involved."

"You were asking about Dwayne," Carter said from the front seat. "I just got the update. No sign so far. They've shut down the hotel and are doing a room-by-room sweep, and, of course, the cops put out a BOLO. But he might just have given them the slip."

"What about the woman you saw in the lobby?" Rico asked.

"What woman?" Carl turned to look at me.

"It's someone I saw standing with the gawkers outside Elizabeth's apartment while I was sitting in the police car. Now that I think about it, I'm pretty sure I saw her outside the police station the next day, when I met up with Phil."

"Wait a minute," Carter said. "You caught a glimpse of this woman twice before, and you say you recognized her today?"

"The first time I watched her for quite a while. Most of the people came and went, but five stayed until the cops took me into the building. Two of them—a man and a woman—were still there when I came out again."

"That right, DiSera?" Carter asked.

"There were people across the street, but I didn't pay attention. What was that you called her?"

"Lies-About-Her-Age. You know, hair, makeup, and clothes too young for the face. The first time I saw her she was a blonde. Today, it was red hair. I think it was a wig. It was like she was waiting for me. But how did she know I was going to be at the hotel? She couldn't have followed my GPS signal, too, could she?"

"Possible, but not likely," Carter said. "We're thinking a leak in the police department."

"And Dwayne? He even knew what room I was in."

"We don't know. Our best guess is that he was sent by the black market gang Kroy dealt with before. Rico gave him a better deal, and Kroy dumped them. Maybe they're unhappy about it. Give me a minute to call this in. You should've told me about her right away."

While Carl murmured on his phone, I turned to Rico. "So that's what you do? Sell things on the black market?"

"It's not really my line of work, but I'm playing it that way for Kroy."

Carl turned to look at us. "I think we caught a break. They have cameras in the hotel lobby and elevators. They're checking them now. See if she shows up."

"Shouldn't be hard," I said. "There wasn't anyone else in the lobby."

"You know, Carl," Rico said. "I'm about to close the deal with Kroy. If he agrees to contract with i-systems for the drop shipment, we'll get a link to the fake pharmaceutical company. So there's really nothing for Valentine to do."

"He hasn't agreed to use i-systems yet, and the clock is ticking," Carl said. "Kroy's big fund-raiser is in two days. From his past pattern, we know he'll arrange the shipments right after that. What if he changes his mind about dealing with you because the crew who sent Dwayne is threatening his life? Besides, you told me Kroy sent you to bring her back, right? You bring her back, that makes you look even better to him. You're resourceful. You're the go-to guy."

"Carter's right," I said to Rico. "You know it. I know it. So please just tell me where to look for the information you need and take me to Kroy's."

"Yes, ma'am," Carter said. He lifted a chauffeur's hat from the passenger seat and put it on. He glanced at me in the rearview mirror. "My cover." He gestured to the hat. "I'm DiSera's driver. That way we don't have to sneak around to meet. Easier that way." He started the car and steered slowly down the alley.

"You haven't told me anything yet," I said.

"Wait till tomorrow. DiSera will brief you in the morning."

I had to be satisfied with that. No one said anything on the ride to Kroy's. I leaned back in my seat and looked out the window at the dark streets. I felt weary right through to my bones. At least Kroy had surveillance, alarms, and a bodyguard so I could sleep tonight without worrying about Dwayne. No bodyguard would be able to protect me from my dreams. I still had the memory of Phil's broken body in the back of my head and now, thanks to Rico, the image of a bound man with his tongue cut out.

Chapter Fourteen

I was wrong about the bad dreams. I slept without a single image appearing, bad or good. And when I woke up, I felt as if I'd been hibernating. The bright sunlight bounced off the stark white walls like a laser beam and made me squint when I tried to open my eyes. Something wasn't quite right. I turned my head on the pillow. Rico lay stretched out next to me, hands behind his head.

"How'd you get in here?" I asked.

He rolled over on his side and propped his head up on his elbow. "Good morning, Sunshine."

I didn't feel sunny. More like a mole yanked out of her burrow. "I asked you a question."

He waited a beat before answering and let his eyes rest on my mouth. "Remember I told you that if I didn't want you to know I was here, you wouldn't?"

I remembered. He'd done that looking at my mouth thing then, too, and I'd thought he was going to kiss me. Again. And I'd wanted him to. But I couldn't want that. Not now. I frowned at him. "We did this thing with me waking up in bed next to you once before. I didn't care for it then. I like it even less now. So let's agree you'll stop before it becomes a habit."

"Can't do that. Sorry."

"Why?"

"Because we need to talk, and this is the best time and place."

"Kroy has cameras all over the place. Connie might be listening in and watching right now."

"Kroy's security system is just to keep intruders out, not to monitor people he's let in. Besides, I checked. No bugs."

"You think of everything, don't you? So talk."

"First, I have a present for you from Carl." He pulled a cell phone out of his pocket.

"Thanks, but tell him I already have one of those."

"Not like this one, you don't. It has everything—not only all the bells and whistles, but beepers and sirens and party noise-makers, too."

"And I assume a tracking device, like the one you used to find me yesterday."

"Of course. And there's a hot button. Just press the pound sign repeatedly. It'll send an emergency call straight to the FBI office. Even if the phone's turned off. It has a camera, of course. Only this one's very high-resolution in case you come across something like documents. You can even take your own picture. Like this." He moved close to me and put his head on the pillow next to mine. He held the phone above our heads. I could see our faces in the little screen, like a tiny television, then the image froze.

"That's it," he said. "Your first compromising photo. Then there's this other feature where you can email it to anyone. Want to send ours to the tabloids?" I watched as Rico pushed sequential buttons until a little message appeared on the screen that said, "Send?" He clicked yes.

"Where did you send it?" I asked.

"To myself. Something to remember you by."

I felt a twitch in my chest. "You're going away?"

"As soon as this deal wraps up, I am. Why? Going to miss me?"

There was a knock on the door as it simultaneously opened. Elizabeth appeared in the doorway and stared at us. Surprised. Or acting surprised. "What are you doing in here, Rico?" she demanded.

Rico propped his head up on his elbow and gave me his lazy smile, the one that made warmth unfold in my belly. He didn't as much as glance at Elizabeth. "What am I doing?" With one finger, he traced a gentle line on my cheek. "Anything Valentine wants me to."

"Valentine," Elizabeth said, "I thought you knew better. You don't want to get involved with his type. Low level gangsters are just errand boys in expensive clothes."

"Go away, Elizabeth." I took my cue from Rico and didn't even look at her when I spoke.

"No. You need to get up. The gala's tomorrow night and you don't have one decent thing to wear. Bobby wants you to perform. Do your little magic act or something. He needs to talk to you about it."

I turned to gaze at her. "I'm busy."

"Too bad. You'll have to be busy later."

I pulled the arm closest to her out from the covers and held it out palm up so she could see the white circular scarred indents on the inside of my upper arm. "Guess what, Elizabeth? I do what I want now. And no one forces me anymore. No one. So you go. And close the door behind you."

She swung around and strode out. She tried to slam the door, but it dragged on the plush carpet and she couldn't get enough momentum for a satisfactory bang. I stared at the ceiling, not wanting to meet Rico's gaze.

"Feel better?"

"Not really."

"First time you stood up to her?"

"First time with no consequences. At least so far."

Rico reached across my body and stroked the scars on my arm. "I wondered about those that first night."

I jammed my arm under the covers. "They're not up for discussion."

"Fine. But what about your rib and your bruises? How are they doing?"

"Just fine, thank you. And don't think you're going to get any free peeks. You had your one and only chance to ogle me."

"No need to be so touchy. I'm just the babysitter here, you know. I don't think you should do this spying on Kroy thing if you're not fit."

"I'm perfectly fit, and I don't need a babysitter. I can take care of myself."

"Glad to hear it." He rolled onto his back and laced his fingers behind his head. "Hope you can take care of me, too, when the shooting starts. You know, this was a quiet deal, until you showed up and people started getting killed."

I flashed on the image of Phil's body and swallowed hard. "That's just coincidence. It's Kroy they're after and you know it."

"That's one possibility."

"So tell me what I need to find out, and I'll do it. Then you can go off to…wherever you're going." I hesitated, then asked. "Are you going to jail?"

Rico barked a laugh. "No. I'm in the clear with the law. Let's get back to you. We need a reason for me to take you out of the house so Carl can talk to you. How about shopping for something to wear to the fund-raiser?"

I made a face. "I hate shopping. For clothes anyway. But if Kroy wants me to do my act, I'll have to go to a magic shop and get supplies."

"Yeah? Like what?"

"You'll see when I do my act. You're going to be there, aren't you?"

"Yeah. I'm supposed to keep an eye on you. So where you go, I go."

"What about your deal with Kroy? Aren't you still working on that?"

"I think we've just about sealed that deal. We talked some last night. He said he was on board with it. When he signs on for my money-laundering service and for using i-systems as an anonymous front to drop ship the drugs, we'll have the evidence we need."

"Evidence?"

"We need the real and the fake drugs to make a case against him, but the fake drugs don't come with a return address. Carl still needs a way to find the supplier."

"I guess that's where I come in."

"You don't have to do this, Valentine."

"That's where you're wrong. I absolutely have to do it." Time to change the subject. Phil's death wasn't a topic I wanted to go into with Rico. "If I'm going to talk to Kroy and get to the magic shop, I need to get dressed."

"Don't let me stop you."

I clutched the covers up to my chin. "I already told you, the ogling is over. Time for you to leave."

"Right now, we're supposed to be an item. And we need to look like we've been doing more in this bed than talk, so you need to get comfortable with me and PDAs."

"What's that?"

"What high school did you go to that didn't have a rule against PDAs…public displays of affection?"

"I was home-schooled. And I'll do fine with your PDAs, but only in public."

"Home-schooled? No way did your mom home-school you. Unless it was special courses in larceny and grand theft."

"Not Elizabeth, my Aunt June. When I got here, I hadn't seen Elizabeth in nine years, hadn't lived with her for four years before that."

"Nine years? So that would make you what—twenty-two, twenty-three?"

"Let's talk about PDAs, because I have ground rules."

"First, tell me how old you are."

"Ground rule number one: hands at waist or back, no copping a feel."

"Valentine, I'm serious. Are you twenty-one?"

"Ground rule number two…"

"Holy shit." He rolled off the bed onto his feet. "You're not even twenty-one?" He ran his hand through his hair. "Okay.

Get up. We're getting out of here now. Carl will have a coronary when he hears this."

I pushed into a sitting position, my back against the headboard, the covers firmly in place under my chin. "Stop being so dramatic. I'm over twenty-one. I just don't know exactly how much over because I could never get Elizabeth to tell me where and when I was born. And when I was living with her, she changed my age depending on the con. When I got to go live with Aunt June because Elizabeth was in jail, Aunt June tried to find a way to get a birth certificate for me, but she couldn't."

"Have you tried asking Elizabeth?"

"Don't be stupid. That would give her leverage over me, and she'd hold out. I have to wait until I have something she wants. Then I'll make a deal. Now, can we talk about the ground rules?"

"Rules? What rules?" He frowned at me.

"For PDAs. Ground rule number two…"

"Hold it right there. I know you like to have rules. We went through this before, remember? No lying, and so on? I'm pretty sure you've broken that rule several times over in the past few days. So just forget about rules."

"These aren't rules for me. They're for you. So you don't—you know."

He came around the bed and sat down next to me. His weight pulled at the covers and made it hard for me to keep them in place. "I don't think *you* get it. This isn't a game. This is real life, and real death."

"Don't lecture me. I saw the bodies. It's more real to me than it could ever be to you."

He hesitated for a beat. "We need to be convincing to everyone who sees us. No dropping our guard, because we won't know who's watching. As far as Bobby's concerned, he thinks that I went after you and brought you back because he wanted you here. And I gave him the idea that you came back because of me."

"So you're supposed to be the irresistible Rico, and I'm putty in your hands."

"Something like that."

A loud knocking on the door. I rolled my eyes. "Go away Elizabeth."

"It's me, Ashley." She opened the door and stood with her arms folded. "I want my book back."

"Sure," I said. "Let me get it. Hand me my robe, will you Rico?"

Rico crossed to the bathroom and tossed the terrycloth robe to me. I pulled it on without dropping the covers. Rico gazed at me with a raised eyebrow and a half smile.

I pulled the book from my duffle and held it out to her. "I haven't had time to read it yet, but I still want to."

"Yeah, right." Ashley didn't move from the doorway.

I crossed to her and she snatched the book from my hand. "Do we have a problem?" I asked.

Her gaze slipped over to Rico and back to me. "No problem. I wasn't sure you were coming back, and I don't like it when people take off with my things."

I sighed. I'd just become another person who flaked on Ashley, and right at this moment, there was nothing I could do about it. "I'm really sorry."

"Whatever." She turned away. "I'm supposed to tell you that Dad wants to see you like right now," she added over her shoulder.

"Thanks—I guess," I said under my breath. I closed the door and leaned against it. "What's up with Kroy? Do you know?"

Rico shrugged. "No idea, except that when you took off yesterday, he asked me to find you and bring you back."

"He wants to use me for something, right?"

"That's what Carl is hoping."

"Okay, let's find out." I went into the bathroom and quickly got ready. Rico walked with me down the stairs. When we reached the foyer, Kroy hailed us from the living room.

"Valentine, it's about time. Get in here."

We crossed into the living room. Elizabeth sat next to Kroy on the wide white sofa.

"Not you Rico," Kroy said. "Val and I have some business to discuss."

Rico turned to me, and before I could say anything, he bent and kissed me on the mouth. Not a lingering kiss, but long enough and thorough enough to make me unsteady on my feet. I had to put both hands on his chest to keep my balance. He drew away and gave me an ironic smile. So much for my rules about public displays of affection. "I'll wait for you outside," he said. "I need a cigarette anyway."

I glanced at Elizabeth, who raised an eyebrow but didn't say anything. She'd already expressed her disapproval of Rico.

Kroy waited until Rico had closed the front door behind him. "He didn't waste any time, did he?"

"What makes you think that it was Rico who didn't waste time?"

Kroy laughed. "Touché." He waved toward an easy chair facing the couch. "Have a seat, Miss Magic."

"Valentine," I corrected him and perched on the edge of the chair.

"No nicknames, is that it?"

"Something like that. What did you want to see me about?"

"You're going to entertain at my fund-raiser tomorrow night."

"Are you asking or telling?"

He narrowed his eyes at me. "You're the one that told me you were interviewing for a job yesterday. So I'm giving you a job."

"Okay. What's the pay?" I asked.

"Depends on how good a job you do. I want you to do your magic thing, but not a kiddie show with stuffed animals. I need the guests to open their wallets wide. There's going to be speeches and slide show about the poor kids with AIDS. Heart-wrenching stuff, but a downer. You'll bring a lighter note. It has to be more sophisticated than the show I saw. Think you can pull that off?"

"I could do a set on string theory or one on Schroedigger's cat. Which one would you prefer?"

"Not cats," Elizabeth said before Kroy could answer. "Bobby just told you no stuffed animals."

Kroy gave me a half smile. "That's okay, Beth," he said and patted her knee. "It's not a real or a stuffed cat."

"Schroedigger's cat is an illustration of the theory of multiple universes," I said. "Very popular in physics currently. And string theory is a concept of how everything in the universe is connected. Sophisticated audiences I've played to enjoyed my take on it."

"Okay, whatever you want, as long as there's illusion and spectacle."

"There will definitely be smoke and maybe fire too. So you'll have lots of spectacle. I have to go buy supplies for the show. I don't have them on hand."

"Okay. How much do you need?" He reached into his pocket and pulled out a wad of bills held by a diamond-studded money clip.

"That's okay. I have money. And you said you'd pay me to perform, right?"

"Look, take the money." He held out the bills to me. "I said I want a big entertaining spectacle, and I don't want you cutting corners to increase your take. And get yourself something to wear. Something that shows off your assets. Know what I mean?"

I took the money from him. The bills were all one hundreds. I peeled off five of the bills and handed the clip back to Kroy. "This is more than enough. And I don't need to buy clothes. I can wear something of Elizabeth's."

Elizabeth rolled her eyes. "Don't worry, Bobby." She placed a hand on his arm. "I know what you want, and I'll take care of it. She'll look perfect when I'm done with her."

"And get something for Ash, too."

"Certainly. We'll get her out of those god-awful Annie May outfits."

Kroy gave me a little smile. "That'll be great." He winked at me.

Elizabeth caught both the smile and the wink and narrowed her eyes at me.

"I'll be back in a little while." I headed out the door. It was good to have a coalition with Kroy, but I'd pay a price later with Elizabeth. I crossed to the Lincoln Town Car parked at the curb.

Carl, wearing a black suit and matching black chauffeur's cap, got out and held the back door open for me. I slid in next to Rico.

I waited until Carl had pulled away from the curb before saying anything. "I don't think I'm going to be much help, Carl. Kroy wants me just to entertain guests at the fund-raiser."

"That's okay," Carl said. "He wants you to stay in his home. That's all we need. We're going to show you what you have to do."

"Who's 'we?'" I asked. "You and Rico?"

"No," Rico answered. "Remember Mike? You met him that night you stayed in the loft."

"Red-haired guy who was building furniture in his spare time? Is he a confidential informant, too?"

"No, he's a federal agent like Carl."

"Nancy, too?"

"Yes, i-systems is the fake company I convinced Bobby to use to ship his pharmaceuticals. They're supposed to set it up so that nothing can be traced back to him."

"And what am I supposed to do?"

"Mike will explain it all." He turned to look out the window.

We drove in silence toward the condemned building where I'd had my fateful encounter with the elevator. Just thinking about it gave me the shivers. I clenched my teeth. There I went again. Going all neurotic and I wasn't even near an elevator. What I needed to remember was that my freak out in the elevator had cost Phil her life.

"You okay?" Rico draped an arm around my shoulders.

"I'm fine," I lied and pulled away from the comfort of his touch. I leaned forward in my seat and asked Carl, "Are you going to find Phil's killer?"

Carl glanced at me over his shoulder. "Not me personally, but the Bureau has pulled out all the stops. The director flew in with a bunch of specialists. All leave cancelled and every available agent working around the clock just to find this Dwayne and the woman you saw. Which reminds me." He pulled his cell from his coat pocket, held it in the palm of his hand and pushed buttons with his thumb while he drove with his other hand. "Here." He handed the phone over the seat to me. "Check out the pics. That's her, right?"

I swiped through a series of photos of Lies-About-Her-Age. They had shots of her in the hotel lobby as a redhead and others of her standing outside Elizabeth's apartment building. "Incredible. How did they get these?"

"Nothing happens anymore without people recording it on their phones. Agents made a canvas of the whole neighborhood and collected everything anyone had taken. And they pulled the hotel lobby cameras. Those weren't great, but our lab can do miracles with fuzzy photos."

"Are you going to give these to the media?"

"Already done. The phones calls are pouring in of sightings of both of them."

"Yeah," Rico said. "And how many of those tipsters saw those two talking to Elvis?"

Carl laughed. "Granted most of the calls won't pan out, but a few will. All we need is one good lead. So stop with the pessimism and give Valentine her present."

"Right." Rico reached into his jacket pocket and held out a small velvet box. The kind jewelry comes in. I just stared at it. No one ever gave me presents that Elizabeth had allowed me to keep. Except Aunt June, of course. And never jewelry. "Go on," he said. "Take it."

I took it and opened it. A heart-shaped pendant lay inside, one half crystal and one half gold. "I don't...I mean, you shouldn't give me anything. It's very pretty, but..." I tried to hand it back to him.

"It's not from me personally. It's for the job Mike wants you to do." Rico lifted the heart from the box and pulled it apart. A small piece of metal protruded from the gold half of the heart.

"It's really a..."

"I know," I interrupted him. "It's a flash drive." My cheeks felt hot. How stupid was I anyway? Thinking Rico would give me jewelry.

"No, actually it's a micro-miniature hard drive," He clicked the two halves back together. "But it works on the same principle. We want everyone to think that it's a special present from me that you never take off for any reason." He unclasped the chain. "So let's put it on you now."

Carl drove us to the back entrance of the building. The back door was propped open with a piece of scrap lumber. Carl kicked it aside once we entered. The woodworking equipment was silent and Mike nowhere in sight. We passed into the hall and on to the i-systems office and found Mike at a computer laughing and swearing. "Think you can pull that ricochet shit with me, you son of a bitch? Think again. Hah, gotcha!" He looked up when we came into his line of vision. "Hey, guys."

"Hey, yourself," Carl said. "Is there a problem?" He gestured toward the computer.

"No problem. Well, kind of a problem, but nothing I can't deal with. Kroy has a ricochet virus on his computer. So whenever his firewall is breached, no matter what you try to see, all you get is this EXE file that once opened fries your motherboard."

"So he fried your motherboard?"

"You kidding? I know the guy who wrote the original program. So I have my own program that sends it right back to him. Only he had the same idea, so it gets sent back to me. Then I send it back and so on. It's like Pong, only played in cyberspace."

"I thought you already got into Kroy's system and couldn't find anything. Isn't that why we brought Valentine here?" Rico asked.

"We found something, only it was crap," Mike said. "He's partitioned his hard drive. So when you hack in and look for anything hidden, you find this partition. Get through the partition and you think, bingo. Only you're wrong. That section is just to fool you so you don't look any further."

"So where are the files we're looking for?" Carl asked.

"In yet another partitioned section."

"So why don't you just hack into it?" Rico asked.

"Because we can't do it without him knowing."

"But he already knows you've hacked into his computer," Carl said.

"Well, he doesn't know it's me, just someone. Which is what we want. Make him a bit paranoid and edgy. But also make him think we haven't breached his last partition. And that's where Valentine comes in."

"I think you have the wrong person," I said. "I don't know anything about computers except how to use the search engines."

"And you don't have to know anything but how to identify a USB port, and I'll show you that. You plug in the pretty little device Rico gave you, and the computer will blast a byte by byte image of Kroy's hard drive to our microdrive. When I have that I'll be able to find and decrypt the hidden partition. And I know that this time it won't be garbage."

"I don't have to tell it what to copy?"

"No. That's the beauty of it. It's programmed, so once it's plugged in, it does it all on its own. Just wait till the little light on the drive goes off and pull it."

"How long will it take?"

"Since all it's doing is taking a picture, so to speak, of the hard drive and not copying it file by file, it'll only take about ten minutes."

"Ten minutes! That's too long. Kroy doesn't let anyone go into his study unless he invites them. And his bodyguard is just as paranoid as he is."

Mike looked at Carl and Rico. "Okay, boys. It's over to you. You said she could do it. The lady doesn't agree."

Carl and Rico exchanged glances. Rico spoke first, "I've said all along it's too dangerous."

"Look, Valentine," Carl said. "If it's not possible, all right. But if you can find a way in, then go for it. Once you've made a copy, you leave immediately."

"That's all you need to nail Kroy?" I asked.

"Kroy and everyone up the line from him in the whole scheme."

Mike opened his mouth to say something, but a look from Carl silenced him.

"If I'm not there," Rico said, "and you sense that Kroy's on to you, walk out. Just go."

"I'll do it." I had to. "Piece of cake," I said with more bravado than I felt. "I am, after all, the Great Valentina." I made a dramatic sweeping gesture with my arm and bowed to them.

With this, tension seeped from the room like a balloon with a leak. "Atta girl," Mike said. "Come over here, and I'll show you what to do." He led me to a nearby cubicle. We sat down in front of a computer.

"This computer is identical to Kroy's. There are USB ports here," he pointed to the front of the hard drive. "And here." He pointed to the side of the monitor. "Any one will do the job." He spoke slowly, as if to a child or a mentally challenged adult. "Okay?"

"Okay," I said, I said slowly, imitating him.

"So give me the microdrive." He held out his hand. When I didn't move, he said, "Here, let me help you. It pulls apart very easily."

He reached for the pendant, but I blocked his hand with one arm and grabbed the pendant with the other. "That's all right. I can get it myself." I pulled the microdrive section free with one hand and palmed it with the other. "Oops." I held out my empty hand. "I must have dropped it." I looked down at the floor. As soon as he bent to scan the floor I pushed the microdrive into the side of the monitor. "Do you see it?" I asked.

He straightened. "No. Maybe it fell in your lap. Stand up slowly and let's see. Don't move your feet. You don't want to step on it."

I stood and staggered as if I'd lost my balance.

"Goddamnit! Hold still. You know what that piece of equipment cost?"

"I'll ask you to watch your language, sir," I said in my best Southern belle imitation, "There are ladies present."

Carl and Rico appeared outside the cubicle. "What's the problem?" Carl asked.

"No problem," I said.

"Oh, yes there is." Mike said, his face nearly as red as his hair.

"This ditz just dropped the microprocessor and she's about to step on it."

"You mean that microprocessor?" Rico said, pointing to the side of the monitor.

Mike swiveled the monitor so he could see where Rico pointed. "What the hell?"

"Thank you, gentlemen," I said to Rico and Carl. "We'll be fine now." They moved away.

Mike turned to me. "What was the point of that?"

"I don't know what your problem is with me, but I'm not a ditz and I resent being spoken to like a child."

"I get that and I apologize."

"Apology accepted. Now maybe you can help me. Kroy's security system monitors all the ways in and out of the house. What if I want to get out, but don't want to trigger an alarm or show up on camera?"

"Can you get access to the monitoring station?"

"At night I can."

"Okay, then," he swiveled his chair to face the computer and typed something on the screen. "Kroy has an ADT system. I'm pretty sure he has the H473HK model and it looks like this." A picture came up of a multiple screen set up.

"That's it. I was in the room for a second. It looks just like that."

"Okay then Miss Not-Ditz, watch closely. This button would turn the system off, but you don't want to do that because that would trigger an alarm. Instead, you need to go through this sequence. Turn off the alarm, turn off the back-up power, then hit these two keys." He moved the mouse and pointed to each button and he described the steps.

"Does that turn off the system?"

"Nope, that's the beauty of it. It will just freeze the picture. It stops recording without being turned off. Normally the system would alarm and switch over to back-up power if the picture freezes for more than two minutes, but if you turn it off in that order, it can't."

"Brilliant," I said.

"Thank you," Mike replied with a grin. "And you'll be beyond brilliant if you pull this off." He removed the microprocessor from the monitor and handed it to me. "Good luck."

I joined the microprocessor to the other half of the heart on the chain around my neck. I'd need more than luck, but I hoped I had luck as well. I rejoined Rico and Carl and we set off for the magic shop. I hadn't decided which routine to do, and since I had plenty of money thanks to Kroy, I bought enough to do both. I needed to practice. I had only this afternoon and tomorrow day. Not really enough time.

Rico and Carl let me do my own thing in the magic shop, but when we got back to Kroy's, Rico got out of the car with me and walked me to the door. "Wait a minute."

"What is it?"

"Make sure you have your phone with you at all times."

"Roger that. And my super spy device," I said fingering the pendant.

"Call me before you go to sleep, okay?"

"Checking up on me?"

He gave me a steady look. "It's not a game."

"Yeah, yeah. You already gave me that lecture." I rang the doorbell.

Rico opened his mouth to say something, but Elizabeth opened the door. Behind her in the middle of the foyer a red-faced Kroy raged at a young man I'd never seen before, while Connie stood nearby, arms folded across his substantial chest. "Listen, you son of a bitch, I don't want any excuses. You said no one could hack into my system."

"N-no sir," the man stammered. "I said no one could retrieve anything of use if they hacked into your system."

Kroy shifted his gaze to Rico and me standing in the doorway. "You," he said, jabbing a finger in my direction. "Where the hell have you been? Get in here. Now. And you," he said to Rico, "get the hell out of here."

Rico gave Kroy an ironic salute and said, "Talk to you later," to me.

Kroy crossed to the doorway and closed the door on Rico. He turned, his face still dark with rage, to the trembling computer tech. "What's going to stop the hackers from getting the real data next time, tell me that." He jabbed a finger at the cringing man's chest.

"Your computer's alarmed so we know whenever there's a breech. And I installed a program that inserts a virus into the hacker's computer, a virus that destroys their computer. It's just that in this case the hacker was very sophisticated and he countered the virus with one of his own."

"What?" Kroy yelled and grabbed the man by his shirtfront. "So now I've got a virus on my computer?"

"No. I blocked it. Nothing's been infected. R-really," the poor man stammered in the face of Kroy's ever mounting rage.

Kroy was teetering on the edge of violence. Time to defuse the situation, if I could. Neither Elizabeth or Connie seemed willing to intervene. "So you used the ricochet virus?" I asked the techie.

Kroy released his grip and frowned at me. The techie staggered backward and turned to me eyes wide in surprise and with a shade of relief. "Yes. It's very effective most of the time."

"What are you talking about?" Kroy asked me. "You know computers?"

"No, but I used to date a computer programmer. That's mostly what he talked about. He knew the guy who wrote the original ricochet program. But it sounds like you put a new twist on it if your program blocked a counterattack."

"Yes, it worked quite well. No important data got compromised."

"This time, you mean," Kroy said. "What about the next time?"

"Well sir, I have some suggestions I'd like to make. One is for a new encryption program that…"

Kroy put up his hand and silenced the man in mid-sentence. He turned to me. "We are going to have a talk. Connie, get that useless twerp out of here." He gestured to the cowering young man with one hand and grabbed my arm with the other.

Chapter Fifteen

Kroy marched me down the hall to his study. I didn't protest or try to pull away. If anything, I deliberately relaxed. Any resistance on my part would just feed his rage. I needed to stay calm and put on what Aunt June always called my "who, me?" face if Kroy accused me of anything. Plenty of time to go all moral outrage if he didn't believe me.

I glanced back at the group in the foyer. Connie descending on the visibly terrified computer tech and Elizabeth, not terrified but worried-looking, watching Kroy march me down the hall. As soon as she saw me watching her, she smoothed the worried frown from her face. Elizabeth worried? That bothered me much more than an enraged Kroy.

Kroy pushed me into his study ahead of him and pointed to a chair. "Sit."

I sat. He remained standing, arms crossed, frowning at me. "I want to know why you're here. I see you in Vegas. I can tell you're related to Beth, but you blow me off. Next thing I know you're on my doorstep. So I invite you into my home, and things start going to hell. So give. And no bullshit."

"I've been looking for Elizabeth for years. She always has a big con going, and I wanted to work with her again. I found out from Ashley where Elizabeth was living, and came straight here from Vegas."

"How do I know you're not lying?"

I shrugged. "Ultimately, you don't. But here's where I've been the past five years." I pulled out my wallet with the twenty-seven library cards. "The dates are sequential."

He grabbed it from me and the long plastic strip of cardholders unfolded. While he looked at the cards, I took in his office setup. Especially the computer. It would be easy to pop the microprocessor into the USB port, not so easy to find an excuse to be alone in the office for ten minutes.

Kroy tossed the wallet back in my lap. "What were you doing in all these places?"

I slowly refolded the strip that held my cards. "Working my magic act, mainly busking—you know, street corner stuff. And working for other magicians, getting paid under the table."

"You forgot to mention running cons and picking pockets."

I nodded. "That too, but nothing with a big payoff."

"And you're here because you think Beth is running a con on me?"

"Hah! Not likely. All I know is that she's running a con *with* you, but she won't tell me anything. And apparently neither will you." I got to my feet. "So I'll do my act tomorrow night as agreed. You'll pay me, and I'll be out of here."

"Sit down. I'm not done with you." He paced the room. The image of a caged animal came uncomfortably to mind.

I sank down into the chair and watched him pace. He stopped in front of the French doors and stared out at the well-tended garden.

"Someone's out to get me," he said without turning around.

"Do you mean 'get you' as in kill you?"

He turned and faced me. "Kill me. Rob me. Ruin me. Or all of the above."

"Who is it?" I asked.

"If I knew that, do you think he'd still be alive?"

"Good thing you have Connie, then. And your security system. No one can get through that."

"Really? Then how did someone manage to hack into my computer? My high-priced tech support, who supposedly set up an unhackable system, doesn't have a clue. Then there's the goon who came after Beth. And guess what? Same guy tortured and killed an FBI agent, and the police don't know jack about it."

I flinched. He knew about Phil?

He narrowed his eyes at me. "You didn't know about that, did you?"

"I heard that someone had been killed, but they didn't mention torture." In fact, I knew the FBI deliberately withheld that detail. "Was that on the news? I must have missed it."

"Hell no. You think the cops are going to advertise their failures? A police commissioner is a pal of mine. I asked him about progress on finding who tried to attack Beth, and he told me the whole situation was bigger than they thought."

I just stared at him. Carter had told me that Kroy had connections, but it hadn't fully registered what that meant.

"So I'm asking you. What do you know about the threat to Beth and the attack on my computer?"

I locked gazes with him. "Nothing." It was partly true.

"I have ways of finding out if you're lying to me, and I have no qualms about using them." He fixed me with a hard look.

My heart rate quickened, but I kept my face blank. I matched him stare for stare. "Good luck with that." I pulled up the sleeves of my shirt and showed him the scars on my arms.

It was his turn to flinch. "What the hell?"

"That's what I say." I stood up and pulled down my shirt-sleeves. "What the hell? If you think I'm working against you, throw me out, but enough with the threats, because I've been there so many times that it just doesn't faze me now."

"What was the number on Rico's credit card?"

I blinked at the sudden change of subject, but answered right away. "8881437273454200. Why?"

He gazed at me for several moments, then crossed the room and lifted a picture. It swung upward on hinges to reveal a keypad and a wall safe. He glanced over his shoulder at me and shifted so his body blocked my view. He punched numbers into the keypad then twirled the dial on the safe back and forth. When he reached the last number, the safe opened without a sound. He reached in and pulled out banded stacks of bills and a sheet of paper. He closed the safe, lowered the picture and turned to me.

"You wanted a job? Okay, you're hired." He approached me and tossed the money into my lap and placed the sheet of paper on his desk.

I picked up the money and fanned through the stacks. All hundreds. At a guess, ten thousand dollars. I lifted my gaze to meet his. "What's the job?"

"I asked Beth about you. She said you were helping her run cons before you were toilet-trained and that you could do that memory trick from the time you could read. Is that right?"

"Yeah, I guess. As far as I can remember, I've always been able to do it."

"Turns out that I need someone with your peculiar talent. I'm going to hire you for two jobs. One as a board member of the Kroy Foundation. The other as director of the BK Trading Company. That money is a good faith payment. I'll give you triple that when you finish the job."

I frowned and held the bundle of hundreds up between my thumb and forefinger. "Hmm. I don't know. You must have gotten the impression that I'm a cheap date. Not true. I know that you're going for a big score, and here you're offering me below minimum wage. This will pay for the privilege of putting my name on the company masthead, but if you actually want me to do something…" I let the sentence trail off.

"How much do you want?" Kroy asked.

"What's Elizabeth's cut?"

Kroy gave me a considering look.

"I can always ask her, you know," I said.

"I paid her one hundred thousand to sign on for the two positions that I'm now giving you."

I whistled. "One hundred K? Does that include her supervising the organizers of the gala?"

"No. That was a separate agreement."

"Does she get a percentage beyond the one hundred thou?"

"No, and she resigned from the foundation and BK Trading as of today. If you're hesitating out of loyalty to her, you should know that it was her idea that I hire you."

I kept my gaze neutral but my heart rate ratcheted up. If Elizabeth had bailed it meant either the deal was too hot or that it was a bust—or about to be a bust. If the deal wasn't going to go down, then all my work and the FBI's would be for nothing.

"And what do you want me to do?" I asked.

"Sign on for those two positions and commit to memory all addresses, account numbers, routing numbers and phone numbers that I give you. I'll retain no other record. Think you can do that?"

"You know I can. Anything else?"

"Your absolute loyalty to me. You breathe a word to anyone—and I mean anyone—about this, and I'll have you killed. Understand?"

I was tempted to make a flip answer, but settled for giving him a serious look and nodding. He loved the feeling of power that holding threats over people gave him. I'd use that against him if I could, but I wouldn't appear to challenge it or undermine it. "In that case, I'll take double what you gave Elizabeth. Half up front. Half when the deal goes down."

"Double? How'd you come up with that figure?"

I smiled. "I'm actually going to work for my money. And I hope that you're not going to pay me all in cash because my mattress isn't big enough."

He laughed and patted me on the shoulder. "Not to worry, Miss Magic," he said, exchanging his threatening tone for his usual bombastic bonhomie, which, weirdly enough, was even scarier. "We'll set you up with your own offshore account." He moved behind his desk and sat down. "We'll do that while we're arranging all of the other paperwork. I'm calling my attorney right now." He reached for his mouse.

"Hang on a minute," I said. "I need some clarification."

He sighed. "What is it?"

"You're turning me into your living safe deposit box, and quite frankly, I don't see you as the kind of man who would trust another person to that degree. How do I know you won't simply kill me after the deal goes down?"

"That's the beauty of it, Miss Magic. My name doesn't show up anywhere on BK Trading documents. Yours will, however, and if anything goes sideways, I won't have to kill you, because you'll be arrested. All I'll have to do is act shocked and indignant because I'm a known and respected citizen, while you are quite literally nobody. Understood?"

I nodded. I understood all too well that Kroy was feeding me a line, but I kept my expression neutral.

"Excellent. Let's get this done." He clicked his mouse and in a second said, "You there, Ted?

A disembodied voice came from the computer. "Hey there, Bobby. How's it going?"

"I'm good. In fact, I'm great. You coming to my shindig tomorrow night? It's going to be the biggest fund-raiser this town has ever seen. People flying in from all over—New York, Paris, London, Hollywood, you name it. Half of them are coming to see all the famous people and the famous people are coming to be seen. All at twenty thousand a head. But I need all my ducks in a row, know what I mean? So are you ready to sign up my new board member and company director, Valentine Hill?"

"Ready and waiting."

"Valentine," Kroy said, "come over here and meet Ted Spears." He pulled a side chair over for me.

I joined him behind the desk and saw the outline of a man's head and shoulders. The figure itself was cast in shadow.

"Hello, Mr. Spears. You know, I can't see you very well."

"That is on purpose. I prefer to keep a certain degree of anonymity because of the—shall we say—delicacy of the work I do for my clients. Did I hear Bobby correctly? Your name is Valentine?"

"Yes, that's really my name. What information do you need, Mr. Spears?"

"Let's see, Bobby said your name was Valentine Hill. Do you have a middle name?"

"No."

"Address?"

"Same as mine," Kroy said. "And phone contact, too."

Spears fell silent, but I could hear him typing on a keyboard. "Social security number?"

I glanced at Kroy and gave a brief shake of my head.

"We'll need you to fix that up for her. That okay, Ted?"

"Certainly. No problem. Just give me a minute and I'll fax the documents to you for your signatures. Before I do that just let me confirm we're talking about BK Trading as the onshore nominee company for the corporation we've set up in Panama. Is that correct?" Spears asked.

"Yes, exactly. But I still want all the banking done in Hong Kong."

"Of course. You know that you can safely bank in Panama, as well. There's complete anonymity and no tax treaties in place, so no one can go on a fishing expedition. But it's as you wish."

"I prefer Hong Kong for now. And make the arrangements with the banks so Valentine can be a signatory on the two accounts. The Foundation's and BK Trading's. And while you're at it, she'll need her own account. Make it in the Caymans. Transfer one hundred thousand into it via today's untraceable route."

"You got it. Hang on a few so I can fax these documents to you."

Kroy swiveled in his chair to face me. "See how I take care of you? Your money will be in your own offshore account before the end of the day. And here's how you'll earn it." He picked up the sheet of paper he'd taken out of his safe and handed it to me. "The top line is Rieman's Pharmaceutical's secure phone contact and the second are the account and routing numbers you'll deposit the money in today, as well as the address you'll give them for the drugs. Ted will fax all the signed authorizations to Rieman's. The third line is the account information of another company we'll call company X. You will authorize payment to them as well, when they call me with the phone number they'll use that one time only. The fourth line is the address they'll use to arrange the drop shipment of the drugs. When I tell you to, you'll call and give them the address. So do what you do to memorize these." He handed me the sheet of paper.

"These numbers aren't in your computer?"

"Hell no. You saw how risky that is. I don't care what that computer geek says. The hell with him and his shadow partitions. They're going to keep trying until they get past his trick partitions. And when they find out it's all encrypted and they can't break the code, they'll come after me for the information."

"Only you won't have it," I said. "I will."

"Correct."

"And if they—whoever 'they' are—try to persuade you to hand over the information, you'll give me up."

"Possibly. Depends on their persuasion tactics."

I stared at the numbers on the paper. I was pretty sure that Phil had never intended for me to get in this deep. And I didn't even know how deep "this" was myself. Oh well, it couldn't be any worse than being trapped in an old broken-down elevator, could it? I lifted my head. Look at me—I'd become so good at lying that now I was lying to myself.

The fax machine whirred softly. Kroy swung his chair around and pulled the pages out of the feeder bin. "Here you go. Sign and date every place Ted's marked." I did as he said, and Kroy faxed them back to Spears. Then I conducted my first duties as a board member and sent three million dollars to Rieman's Pharmaceuticals and the same amount to an anonymous account while Kroy held the page and checked that I had the numbers right.

He and Spears ended their conversation with another jovial exchange, and Kroy shifted his gaze to me. "Good job. How about the other numbers?"

"You can test me if it'll make you feel better," I said.

He blinked as if considering it, but shook his head. "You wouldn't say that unless you were positive." He fed the sheet into the shredder and transformed it into bits of confetti.

I stood up to leave.

"Oh, and one more thing," he said. "You're to have no contact whatsoever with Rico or anyone else outside, for that matter. You won't leave the house until we go to the gala. And I'll need your phone."

"My phone? Why?"

"I need to guarantee that you follow my rule. No contact."

"I don't understand. I thought you were doing a business deal with Rico."

"I was. Just not the business he thought. He made an offer to help me ship some product and manage the profits. He came up with a very good rate of return and I used his offer to negotiate a better deal with the guys I used before."

"So you double-crossed him."

"Don't be naïve. It's just the way things work in business. But he doesn't need to know until the deal's gone down."

"What if he comes here?"

"Connie has his orders. Rico won't make it through the door. You can make up with him later." He held out his hand. "Phone."

I gave Kroy my phone and stuffed the stacks of hundred dollar bills into the back of my pants waistband. "Why are you buying the medicines now? Aren't you going to raise more money at the gala?"

He fixed me with a steady gaze for a moment. "You're a smart girl. I can see that. But the smart thing to do right now is don't ask questions. Not of me. Not of anyone else. Understand?"

"Got it." I made the motion of zipping my lips.

"That's the way," he said. "Now get out of here and let me get some work done."

I left and went upstairs in search of a phone. I hesitated a moment in front of Ashley's door before I knocked. She hadn't been too happy with me that morning. What were the odds I could talk her into letting me use her cell phone? I knocked and waited until I heard her sulky, "Who is it?" I opened the door a crack. "It's me, Valentine. May I come in—please?"

"Whatever," Ashley said. I chose to view it as an invitation.

I stepped into her room and closed the door behind me. Ashley lay on her bed reading and didn't acknowledge me.

"I have an emergency, and I need your help."

"What's the emergency?" She asked in the tone of someone who couldn't care less.

"Your dad confiscated my phone."

Ashley lowered her book. "Why?"

"He doesn't want me talking to Rico. Their business deal fell apart. He thinks I might pass on information about the deal he's cut Rico out of."

"Would you?"

"Of course not! But your dad's really paranoid. Know what I mean?"

Ashley gave me a long considering look. "Maybe he has his reasons."

"You're right. He does, but I'm not one of them. What do I care about his stupid business deals? I just want to phone my boyfriend and tell him I won't be able to talk to him or see him until after the gala."

"Do you love him?"

The question was so unexpected that I didn't have a ready answer.

Ashley gave me a knowing smile. "That's what I thought." She got up from the bed and crossed to her desk. "I wasn't sure I was going to show you this." She handed me a flyer, a sheet of pink paper covered in smudgy black print in various fonts surrounding an image of hands playing a guitar. "Rico's good-looking if you like his type, but he's not Jeff."

I looked from the flyer to Ashley's face. "What's Jeff got to do with anything?"

She gestured to the flyer. "He's here. Just like he said. See? Ghoul Food. That's the band he told you about."

I peered at the flyer again and saw Ghoul Food listed along the right hand margin along with seven other ridiculous names.

"They're playing at 924 Gilman," Ashley said, an undertone of excitement in her voice. And when I just stared at her, she went on. "Gilman? In Berkeley? God, don't you know anything? I knew about Gilman even before I moved here. Bands like Sabertooth Zombie and Rancid play there. It's going to be his big chance."

I handed the flyer back to Ashley. "Look, I don't think you understand. Jeff and I—actually there isn't a Jeff and I. There never was." I might have added "even before he stole all my money," but I didn't need to get into a long tale about Jeff. What I needed was a phone.

"Why won't you admit it? You still have feelings for Jeff. And Jeff loves you. I was there, remember? Can you say the same about Rico?"

Where did Ashley come up with this stuff? Was anime a Japanese version of American soap operas? "Yes—I can." I pointed to the gold and crystal heart that hung around my neck. "He gave me this today. And told me he wanted us to be exclusive. He told me he's never said that to anyone else."

"But do you love him?"

"Look, this is all new to me," I said. "I've never been in love before. But, yes, I think I love him. And I know he'll be upset when he calls and I don't pick up or call him back. So please let me borrow your phone. Just for a few minutes, that's all." I acted the role I thought Ashley would believe, but I put all the desperation that I in truth was feeling into my voice.

"Okay." She pulled her phone from her jeans pocket and handed it to me. "But I want it right back."

I took the phone. "I promise. And thank you." I hurried into my room and closed the door, then on into the bathroom and closed that door too. Rico told me he'd checked the room for bugs, but that was in the morning. I couldn't take any chances. I turned on the water in the sink and opened the phone. My index finger hovered over the numbers as it gradually came to me. I didn't know Rico's number. He'd put it on speed-dial on the phone he'd given me, so I'd never actually seen the number.

I paced the short length of the bathroom several times. If I'd been in the habit of cursing, now would be the time for it. I had to think. Wait. I stopped pacing. I knew a number I could call. The one Phil had written on the back of Lopez's card. She'd told me I could call it anytime and someone would always answer. And that number I had seen. I punched it into the phone.

A woman's voice answered curtly, "Who's speaking?"

"This is Valentine Hill," I whispered into the phone.

"Please speak up. Who gave you this number?"

"Agent Philips did. The day before she died. You must have a report there with my name in it. Valentine Hill," I repeated a little louder in case she'd missed it.

"One moment." She must have put me on hold, but there was no sappy music, or message thanking me for my patience, just dead air. I waited. Finally she came on the line again.

"Ms. Hill?"

"Yes?"

"What can I do for you?"

I let out the breath that I hadn't realized I'd been holding. "I've been working with Carl Carter and it's urgent that I reach him."

After a pause, during which I heard the tapping of computer keys, the woman said, "Special Agent Carter is in the field and can't currently be reached. Leave your number and I'll have him call you."

"No, that won't work. They took my phone away. I borrowed this one, but I have to give it right back. If I can't talk to Carl maybe you can give me a number for Rico DiSera? He's working with Agent Carter, so possibly you have his information on file?"

Another pause accompanied by tapping, then, "Special Agent DiSera is also in the field and can't be reached. Do you want to leave a message?"

"*Special Agent* DiSera," I echoed.

"Is there a message?"

I sank onto the rim of the bathtub. "Message…yes." I couldn't focus.

"Can you speak up? I can't hear you."

Rico had lied to me. Repeatedly. The phony cab driver and pretend gangster who teased me with his fake seduction. And while I kept trying not to like him too much, he coldly and deliberately played me.

"Ms. Hill? Are you still there?"

I cleared my throat. "Yes. I'm here. The message for Agents Carter and DiSera is—I'm working for Kroy now and have information, but he took my phone and won't let me leave the house. I'll find a way to make contact again tomorrow night during the gala. Got that?"

"Yes."

I ended the call without saying good-bye. I turned off the sink tap, and walked slowly out of my room to Ashley's door. I knocked lightly and opened the door. "Ashley? Here's your phone."

Ashley had returned to her book, but she looked up when I came in. "Whoa. You don't look so good. What happened?" She put her book aside.

"Nothing happened. He didn't pick up, so I left a message. Thanks for letting me use your phone. I really appreciate it." I held the phone out to her.

"Something happened. Your hand is shaking." She took her phone from my fingers.

"Just tired, that's all." I turned, went out the door, and nearly collided with Elizabeth, who was carrying several oversized shopping bags from Saks and Neiman Marcus.

"There you are," Elizabeth said. "I was looking for you. You're going to love what I bought for you."

"Can we do this later? I'm really tired." I didn't want to deal with Elizabeth, particularly not when she was playing Lady Santa. Her "gifts" always came with big price tags. I needed time to calm down and think about rotten Rico the fibbing fed. He probably had a 'The ends justify the means' poster hanging on his office wall.

"There is no later, Valentine. We need to do this now." She leaned into Ashley's room. "You too, Ash. Come try on your dress." She continued down the hallway to my bedroom. Ashley slid off the bed and joined me, trailing behind Elizabeth.

Once in my room, Elizabeth arranged the shopping bags on my bed. "You girls should have come with me. I had so much fun. Wait till you see." She rummaged in one of the bags and pulled out a long black dress. "For you, Valentine. It looks like a rag on the hanger, but wait till you see it on. It's stunning. Of course you'll want to wear something different for your performance, and I thought this would be perfect." She produced a second dress, black like the first but with about a fourth of the material. To call it skimpy was an exaggeration.

"Wow," Ashley said. "Does that come with its own stripper pole?"

"Ashley! What a thing to say," Elizabeth said. "It's perfectly appropriate for a stage performance. I'm sure Valentine's used to wearing dresses like this when she's onstage. Right, Valentine?"

"It's fine, Elizabeth. Thanks." I tried for tact. The last thing I wanted to do right now was antagonize Elizabeth. I'd wait until I tried it on in private before I decided if it was too skimpy. I had a backup costume I could wear, and Elizabeth didn't need to know about it until I was onstage.

"Bobby thinks it'll be perfect," Elizabeth said, as if that ended all discussion. "And wait till you see what I got for you, Ashley. I couldn't decide which one I liked best, so I bought them both so you could choose. She pulled out two dresses, one pink chiffon, one lilac lace. Neither one had the drama of the dresses she'd bought for me. In fact, the styles were more appropriate for a pre-teen than for a fifteen-year-old.

Ashley stared at them. "Are you out of your mind?"

"Not at all. Which one do you like?"

"I wouldn't wear either one to my own funeral."

"These are exactly what your father would like to see you wear to his gala."

"Well, screw him and screw his gala," she said and whirled out of the room.

"I think you should tell her that tantrums aren't going to cut it with Bobby," Elizabeth said.

I shook my head. "She wouldn't listen to me. Besides, I agree with her. These dresses look like a bridesmaid's nightmare. And you knew she'd never go for pastels."

Elizabeth shrugged. "It's not about what she likes. It's what Bobby wants. My job is to see that everything goes smoothly and just the way he wants it."

"That so? And what do you get out of it?"

She flashed an enigmatic smile and didn't answer my question. "And it looks like now you're helping Bobby, too?" She posed it as a question.

I was suddenly extremely aware of the bundles of cash I'd tucked into the back of my pants waistband. I gave a tug at the hem of my shirt to make sure it hadn't ridden up. "I think you know that Mr. Kroy would be very upset if I commented on that."

"You can tell me. After all I'm the one who gave you a glowing recommendation."

"Including praise for my unyielding discretion?"

She gave me a considering look. "I hope that's true, because there's something I need you to do for me."

My heart skipped a beat. That was how Elizabeth had always introduced me to a new scam. "What is it?" I asked, trying for a casual tone.

"Can I count on you? Completely? Decide now, because there will be no backing out. At least, not without consequences," she said with ice in her eyes and in her words. This was the old familiar Elizabeth. The mother from hell.

"You can count on me." I met her gaze straight on. "Why do you think I'm here in the first place?"

She gazed at me for a beat, as if she was still making up her mind. I held steady, giving away nothing in my expression or body language. She blinked first.

"Wait till you see what I have." She turned and pulled two rectangular velvet boxes out of one of the shopping bags. "This one is for you." She opened the first box and held it out for me to see. A diamond necklace lay nestled in the velvet folds of the box. The stones were gradated in size. The one in front had to be at least four carats.

"Are they real?"

"Of course they're real," she said with a laugh. "Have you ever known me to wear fakes? And you have to agree they're much more stunning than that little thing you're wearing. Swarovski, right? Where did you get it?"

"Rico gave it to me."

She rolled her eyes. "Well, tell him he'll have to do better than crystal. Now look at mine." She opened the second box to display a three-strand diamond necklace with a large diamond pendant hanging from the longest strand. "Three hundred carats total, worth ten million. What do you think?"

"Where did you get them?"

"They're on loan from Bulgari for the gala. Bobby arranged it. Insured to the max, of course, which is a good thing because they're going to be stolen."

"Are you nuts? With your record, they'll nail you for it for sure. And for what? You couldn't fence it for one-tenth of its value."

"I already have a very eager buyer who's going to give me three point five million. And no one will accuse me, because I'm going to be in the hospital with a heart attack."

"So what does that make me? The fall guy? Because if both necklaces are stolen, and you aren't on the short-list of suspects, I definitely will be."

"No, no. Would you just listen for a second? Your necklace isn't part of the deal, just mine. I'll need you for a brief time only. I'll have a heart attack—not a real one of course, but an excellent imitation. I have a little pill that will make it look very believable. You'll rush to my side, go with me to the hospital and on the way the you will help me lose the necklace."

"No one loses three hundred carats, Elizabeth."

"I know you'll find a way. You always did."

"And what do I get out of it?"

She tilted her head to one side. "How does five percent sound?"

"You must be kidding."

"All right then, ten percent."

"Still not enough for the risk I'll be taking." I folded my arms across my chest.

"Okay, fifteen and that's as high as I go."

"I thought I was crucial to your plan."

"You are, but if you act like a brat I'll just have to make other arrangements."

I tapped my foot and stared off into space, giving the impression I was debating her proposal. I'd been waiting for this moment for a long time. I might never again be in a position to negotiate with her, so I had to put it just right. "Okay, I'll take the fifteen percent, but only if you give me some information."

"What?"

"I want to know exactly where and when I was born."

"Are you serious? But you know your birthday—February 14th." She closed the jewelry boxes and returned them to the bag.

"Is it really?"

"Of course." She turned her attention to Ashley's dresses, folding them carefully and replacing them in the shopping bag.

I gritted my teeth. She wasn't even pretending to be telling the truth by giving me her full insincere attention so I'd believe her. "What year?"

"Oh dear, now you're asking a tough one. You know I've never paid much attention to years, except to subtract them from my age," she said with a light laugh. "But I can probably figure it out. And you want to know where? You're going to force me to rack my brain."

"Don't play with me, Elizabeth. If you want me to help you, you'll have to tell me what I want to know, or it's no deal. Date, year, and place of my birth, *and* everything you know about my father, beginning with his name."

She stopped fiddling with the shopping bags and faced me. She looked caught off guard. "Your father? Why? And why now? It's never come up before."

"You used to talk about him."

"I did? When?"

"Right up till you were sent to prison, and I went to live with Aunt June."

Her eyebrows drew together in puzzlement. "What did I tell you?"

"I'd do magic tricks for you, and you'd say I reminded you of him. I asked you if he was a magician, too. You said he was."

Elizabeth laughed. Not the tinkly laugh of supposed genuine amusement she'd perfected over the years, but her primal harsh laugh. Not a sound that invited others to share in her amusement. Once she'd started, she couldn't seem to stop. She sat down on the edge of the bed, took some deep breaths and finally stopped. "Don't look at me like that," she said.

I could feel the heat in my face and struggled to keep the anger that surged through me in check.

"God, I haven't laughed like that in years. Poor Valentine. Is that why you took up this magician shtick? To be like daddy?" She nearly broke out into laughter again. "Okay, I'll tell you right now. I don't know who your actual father is. The man you reminded me of was a magician in bed. Not something I wanted to share with a little girl. Besides, it worked better for the con if you believed there was an actual daddy out there somewhere. Sorry to disappoint you. I hope that's not a deal-breaker."

Chapter Sixteen

I spent the rest of the afternoon and evening bouncing between my rage at Elizabeth and my anger at Rico. How could I have been so stupid, so naïve? They had both conned me. Me! The one who could spot a scam before it even launched. Elizabeth's laughter still echoed in the room. Was Rico the rat laughing at me too? I paced and stewed. Finally, I managed to bring my fury down to a slow simmer, which left room for anxiety to creep in. I had to perfect my routine for the gala. I hadn't practiced anything for days now and my plan included some new twists on an act I'd performed only twice.

I pulled out my magician's cape and stowed the smoke bombs, the balls for juggling, and all my ropes in its secret pockets and began a run-through. After a few miserable efforts I threw down the rope I was trying the split-and-reconnect illusion with. I wasn't a magician. I was a joke. I was about to take off my cape and throw it on the floor too when I heard Aunt June talking to me. "Don't perform for yourself. You can't be a magician and an audience at the same time. Do it again now, for me." I could almost see her, sitting very straight in her chair, eyes bright and focused completely on me. I started over from the beginning, not stopping when I messed up, but noting the rough spots. Then I repeated each misstep again and again until I could do that part ten times in a row without a glitch.

I was ready for a complete run-through but knew I needed a break. I'd long ago recognized the importance of allowing time between practice sessions. And food as well. All part of being a professional, Aunt June would have said.

I took the back stairs to the kitchen, grateful for the hidden passageway because I didn't want to see Elizabeth or Kroy. Carmela stood next to the dishwasher carefully stowing dirty dishes into the racks and gave me a sour look when I came through the door. "Don't let me interrupt," I said.

She snorted and turned away.

I found a plate and fork, crossed to the refrigerator, and helped myself to only obvious leftovers. I took my loot upstairs and ate everything I'd stacked on my plate. Now I understood why Kroy called Carmela "Miss Carmel Candy." She had a dour personality, but could she ever cook.

I did one more run-through and nailed it. Or at least didn't mess up even once. Time to stop and get some rest. I'd practice more tomorrow, maybe tweak the pacing. I fell into bed and slept without dreams until some small hour of the morning when memory of my real job brought me wide awake. I was supposed to get information from Kroy's computer. If Kroy hadn't locked his office, I had a good shot right now at plugging in the device and getting copy of his hard drive.

I pulled on some sweats, grabbed my dirty plate for an excuse to be downstairs if people were still up and headed cautiously down the staircase. I paused at the foot of the stairs. The outdoor porch light cast a dim glow into the foyer, but otherwise everything was dark and quiet. I felt my way in the dark from the foot of the stairs down the hall to Kroy's office. I'd just reached out for the doorknob when the hallway flooded with blinding light. I jerked around and dropped the plate. It shattered on the white marble tiles.

The giant figure of Kroy's bodyguard loomed at the end of the hall. He held a gun in his hand and pointed it at me. "What're you doing?"

"Connie! You nearly scared the life out of me." I bent to gather up the shards of broken china.

"What're you doing?" he repeated.

"I was just bringing my dirty plate back to the kitchen." I kept my head down and continued to clean up the broken plate with shaking hands.

"Kitchen's at the end of the other hall."

"I got turned around in the dark. I was trying to be quiet. I didn't want to disturb anyone, but I guess I wasn't quiet enough."

"You set off the motion detector alarm."

"Mr. Kroy never mentioned motion detectors to me." I balanced all the broken pieces with the larger ones on the bottom.

"No one's supposed to be downstairs after Mr. Kroy turns on the motion detectors."

I sighed. No point repeating myself. Kroy apparently hadn't hired Connie for his mental acuity. But that could work for me if he bought my story about looking for the kitchen. I stood up and faced him. He still had the gun leveled at me. "Would you mind not pointing that at me?"

He lowered the gun.

"I feel like I really messed up, setting off the alarm, waking you up, and then breaking a piece of china. I hope Mr. Kroy doesn't get too mad at me."

"He will if you don't clean it up real good. There's a broom and dustpan in the kitchen." He led me down the hall to the kitchen and pointed to the broom closet. I put the broken plate in the trash, burying it a bit so it wouldn't be too obvious to Carmela, then went back to sweep up all the tiny bits under Connie's watchful eye. When he was convinced I'd swept up every last piece, he let me dump the last of it and go back upstairs.

"Good night," I said. "Sorry I woke you."

He grunted in reply and waited until I was at the top of the stairs before dousing the lights. I sank down onto the bed. That was a close call. My heart was still beating faster than normal. It hadn't occurred to me that Kroy would have motion detectors. Lucky for me that Connie was fast to respond to the alarm, or he'd have found me in the study and I'd never have convinced him I was just looking for the kitchen. Lucky too that it had been Connie and not Kroy. I'd never have fooled him about my intentions. What if Connie felt he had to tell Kroy? As paranoid as Kroy was, he'd think I was after something in his study. Maybe I'd use my "who, me?" face again. It had worked once. I rolled over and stuffed the pillow under my head. Better to concentrate on the real problem. How was I going to get into Kroy's study unseen for ten minutes? What if he had other kinds of detectors that I didn't know about? I tried to imagine what those might be, but couldn't keep my focus. Elizabeth's laughter continued to break into my thoughts and the reminder that I'd never know who my father was. Why had I been so stupid to hang onto that belief all these years?

Except for a brief foray into the kitchen, I stayed in my room the next day and practiced. In between run-throughs I put the money Kroy had given me into the secret spaces in my cape that Aunt June had designed. A few thousand dollars stiffened the stand-up collar even more, and most of the remaining bills fit smoothly into the wide hem.

I tried on the dresses Elizabeth had left for me. They were both more low-cut than what I usually wore, but not impossibly so. She'd left some shoes as well. I put those on with the skimpy dress and practiced again to make sure I was completely comfortable. I took a shower, washed my hair, and took a nap. Or tried to.

Elizabeth came in without knocking, followed by a man and a woman I'd never seen before. "Get up. Get up," she ordered. "Giancarlo and Pam are here to do your hair and makeup."

I jumped up from the bed. "That's okay. I can do my own makeup, and there's nothing to be done with my hair."

"Don't argue with me," Elizabeth said and directed Giancarlo and Pam where to set up. "They need to hurry and get you done so they can do me. Ashley completely refused anything. Wouldn't even open her door." She pushed me into a chair and backed away to watch. "You can do something with that hair, can't you Giancarlo? Don't even try to straighten it. That would take too long. Just put some product on it. Tame it into something less feral."

I submitted. I always hated this kind of fuss, but Giancarlo and Pam were very fast and professional. And I had to admit quite good at their jobs. Looking good would make the audience receptive to me and my act. And that would keep me on Kroy's good side, if he in fact had a good side. If Connie ratted me out about last night, Kroy could well decide he couldn't trust me. And it didn't take a vivid imagination to guess what would happen to someone he'd given super secret information to if he felt she wasn't to be trusted. So I didn't go downstairs until Elizabeth knocked the second time on my door, sounding very exasperated. "Valentine, you're keeping everyone waiting."

I'd packed all my gear and change of clothes. If things went well, I'd come back here and try to copy Kroy's hard drive. But if they didn't go well, I needed an escape plan or two, which meant I'd keep my gear close at hand.

I could see Kroy, Elizabeth, Connie, and a heavy-set man in a chauffer's hat standing in the foyer. I descended the stairs slowly and waited for Kroy to spot me. When he did, I got the double-take I'd hoped for. Nothing like a low-cut dress and some well-applied make up to distract attention.

The chauffer met me halfway up the stairs. "Here, miss, I'll take that," he said and relieved me of my gear.

When I reached the foot of the stairs, I did a twirl and asked, "What do you think?"

"Beth did a great job," Kroy said.

Elizabeth looked me up and down with a critical eye. "You're not wearing your necklace."

"I want to wear the one Rico gave me. I feel it will bring me luck tonight. Here you go." I handed her the velvet box. "I think Ashley should wear it."

"Where is Ash, anyway?" Kroy asked. "We can't be late tonight."

"Here I am," Ashley said from the top of the stairs. We all turned and looked at her and stood in frozen amazement for several seconds. She had dyed her hair vivid red and styled it into a wind machine side sweep effect. She wore full anime regalia, from the lace-edged striped knee-high socks to the micro-mini pleated plaid skirt, to the white blouse and school tie, to the painted design on her face.

Kroy spoke first. "What the hell do you think you're doing?"

"Going to the gala," Ashley said as she descended the stairs.

"Not looking like that, you're not. I thought I made it clear no more crazy hair colors. You're grounded. No gala. No nothing. Go to your room." He didn't raise his voice, but his rage was a palpable presence.

Ashley seemed about to stand her ground then spun around and ran back upstairs. Her departure was punctuated by the slam of her bedroom door.

"All right," Kroy snapped, "let's go."

Connie moved ahead of us and opened the door. Another large man stood outside. The chauffeur hurried to open the doors of the limo and the second man followed us. Connie watched us get in the limo, then closed the door of the house.

"Connie's not coming?" I asked.

"Have to leave someone on the property. Everyone will know that no one is home. Makes me a prime target."

He seemed to have forgotten about Ashley. We drove in silence to the hotel, but as we pulled into the drive to the main entrance, Elizabeth smiled and said brightly, "All right, boys and girls, show time!"

We were quickly ushered through the foyer and into the ballroom. Although beautifully decorated with huge vases of flowers everywhere and brilliantly lit, it felt empty. There were only about fifty people hanging around the bar and the buffet table. You'd never guess that this was supposed to be a gala. But as soon as Kroy walked in, the energy level amped up to high. He went from person to person, shaking the men's hands and kissing women's cheeks. He had a way of seeming to focus on that one person, although I could tell he was aware of everyone on the periphery. I was introduced simply as "Beth's daughter." I put on my performer's face as well, and smiled, nodded, and spoke in all the right places as we trailed Kroy from person to person and group to group.

Kroy's arrival served as a signal for the festivities to begin. A small band took the stage and began playing jazz classics. The lighting subtly shifted to brighter on the band and the buffet and dimmer elsewhere. And almost as quickly, the room filled with people. As part of Kroy's entourage, I had freedom to scan the crowd while I smiled and nodded and pretended to listen to Kroy's bull. The two bodyguards who escorted us to the gala stayed nearby but not intrusively. A third guard, apparently sent by Bulgari specifically to look out for Elizabeth's necklace had looked very relieved when she handed over the necklace I'd rejected. I spotted a number of other outrageously jeweled women who probably had their own jewelers' reps keeping an eye on the goods.

Kroy caught my eye and with a jerk of his head, directed me to a place outside of the current group. "Listen up. I'm going to talk to the crowd now, do the slideshow and I want you ready to go on right after that. Your stuff is in a room right next to the ladies' restroom behind the stage, so you can change undisturbed. Okay?"

I nodded. "Sounds good."

"But pay attention. Never get too far away from me. I just got the first phone call that they're shipping the product out tonight."

"Okay."

I watched Kroy take the stage and give his set spiel about the children worldwide suffering from AIDS and how his foundation guaranteed that every cent donated went to purchasing and delivering the drugs that would save the children's lives. He put just the right degree of intensity and sincerity into his talk. Altogether very convincing, if I didn't know better. As he spoke, faces of the affected children were projected onto a huge screen behind him—horrific images of pain and suffering. The hypocrisy of it all made my stomach heave.

I turned to head for the changing room, when Elizabeth crossed my path. "Are we all good?"

I had to laugh. "Not an adjective I'd have chosen for the two of us. But I'm with you on your plan, if that's what you mean."

"Timing is crucial," she said. "It's all set for the moment you finish your little magic act. I'll be over by the north exit, so you'll have to get to me quickly."

"Okay. Can do."

A group of women called to her. "Must go talk to the ladies," Elizabeth said and was quickly swept up in a throng of women in designer dresses and bling.

I had nearly reached the changing room when I was accosted a second time. "Valentine." I turned.

"Uncle George. What a surprise to see you." Surprise hardly covered it. Stunned was more like it.

"I'm certain it is, since you've done your best to avoid me. I must have left ten messages for you and you didn't have the good manners to answer any of them."

"I'm sorry. I lost my phone. I haven't been able to contact anyone."

"I see," he said. "Fortunately for me, while waiting for you to return my call, I had time to read the local paper and saw the society news about this fund-raiser put on by Mr. Kroy. I had good reason to believe that Betty would be here as well. And I see that I was correct."

"So you're here to what—find Elizabeth and tell her that you forgive her? Seriously?"

"Yes, that's my goal. I know she's here, and even though it's quite a throng of people, I know I'll have my chance."

This was one very strange man. I was glad to have an excuse to get away. "I'm about to perform a magic act, but I have to change first. If you wait out front you can catch it. Sorry, I really do have to dash." I hurried off before he could say anything else, found the changing room and ducked in before anyone else could waylay me.

I locked the door and turned around.

"Hi, Valentine," Rico said. He was lounging on a sofa and looking even more gorgeous than I remembered. He'd shaved, but still needed a haircut. He was dressed in black tie that clearly wasn't a rental.

I put my hands on my hips. "Special Agent Rico DiSera, I believe? Or do they have a different title for lying rat bastards? What do you want?"

"To give you your phone." He held out a phone to me. I didn't take it. "They passed your message along. We've been pretty worried about you. I couldn't tell you who I was because it would have put you in more danger than you're already in."

"Yeah, right," I said. "You can leave the phone and go. I have to change. I'm just about to go on."

"I don't blame you for being angry at me. Were you able to copy Kroy's computer?"

"Not yet. And I may not need to. Kroy has taken me into his confidence."

"Look, just forget it. I don't think you should go back there. It's too dangerous."

"I don't work for the FBI, so stop giving me orders. And I mean it. Get out. Now."

He slowly rose to his feet. "You look absolutely stunning."

"Whatever," I said as rudely as possible.

"And you're not leaving here tonight without me."

"Dream on. But do it outside."

He left the room. I had to hurry to get into my other dress. I didn't have time to do any of my usual prep work before there was a light tap on the door and a voice telling me it was time.

I pulled my cape on and fastened it, took a deep breath, straightened my shoulders and opened the door. I came to the small stage from behind and out of view of the audience just as I'd planned. The stage helper attached the lavalier mike to the front of my dress. Kroy finished introducing me and retreated down the steps. I didn't look at him as he passed me. I'd already transformed myself into the Great Valentina.

I began speaking before I ascended the steps so that the audience couldn't locate where the voice was coming from. "Do you ever stop to think that we are all, every one of us, linked together?" I paused a beat. "And how can that be?" Another pause. "Because first came the big bang." At the word "bang"

I tossed the smoke bomb onto the stage. The audience gave a gratifying gasp. I stepped onto the stage and stood with my head down and cape wrapped around me and waited for the smoke to clear. I raised my head, tossed my cape open and over my shoulders, and began tossing a small ball from hand to hand while holding four more, two in each hand. "And matter took form in the shape of particles, like quarks, and neutrinos," I tossed a second ball into the air and juggled the two. "And electrons, and muons and tauons," I said adding a ball to the juggled rotation as I named each particle. "And, as everyone knows, I'm talking about the Standard Model of particle physics." A few giggles here and there from the audience. "And you also know that the Standard Model can predict the behavior of all subatomic particles." I paused in my patter, and, as I juggled, I tossed each ball higher and higher. "With one…very…big…exception." I paused again. "The model can't predict how particles respond to gravity." I covered my head with my arms and all the balls fell on me one by one and bounced away. That got the big laugh I was looking for.

"So they came up with a new theory." I pulled the end of a cord from my inner pocket, taking my time. "What if particles aren't separate entities after all, but simply different manifestations of one basic object—a string?"

I continued to pull the cord from my pocket. After a few yards had appeared I gave the audience a mock look of surprise that it was taking so long. Then I shrugged my shoulders and rolled my eyes, all while the unending cord piled up at my feet. The audience was with me and laughter sprinkled around the room as the rope continued to pile up on the floor. I scanned the room, making eye contact with as many people as I could, pulling them into the fun and making it personal. Finally I gave an exaggerated sigh of exasperation, reached into another pocket, produced a pair of giant scissors, and cut the cord. "I apologize for the drastic measures, but I can't keep you here all night, can I?" I approached the edge of the little stage and handed the scissors out to a young woman who stood closest to the stage.

"Do me a favor and hang onto these for a minute, would you? In case I need them again."

I straightened and flourished the end of the cord that remained in my hand. I was ready to launch into my spiel about string theory, when someone on the other side of the room screamed.

"Call 911," someone yelled.

"Any doctors here tonight?" another person called out.

Everyone in my audience swiveled around to see what the commotion was all about. I could hear them asking each other, "What happened?" "Is someone hurt?"

I knew immediately what had happened. Elizabeth, curse her black soul, had started her heart attack act earlier than planned. Or earlier than she'd led me to believe. She'd probably planned it that way all along. I never intended to let her get away with the necklace, and she must have sensed it.

I snatched up my pile of cord, jumped down from the stage and headed in the direction of the commotion. She still wasn't going to get away with it. Not with me around.

I had to struggle to get through the crowd. "Excuse me, please. That's my mother." Apparently "mother" was a magic word. People turned this way and that to make room for me to squeeze through.

As I got closer, movement became nearly impossible. Kroy's bodyguards had bulldozed their way to the front of the crowd and pushed back against the throng. I could hear them growling, "Get back. Give her room."

"I'm a doctor," one man announced. In this situation, doctor trumped daughter, and everyone pressed against me on all sides to make room for him.

"Please, please let me through to my mother," I said in my most pathetic voice and dug my elbow into the linebacker-sized man blocking my path. It took a while, but I finally wriggled my way into the front ranks. EMTs had already arrived. A fast response time to the 911 call. They knelt on either side of Elizabeth, who looked awful—eyes closed, face ashen and lips with a bluish tinge. A voice in the crowd asked, "Is she dead?" echoing my own thoughts. One of the EMTs put an oxygen mask over her mouth and nose and adjusted the knobs on a portable tank while the doctor leaned over his shoulder and checked her pulse. The other EMT rolled a gurney next to Elizabeth and pushed a lever to lower it. He moved next to her head and the other one to her feet. "On three," the first one said and counted, "one, two, three." They lifted her onto the gurney, raised it to waist height and fastened straps around her waist and legs. And just like that the two EMTs and the doctor were moving her to the exit.

I ran after them. "I'm her daughter." I caught up with them as they were wheeling her into the elevator. "Please, let me go with her."

One of the EMTs said. "You can't ride along in the ambulance. No room with the doc along. Just follow us in a taxi. San Francisco General. And take the next elevator please, we need the room to attend to your mom." And with that, the elevator door swished shut.

I ran toward the stairs. Fortunately, the ballroom was one floor below the main level so I didn't have to endure an elevator ride. I was upstairs and in the lobby and out the front entrance in just under a minute. No ambulance. No paramedics. No Elizabeth.

"Help you, miss?" the doorman asked.

"Was there an ambulance here just a minute ago?"

"No, miss. Is there an emergency? I can call 911 for you."

"What about two EMTs with a woman on a gurney?"

He shook his head no.

In the distance I heard a siren. The real EMTs were on their way. And Elizabeth and her crew of fake first-responders were in the wind.

Chapter Seventeen

"Are you sure I can't call 911 or the police?" the doorman asked.

"No thanks," I said. "It isn't necessary. And when the ambulance that's headed this way gets here, tell them they aren't needed. It was a mistake."

I turned and headed back into the hotel and was met in the doorway by one of Kroy's bodyguards. "You need to come back to the party. Mr. Kroy wants you."

"For heaven's sake, leave me alone, will you?" I could see the Bulgari man bearing down on us wearing an expression of determination mixed with panic.

I moved to meet him. "I'm really sorry. She's gone."

He jolted to a stop. "Gone? They couldn't revive her? Are you sure? That's terrible. Please forgive me, but where did they take her? I really shouldn't have let her go unattended. It's against all policy, but I've never had a client...." He stopped abruptly apparently unable to say the word "die."

I jumped in as soon as he halted. "Not dead. Gone. Decamped. Absconded. Flew the coop."

The Bulgari man's face went white. He opened his mouth and closed it several times giving a pretty good fish-out-of-water impression.

The bodyguard took my upper arm in a firm grip.

"Hey," I protested.

"We have to go back—now." He pulled me away from the stunned jeweler's rep.

I had no choice but to let myself be hauled away. Not that I wanted to stay there and try to explain to the Bulgari man how Elizabeth had pulled off her theft, but I wanted even less to return to the scene of my interrupted performance.

"Not the elevator," I said to the bodyguard who persisted in holding my arm even though I was going along with him. I led him to the stairs and headed down to the ballroom. Kroy met us at the door.

"What the fuck did you think you were doing? I told you to stay close."

I pulled my arm free from the bodyguard's grip. "I was trying to save you from scandal since that would probably affect the amount of money people would be willing to donate."

"What the hell are you talking about?

I leaned forward and whispered. "Elizabeth's gone. With the necklace. The heart attack, the EMTs, even the doctor were all phony."

"Not possible. I saw her myself. She looked bad."

"Anything's possible where Elizabeth's concerned. There was no ambulance. The EMTs must have been in a room upstairs and came down at her signal. I bet they went back that way. She's undoubtedly in disguise and out a service entrance by now. With the necklace."

To my surprise, Kroy barked out a laugh. "The bitch. She told me she was good. I didn't believe her." He sobered. "The necklace is insured, so I'm only out that money. And as far as I'm concerned, she's dead and that's how I'll play it. The jeweler will go along. He won't want it known they've been scammed." He checked his watch. "I have to keep the party going here, so she's not dead yet—just critical. You got that?"

"You're not going to make me go back in there, are you?"

He considered for a moment. "No. That wouldn't look good." He spoke to the bodyguard. "Take her the back way to the dressing room and see that she stays there."

The bodyguard did as he was told and in a few moments I was back in the dressing room. He left me there, but indicated he'd be just outside the door. Once alone, I paced for awhile. I should have guessed Elizabeth would pull a switch on me. She'd never willingly tell me what I wanted to know. Not unless there was something in it for her. My instincts about people were all messed up. My gaze fell on the new cell phone Rico had given me. I crossed the room and picked it up. Case in point—Rico DiSera—if that was his real name. He'd lied to me repeatedly and each time I'd believed him.

I stopped pacing and slumped down on the sofa. Time to face facts. I'd believed him because I wanted to. I hadn't lost my liar radar. I'd simply turned it off when I was around Rico. He'd saved me from the elevator and hadn't said how stupid I was to have freaked out so much I couldn't even move. And he'd kissed me. My fingers drifted to my lips and I sighed. No question, he was an amazing kisser, which led naturally to thinking about what other special skills in that direction he might have.

I eyed the phone and my finger hovered over the speed-dial number to Rico's phone. So tempting to call on the pretext of telling him about Elizabeth. After all, she would never have been in a position to pull off a ten million-dollar jewel theft if the FBI hadn't made her their confidential informant. But he'd know about Elizabeth soon enough, and he might well guess that I was calling only to hear his voice. And how pathetic was that?

I shoved the phone into a pocket of my cape. I had to push all thoughts of Rico out of my mind. I had a big decision to make. And I couldn't let the fact that Rico might not like what I decided influence me. Or even the fact that he might not like me at all once he found out about it. I stretched out on the sofa and wrapped myself up in my cape. I'd change back into my long dress when I'd thought it all through.

The bodyguard banging on the door woke me up. My hard thinking had led immediately to hard sleeping. The door reverberated with more pounding. "What is it?" I asked.

The bodyguard opened the door. "Party's over. Time to go. Mr. Kroy is waiting."

I looked down at my short dress, creased and rumpled from being used as pajamas. I looked a mess, but it didn't matter. I looked good enough for what I had to do. "What time is it?"

"Four a.m."

"Okay, I'm coming." I heaved myself from the sofa, grabbed my duffel and my long dress and followed him out. We took the back stairs to the garage. Maybe this was the very route Elizabeth had taken when she made her getaway.

I climbed into the backseat of the limo where Kroy was already ensconced, tapping on his cell phone. He glanced up briefly, nodded at me and returned to his cell. We continued on like this almost all the way back to his house. His silence occasionally punctuated by a grunt. Finally he said, "The early news on the gala is good. Only one blogger mentions Beth. Columnists are bound to pick it up, but we had some big names there tonight. I'm betting that gossip about them will beat out everything else."

"And the phone call you've been waiting for?"

"Not yet." He looked out the side window. Clearly not wanting to continue the conversation.

He called Connie just as we turned onto his street, and Connie was at the door to greet us when we walked in.

"Everything okay?" Kroy asked.

He didn't answer but looked past us through the still-open doorway with a look of alarm.

I spun around and saw a giggling Ashley coming up the front steps pulling Jeff after her.

"Surprise!" Ashley announced as they came into the foyer.

Jeff, my ex-hat man who'd robbed me of two thousand dollars and destroyed my most precious possession, looked stunned to see me. "Babe," he said weakly.

"Don't 'babe' me, jerk." I marched up to him and socked him in the jaw, just as I promised myself I'd do the next time I saw him. He staggered backward but didn't fall down. I mustn't have hit him hard enough.

"What the fuck is going on? Where were you?" Kroy shouted at Ashley.

"Out," Ashley replied with a stubborn set to her jaw.

Kroy looked on the verge of having a stroke. He swung around to face Connie.

"You let her go out? I told her to stay in her room."

"I'm sorry, Mr. Kroy. I didn't see her leave."

"Sleeping when you were supposed to be on watch, I'll bet. Get out of my sight. I'll deal with you later."

Connie ducked his head as if he'd been struck and returned to the monitoring room, closing the door behind him. Seeing the large man cowed by her father's rage seemed to have a sobering effect on Ashley. Or maybe it was my immediate physical attack on Jeff. Whatever the case, she adopted a placating tone. "Daddy, Jeff is Valentine's boyfriend. That's why I brought him home. He's in a band. They were playing at Gilman's."

Before Kroy could answer, his phone chirped. He pulled his phone out with one hand and pointed to Ashley and Jeff with the other. "You two, stay where you are."

Jeff had been backing toward the open doorway but halted at Kroy's command. Kroy answered his phone and gestured for me to join him. We moved a few yards away from Ashley and Jeff with Kroy speaking softly into his cell. He handed the phone to me and said. "Listen. It's a new phone number." I took the phone, listened to a man's quiet voice recite a number, then handed the phone back to Kroy. "You got that?" I nodded and he ended the call. "That's our go-ahead. Now you call the bank. That's the first number on the list. Give them the signal to transfer the funds. Then you call the number you just heard, confirm the money transfer and give them the address." He handed me the phone. "After you do that, make arrangements for the other shipment."

A voice from the doorway made me freeze. "I'm here for the bitch." I spun around. Dwayne the dodo—back again.

From that point on everything happened very fast, but I experienced it in slow motion, the way I did when I juggled and was in the zone. Since Jeff was right by the doorway, Dwayne focused on him first. "Where is she? And don't give me any shit about a hospital. I know she's not there."

Jeff put out a hand toward Dwayne. "Hey, dude, chill for a second, will you?"

I don't know if it was being called "dude" or being told to "chill" that bothered Dwayne more. Whichever it was, his response was immediate. He pulled out a gun and shot Jeff between the eyes.

In the same moment, Ashley screamed and Connie exploded out of the monitor room. As soon as Dwayne turned his gaze to Connie, I stepped forward, grabbed Ashley by the arm and ran, nearly dragging her with me, down the hall and around the corner into the kitchen. Kroy was nowhere in sight. "Get into the back stairway." I pushed her in that direction. I heard two more gunshots, which I hoped meant that Connie, or even Kroy, had stopped Dwayne—permanently. But I wasn't going to bet on it. I dashed over to the door to the garage, opened it and hit the garage door-opener button. Try to make him think we ran out that way. Then I ran toward the door to the back stairway where Ashley stood frozen. I opened that door and shoved her in. Ashley began to sob.

"Hush," I whispered. "You have to be quiet." I closed the door behind us and led her halfway up to the curve in the stairway.

Ashley kept crying and making little whimpering noises. "He shot Jeff. For no reason. Is he going to shoot us too?"

"No. He won't find us if you keep quiet." Or at least I desperately hoped he wouldn't. I put my arm around her shoulders and we crouched together on a stair step. In a short while we heard Dwayne yelling, "You fucking bitch, I know you're here." He was in the kitchen.

Ashley trembled but kept silent. I held my breath.

"What is this fucking shit?" Dwayne screamed in his usual limited vocabulary, then came the sound of breaking glass and pottery. This continued for nearly a minute followed by silence.

I breathed in and out slowly trying to slow my racing heart.

"Is he gone?" Ashley whispered.

"We have to wait awhile," I whispered back, "to make sure. I didn't see your dad when we came in here. Do you think ran away or went to get a gun?"

"He's probably in his panic room. It's behind a panel in his study. I saw him running down the hall as soon as that awful man showed up. He didn't even wait for me." She started crying again and I immediately shushed her.

Panic room. I'd heard about those, but never seen one.

"Does it have monitors so he can see what's going on?"

"Yes."

"What about a phone?"

"I don't think so. But he'd use his cell anyway."

No, he wouldn't. I had Kroy's cell phone. So if that's where he went he hadn't called for help. And I didn't want to make the noise a call would make until I was sure Dwayne was gone.

I sat and breathed for what seemed a very long time and thought about what to do next. Dwayne was vicious and cunning, but also impulsive and impatient. He had to imagine that someone must have called the police by now. "Wait here," I said, I crept down the stairs and cracked the door a fraction. The sliver of the kitchen I could see was totally smashed. And I saw something else—blood. That had to be Dwayne's, which meant he was wounded. Not mortally, judging from the amount of damage he'd done, but eventually he'd be weakened by loss of blood. I pushed the door further open and scanned the entire kitchen. No sign of anyone and no sounds either. Although in a house this big, it would be easy to go unheard. I closed the door and climbed up the steps.

"How did you get out last night without Connie seeing you?"

"Down these stairs to the kitchen. There's another door that goes to the backyard. I pulled out the wire that sends the 'door open' alert. Outside there are places where the bushes are overgrown so you don't show up on the monitors. Then it's sort of a climb uphill through the trees to the road."

I could just picture it because I'd seen that view from the other end on the day Phil and I scoped out the house. "Okay, this is what I want you to do." I pulled a couple of bundles of cash from the hem of my cape and pressed them into her hands. "Take this money. Stow most of it in your shoes and the rest in your pocket, if you have a pocket. Go out the way you went last night. Dwayne's not in the kitchen…"

"Dwayne?" she recoiled from me. "You mean you know him?"

"No. Not know. He tried to kill me once. He's not in the kitchen and even if he's looking at the monitors, he won't see you. You get out of here. Go to a neighbor. Someone way up the street. Call your mom and tell her what's happened. She'll get you home safely. Can you do that?"

"Yes. You're sure he's gone?"

"I'm sure that if he's not gone, he won't see you."

I led her down the stairs and saw that she got safely away. I went back to my hiding place in the stairway and called 911. Then I made calls to the numbers Kroy had given me. Finally, I ventured back into the kitchen, stepping carefully to avoid the blood drops and smears. I moved slowly down the hall to the foyer. Jeff's body lay where he'd fallen. A few feet away lay Connie's body, his gun a few inches from his lifeless hand. I could see two blood trails on the stairs. Dwayne had gone up and come down again. I stepped into the monitor room and switched off the monitors the way Mike had shown me. Kroy wouldn't see the cops when they came in the house and know he was safe. Then I followed the trail of blood drops to the open front door and in the dim dawn light I followed it all the way to the sidewalk, where it stopped. He must have gotten into a car.

At last I could make the call I'd wanted to make for hours and hours. But when Rico answered the phone, I couldn't speak for the tears that choked me.

Chapter Eighteen

I sat on the curb in the dim dawn, huddled in my cape, the phone clasped in my hand like a life line. Only I couldn't be sure that I'd be pulled to safety. Dwayne was gone—for the time being. It was clear now that he was after Elizabeth and had been all along. And Elizabeth had already made her getaway. I hoped that he'd figured that out by now and was chasing after her. I could only wish I'd never see him again, because it didn't look like the cops were ever going to stop him.

The vehicles arrived in a constant stream, lights flashing. Cop cars, ambulances, and unmarked cars one after the other. The street and sidewalk were soon flooded with people, some in uniforms, some in blue nylon jackets with FBI in yellow on the back, some in street clothes with badges on their belts. Lights came on in the houses up and down the street. A uniformed cop approached me. "Watch out for the blood," I said as he nearly stepped on the trail of droplets Dwayne had left on the sidewalk.

He halted, looked down, and stepped over the red marks. "Did you make the 911 call reporting a homicide?"

I nodded. "They're just inside the front door."

Rico came running toward me. He was still wearing his tuxedo but had a blue nylon jacket over it, with a yellow insignia and TEA on the left front. I got shakily to my feet.

"Valentine, are you okay?" He took me in his arms.

I opened my mouth to reply but my throat closed up and tears started again. I wasn't okay and didn't know when, if ever,

I would be again. I'd done what I had to do, but once I told Rico, he wouldn't want to hold me so gently. So instead of telling him, I asked. "What's TEA? Some kind of political statement?"

"It stands for Treasury Enforcement Agency. It's who I work for. I'll tell you about it later. I have a lot to tell you, but let's deal with this situation first." He released me from his embrace, but kept one arm protectively around my shoulders.

The uniformed cop had stood aside when Rico came up, but now stepped forward. "Sir, this lady made the 911 call and we need to ask her some questions."

"Special Agent in Charge Williams will have to speak to her first. This is an FBI investigation." Rico told him. "But you can find whoever Homicide sent and bring him over."

"Where's Carl?" I asked. "I need to talk to him, too."

The officer turned to do as Rico had asked. Rico pulled out his phone and made the call. "Carl, why aren't you here yet? I know octogenarians who drive faster than you."

I sensed a change in the scene and immediately saw why. Williams had arrived with two agents in tow and was barking orders left and right as he strode in my direction. Vehicles were reparked to clear a lane. A crew of uniforms began to unroll yellow crime scene tape. Onlookers, mainly neighbors in bathrobes and slippers, were herded a good distance away. Finally he reached me and gazed at me with concern. "Ms. Hill, are you all right?"

〉〉〉

I didn't know how to react to this version of the Special Agent in Charge, so I just blurted out. "Dwayne did it. It's Elizabeth he's after. He killed Connie and Jeff."

"Jeff?" Rico broke in. "You mean lover boy Jeff who stole your money? What the hell was he doing here?"

"It's a long story. They're just inside the front door. I'm pretty sure that Connie wounded Dwayne. There's a trail of blood all over the house and it leads out to the curb." I pointed to the blood on the sidewalk. "He must have had a car here, or someone picked him up. It looks like a lot of blood, so maybe he's gone to a hospital."

Williams pointed to one of the two agents who'd accompanied him. "Check all hospitals." The agent immediately broke away and gathered a crew of agents and cops around him. "Anyone else hurt?"

I shook my head.

"What about Kroy and Ashley?" Rico asked.

"I helped Ashley escape out a back way. Kroy's in his panic room. That's why I need to talk to Carl. I turned off the monitors. He doesn't know you're here. You can't let Kroy know it's safe to come out until I tell Carl everything. I have all the information he'll need to put Kroy away for life."

"What are you talking about? You inserted yourself into an FBI investigation?" He turned to Rico. "You permitted this?"

"Reports were submitted daily, sir. You may not have had time to review them since the Kroy investigation took a backseat to the agents' murders."

Williams gaze hardened. Much more the expression I was used to. But I didn't want Rico to be at the receiving end.

I stepped in front of Rico. "I got myself into this situation and then offered to give the FBI information. Special Agent DiSera tried to discourage me, but I didn't know he was Special Agent DiSera because he was undercover as a taxi driver, but actually as a gangster and as a CI for the FBI. Only he doesn't work for them. He works for TEA, whatever that is." I paused to take a breath.

Williams put up his hand palm outward. "All right, hold it right there. Let's just stick to what happened tonight." He gestured to the other agent who'd accompanied him. He pulled out a cell phone and turned on the video function. I recounted what had happened from the time of my return from the gala with Kroy to my 911 call. Only I left out the part about the phone calls. I'd wait until Carl arrived for that confession.

They let me talk without interruption. When I'd finished, Williams said, "I might have some questions for you once we view the scene. Do you have some place safe you can go? Got to figure this Dwayne will still be looking for you as a way to your mother."

"I'll make sure she's safe, sir," Rico said. "I know the investigative focus is on Dwayne and whoever's working with him, but could you appoint a team to detain Kroy and keep him isolated until Special Agent Carter and I can review the evidence that Valentine has gathered? The Treasury Department will be very grateful."

"Of course. It's an important joint-task force operation. I'll be glad to see it successfully completed."

Rico nodded in acknowledgement.

⟩⟩⟩

I looked at Rico out of the corner of my eye. He sounded different. Authoritative. He even held himself in a different way. He looked at me. "What's the matter?"

"Nothing."

He raised an eyebrow as if he didn't believe me. I spotted Carl, wearing a blue jacket with FBI on the front, making his way toward us. I waved and distracted Rico's attention away from me and toward Carl.

"Finally," Rico said when Carl drew near. "Where are you parked? Let's get Valentine out of here."

"I'm down the street," Carl said and led the way to his car.

I didn't exactly drag my feet, but I didn't hurry either. The moment I'd dreaded had arrived. I couldn't stand the tension and started talking before we reached Carl's car.

"I know everything about Kroy's dealings. I'm on the board of directors of the Kroy Foundation, and I'm director of BK Trading. You know, the onshore shell company that sends the money offshore and no one can track it?"

Carl and Rico stopped in their tracks and stared at me. Then Rico grabbed my arm and hurried me into Carl's car. He got into the backseat with me while Carl climbed into the driver's seat. "Okay," Rico said. "Back up. When did this happen? Why didn't you tell me?"

"It happened yesterday, and I couldn't tell you because Kroy took my phone away."

"Damn it, Valentine, you know what this means?" He ran his fingers through his hair. "You're criminally culpable for every crime that can be traced to the shell company."

"That's what Elizabeth said. She was the director, but Kroy had her resign and named me. But it's okay because I'm a CI now. Like you. Or like you pretended to be. And I have all the numbers. Phone numbers, account numbers, addresses. Up here." I tapped my head. "That's why Kroy wanted me, because the numbers aren't on his computer. And here, "I reached to the back of my neck and unfastened the chain and handed the crystal and gold heart to Carl. "I didn't get to use this, but it doesn't matter now because you have his computer, right?"

"What do you think, Carl?" Rico asked. "Will they have to include her in the case against Kroy?"

"Let's all just take a breather," Carl said. "I picked up some coffee for us. The good stuff too. That's what took so long." He handed me a lidded paper cup and passed another to Rico. I held the cup in both hands and let the warmth seep into them. I hadn't told them the bad part yet. The part that would make Rico really angry at me. I slanted a look at Rico.

"What is it Valentine?" Rico asked. "Come on out with it."

"I don't want you to be angry with me."

"I'm not angry, just concerned. And don't worry. Carl and I will sort it out. You won't be prosecuted."

"Not angry about that. About what I did."

Silence fell in the car. Rico and Carl's eyes were riveted on me. Finally, Rico asked, "What did you do?"

"I sent the money from the black market drug dealers to my offshore account. So you can recover the money and trace it backwards to them. Kroy had already sent the foundation money to pay for the real drugs, but I changed the shipping address to the real AIDS relief organization. And…" I paused.

"Go on," Rico said.

"I sent the fake drugs to the black marketers." I said softly and ducked my head.

Carl's deep laugh greeted my admission. In a second Rico joined in.

"You're not mad at me? I know you needed all the drugs for evidence, but the children need them more."

"Who could ever be mad at you?" Rico said. "Exasperated, sure. Terrified for you, definitely. But not mad."

"Thank you. Thank you." I threw my arms around Rico's neck and hugged him as tight as I could. He drew me close and put his face next to mine.

"Tell me what I did," he said with a laugh, "so I can do it again."

I nestled my face in the crook of his neck. "I was just so scared you'd never even speak to me again."

"Sorry to interrupt," Carl said, "but we have work to do."

I pulled away from Rico, but he kept one arm around my shoulders.

"Right," Rico said. "Let's get the information from Valentine and we'll decide which part is yours and which is mine. You still have that voice recorder, Carl?"

"Right here." Carl pulled a little device out of the glove box and passed it back to Rico.

"First, you said you had Kroy's phone. Why don't you hand that to Carl. He'll get traces out on those numbers. And then let's start with the phone numbers and addresses, then you can give us the bank info. Okay?"

I handed the phone to Carl, and Rico spoke into the voice recorder giving the date and time and identifying himself and Carl by their titles and me as the confidential informant. He gave me the recorder and I did as he asked. When I finished I gave a big sigh and let my head fall back against the headrest.

"You okay?" Rico asked.

"It's such a relief that it's over. No more secrets. No more lies."

"You were amazing, Valentine," Rico said. "You definitely have the thanks and recognition of the Treasury and of the FBI. Okay, Carl, let's agree on how we'll proceed from here. It looks like you have enough information to pull a raid on the black marketers when they take delivery of the drug shipment. I have to get to the office to follow the money trail."

"I don't understand. You're going to follow the money yourself? I thought you were like an action-type agent. Undercover and all that."

"I was recruited to work undercover for this operation. But my usual assignment is as a forensic accountant."

"You're an accountant?" I was stunned.

"A forensic accountant. There's a difference. I'll explain more later. We have to go now."

"Valentine going with you?" Carl asked.

"Yes, I'm her protection detail. Come on, Valentine," Rico said. He got out and held the door open for me. The crowd had increased while we'd been talking. The neighbors, curious about the police action on their block, were heavily outnumbered by news crews. Someone from the crowd called out, "There she is," and in seconds a wave of news people with microphones, cameras and other paraphernalia shifted from the edge of the crime scene-tape barrier to me.

Rico put one arm around my shoulders and held the other out like a traffic cop. "Stand back," he said in his new persona as an authority figure. Voices yelled my name and shouted questions at me. Cameras flashed in a crazy pattern of light. I pulled my cape tightly around me and put my head down. I wasn't prepared for this. We made our way to Rico's car and he stowed me in the passenger seat while maintaining a stony face in front of the cameras.

"Sorry about that," he said as he slid behind the wheel.

"How did they know who I was?"

"You did perform at the gala last night in that very outfit." He slowly edged the car past the news crews. We had to wait a few minutes while police moved cars that had arrived after Rico and parked at all angles. Photographers continued to take pictures of us through the windshield.

"It's really creepy," I said through clenched teeth so no one could read my lips.

"I'll keep them away from you as soon as we get out of here. But you'll have to face them again when you testify in court."

"I'll be better prepared. Maybe I'll work up a little magic show for them."

"But now that you mention it, since they know that both Treasury and the FBI are involved, they'll probably stake out the Federal building."

"Is that where you need to go to track the money?"

"Yes. I need a secure, encrypted computer. Let me think. Would you mind going back to i-systems with me? I could use one of those computers."

"No, I don't mind, just as long as I don't get trapped in the elevator." I smiled to show I was kidding.

He glanced at me, his face serious. "That is not going to happen to you again, if I have anything to say about it."

"Do you want to have anything to say about it?"

He didn't answer me. He pulled the car over to the curb and turned to face me. "Valentine, we have a lot to talk about. I need to tell you some things. Important things. But right now I only have time for one of them. I'm crazy about you. Since I met you, it's taken all my willpower to keep my hands off you. So, yes, I do want to have something to say about everything that happens to you."

"You're crazy about me? Really?"

"Oh yeah."

"Prove it." And he did for several heart pumping, body melting, mindless minutes.

When he pulled away and gazed at me with smoldering brown eyes, I smiled and said, "Okay, I think I believe you. And know what? You're the most amazing kisser. Undoubtedly the best I've ever kissed."

He pulled me into his arms again and showed me again just how amazing he was. He kissed me until I was completely breathless and wanting more, much more. He drew away slowly. "We can't do this now, or here."

"And you have to find that computer and get the evidence to nail Kroy and everyone else he's had dealings with, right?"

He drew a deep breath. "Right. But after that, watch out." He started the engine and pulled into traffic. I smiled to myself and snuggled into the seat.

We arrived at the back of the building just as before when he'd been playing cab driver. We walked up the loading dock, Rico pulled out some keys and unlocked the back door. "I don't think anyone's here."

He flipped on the lights, illuminating the large workshop and the woodworking equipment.

"Mike's going to miss all this." I followed Rico to the doorway where he flipped a few more light switches for the hallway ahead.

"Hold it right there," said a familiar voice from the doorway behind us.

I turned to face Uncle George and Dwayne. Both holding guns pointed at us.

"Uncle George? You?" I was stunned.

"What the hell?" Rico said. "How'd you find us? I know we weren't tailed."

"Tracking devices aren't difficult to affix to a vehicle in a crowd of people," Uncle George said.

"But I don't understand, Uncle George. You and Dwayne?"

Dwayne took a threatening step toward us. "Shut your face, stupid bitch. He's not your uncle. He's my uncle."

"It's okay, Dwayne," Uncle George said. "She can call me whatever she pleases as long as she tells us what we need to know."

"You're talking about Elizabeth, right?"

"Bingo," Dwayne said.

"And I shall not tolerate your lies this time," Uncle George added.

"You better believe it," Dwayne said. "And we can do it the easy way or the hard way. I don't mind the hard way myself, but we're kind of running out of time. We spent a coupla hours on that other bitch."

Rico shifted his position so he partly blocked me from the guns pointed at us. "You mean Special Agent Philips? Or did you know she worked for the FBI?"

"She informed us of that fact," Uncle George said, "after Dwayne employed some of his persuasive techniques. However, she didn't reveal Elizabeth's location. I believe now that she didn't know. You, my dear, are a different story."

When he called me "my dear" my skin crawled with revulsion. "Don't talk to me about lying. You're the biggest liar of them all." I took a step toward him. "You said you wanted to forgive Elizabeth and complete your journey. What a load of crap."

Rico put a restraining arm around my shoulders and pulled me back.

"I quite agree," Uncle George said. "I acquired that very peculiar line of thought from one of Betty's other victims. You mentioned him the other day—Harold Costello."

"Uncle Rocky," I breathed.

"Stupid name for a stupid man. He forgave Betty for stealing his money, but not for taking you away. It's quite unbelievable. He searched for you. Planned on adopting you. He had them put your face on milk cartons for years using a computerized age progression photo." He tilted his head to one side and considered me. "You actually do look like that picture. But of course the strongest resemblance is to your mother, and I'm not referring to looks but to character. I'm going to give you one chance to separate yourself from her evil nature. Lie to me and you'll face the consequences." He jerked his head in Dwayne's direction.

Dwayne must have taken this as a signal to assert his power to inflict pain. He crossed a few steps to the nearest woodworking machine, a table saw, and flipped the on switch. The motor noise reverberated in the high-ceilinged space. I studied Dwayne. He'd flipped the switch with his right hand. The one that also held the gun. I'd seen the trail of blood at Kroy's. Dwayne had to have been wounded in the exchange of gunfire with Connie. How badly, I had no clue. I'd bet that it had to be his left shoulder or arm, but he stood at an angle so I couldn't see his left side at all. I looked at him more closely. His face shone with sweat, and he leaned against the machinery as if for support.

"I only lied once. The other times I really had no idea where she was. You know that she staged a fake heart attack, right?"

"Yes. Don't waste time telling me what I already know."

"Okay. I'll tell you. She's here, in a loft apartment upstairs."

"Really?" Uncle George asked with raised eyebrows. "Somehow that doesn't seem likely." And with a speed and strength I didn't expect from his pudgy build he stepped toward me, grabbed my wrist, dragged me to the table saw and slammed my hand down within inches of the whirring blade. The vibrations from the motor ran from my palm all the way to my shoulder. "I don't believe I've ever seen a one-handed magician."

Dwayne laughed. "Me neither."

"She's telling the truth," Rico said quickly. "Elizabeth cut a deal with the FBI. She's going to be a prosecution witness at Kroy's trial. We're here to take her to the U.S. Marshals who're going to put her in witness protection."

Uncle George did his head-tilting thing and gazed first at Rico and then at me with narrowed eyes. "Very well," he said. "You, Valerie, will take me to her. And Dwayne, if this one gives you any trouble, shoot him."

He released his grip on my wrist and gestured at me with the gun.

"Fine." I knew what I had to do.

"No," Rico said. "I'll take you."

Uncle George eyed Rico. "I think not."

"Valentine?" Rico said.

Would Rico remember that Dwayne had been shot? I had to tell him what I'd figured out. "He doesn't like being *left* with *Dwayne*," I said. "Am I *not right?*" I gave Rico an intense look.

Rico blinked a couple of times and nodded. Neither Uncle George nor Dwayne reacted.

"It's this way." I led him out of the workshop into the hallway and to the elevator. I grabbed the handle of the folding gate and slid the elevator door aside. I glanced at Uncle George.

He gestured with his gun for me to go in first. He followed closely on my heels.

"The gate has to be all the way closed or the elevator won't go," I said.

He pointed the gun at my mid-section. "Then close it."

I closed the gate with force so that I made it clang shut as loudly as possible. I needed Rico to hear it over the noise of the table saw so he'd be ready to deal with Dwayne when the lights went out. I pictured the precise movements I'd have to make. Just as with every performance, timing was everything. I slowed my breathing and tried to ignore my racing heart. "Ready?" I asked Uncle George, my hand poised over the antique control panel. "It jerks a little when it starts and stops."

"Enough of your delaying tactics, Valerie. Get on with it."

I kept my gaze fixed on him as I pushed the button with my left hand and made a fist with my right. *One*, I counted silently. The elevator motor started and the car jerked into upward movement. *Two.* The gun in Uncle George's hand wavered as the car moved. *Three.* The elevator jerked to a halt, the lights went out and I landed a right uppercut on Uncle George's chin, swinging from my toes the way I'd been taught by my real Uncle Rocky, who wanted to be my dad. He'd have been so proud of me. In the darkness I felt the elevator car shudder as Uncle George crashed to the floor. I jumped with my full weight onto Uncle George's still form, just in case he wasn't actually unconscious. No reaction. Good. He was out cold. I felt around for his gun, but when I found it I was afraid to pick it up. What if it went off? I pushed it toward a corner of the elevator. Then I sat on Uncle George's chest and waited for the lights to come on. Come on, Rico, turn on the lights. I repeated these words in my head like a mantra. If I pictured Rico I could keep the panic at bay.

The lights came on. I immediately pulled out the cord I'd planned on using in my act from an inner pocket of my cape and tied Uncle George's hands and then his feet using knots that few people would know how to untie.

"Valentine, Valentine," I heard Rico's voice coming near. The elevator had stalled before it had completely cleared the first-floor opening. I peered through the metal grid of the folding gate and saw Rico looking up at me.

"I'm here," I said. "Uncle George is out cold."

"Open the gate. You can squeeze through that opening and I'll lift you down."

I did as he said. I never thought of myself as a lightweight, but he lowered me to the ground easily. "You're okay? God, you scared me. What happened to George? Here, step away from that elevator shaft. I've had enough disasters for one day." He pulled me some feet away from the black opening below the stalled elevator car. "How did you do it? Where's the gun? Damn it Valentine, never do that again. You hear me?" He pulled me against his chest, and I snuggled there.

"Uncle George has a glass jaw, which I found out when I was little and punched him. The gun's still in the elevator. He can't reach it because I tied him up. What about Dwayne?"

"Dwayne deprived me of my chance to play the hero. He passed out before the circuits blew. You were right. He had been shot. By the time I checked his pulse, he was gone. Bled out."

"Couldn't have happened to a nastier psychopath."

Rico's laugh cut off abruptly. He dropped his arms to his side and crashed to the floor revealing Lies-About-Her-Age standing behind him holding a gun by the barrel.

"What did you do to him?" I demanded and sank to my knees next to Rico's unconscious body. His chest rose and fell in even breathing. I pressed my hand against his cheek. No response.

"Just gave him a good concussion. I would've shot him, but I was afraid the bullet would pass through him and hit you. And I need you alive." She shifted her hold on the gun from barrel to grip and slid her finger onto the trigger.

"Who are you, anyway? I've seen you everywhere."

"I knew you didn't remember me. Denise Hunsinger. I met you when you were little. George is my brother."

"And Dwayne?"

"My son. And they're both useless. I've had to do everything. When they didn't come back to the car with your bitch of a mother, I knew it was up to me to get the job done—again. Now stand up and stop asking questions or I will shoot your boyfriend."

What was it with this family? All of them gun-carrying crazies. Scary crazy at that. I slowly rose to my feet. What could I do now? Even if a glass jaw was a family trait, I'd already used the black-out option. I could only hope that Rico had called the cops before he came to get me out of the elevator. I needed an advantage, an edge.

"What I don't get is, what do you want with Elizabeth, anyway?"

"I want my money."

"*Your* money? Don't you mean your brother's money?"

"It's my money. I earned it. I'm the one who ran the business while George nursed his wife. Never understood what he saw in that silly bitch anyway. When she finally died, did George come back and help me? No. He fell for your mother's scam. Followed her around like a lap dog, while I put in sixty-hour weeks. I said 'I told you so' when she made off with everything. It's taken us years and years to find her, and I'm not going to let her get away again without handing over *my* money with interest. And I'm done talking. Take me to her now." Her voice rose to a screech.

I'd hoped to get her worked up so I could distract her, but she seemed maniacally focused, the gun rock-steady in her hand. There was only one thing for me to do—I had to be The Great Valentina. For real.

I pulled my shoulders back and straightened my cape. "I'll do better than that. I'll bring Elizabeth to you. You know that I am one of the greatest magicians in the world, don't you? I'm the one who made Elizabeth disappear. She exists now only in the ether." I lifted my hand in a dramatic gesture. Her eyes followed my hand. "And I can bring her back to this plane. Just like this." I made a fist, lowered my arm and opened my hand palm up to show a fluttering butterfly. I heard her quick intake of breath. I gave a flick of my wrist and the butterfly disappeared. She blinked and stared at my hand. While her attention was fixed on my empty hand I surreptitiously palmed my second smoke bomb, the one I'd planned on using to end my act.

"I won't waste your time," I said quickly before she could speak. "Elizabeth! I command you to appear." I stepped back toward the elevator shaft and threw the smoke bomb at her feet. She gave a little scream as it exploded.

I knew I had at most two seconds, maybe only one, but I'd practiced my maneuver over and over. My act's grand finale. I'd already unfastened the snap at the neck of my cape. Holding the cape by the collar I snapped my wrist twice, releasing the clever extension rods that allowed me to kneel down and hold my cape up and away from me. To the audience, it looked as if I'd turned my back and held my cape out with my arms.

She fired her gun. The sound hit my eardrums with physical force, but the bullet passed only through my cape. I crouched and tried to make myself as small as possible. If I were on the stage at the hotel, I would've been down the exit steps backstage and not visible at all. The smoke and part of my cape kept most of me hidden from her view, but probably her rage gave her tunnel vision so all she could see was the cape and the illusion of me standing there unharmed by her bullet.

"You bitch!" she screamed and dived for the cape.

I released my hold on the extension rod and she pitched forward into the open maw of the elevator shaft. Her body hit bottom with a thump and I was on my feet, running toward Rico.

"Rico." I put my hands on either side of his face. "Rico, please wake up."

He opened his eyes. "Did I just hear a gunshot?"

"Yes, but I'm fine. It was Uncle George's sister. She knocked you out."

"Is that what happened?" He struggled to a sitting position and put his hand to the back of his head. "What's that sound?"

I cocked my head to listen. My ears were still ringing from the gunfire. I could hear faint moaning. "That's her. She fell down the elevator shaft."

"She fell?"

"With a little help from the Great Valentina," I said with a grin.

"Come here Great Valentina." He drew me into his arms. "I have something important to tell you."

"You already told me. Don't you remember? You're crazy about me."

"Not that. Although I'd like to tell you that again when I can show you just how crazy. This is something else. You, Valentine, are twenty-four years old. You were born in Ann Arbor, Michigan, on February fourteenth."

I gasped. "I am? I was?"

"Want to know how I know?"

"Yes, please tell me."

"I knew Elizabeth was up to something. The EMTs got there too fast, and I knew Kroy didn't have an ambulance waiting outside. So I followed her and her phony EMTs and saw that they went up to the third floor. It was simple to track them and put them all under arrest."

"How did you convince her to tell you my birth date? Please don't tell me you let her go free."

"Not exactly. I told her that if she didn't tell me she would be charged with obstruction of justice and accessory to murder in Phil's death because Phil wouldn't have been killed if Elizabeth hadn't disappeared."

"So you did let her walk away."

"As I said, not exactly. I handed her over to the cops and she was charged with grand larceny for stealing the diamonds. She'll be held without bail because she's a flight risk. Plus, when the national media cover the story, we'll ask other victims to come forward and press charges."

"You conned her. I can't believe it. You scammed Elizabeth. No one has ever done that before." I threw my arms around him. "Now I can get a birth certificate and a social security number. How can I ever thank you?"

"I'll think of something," he said with his incredibly sexy smile. And he did.

Author's Note

If you have any thoughts, comments or questions about *The Magician's Daughter*, I'd love to hear from you. You can contact me at judith@judithjaneway.com. For information about events and upcoming books or to sign up for my newsletter, please visit judithjaneway.com.

To receive a free catalog of Poisoned Pen Press titles, please provide your name and address through one of the following ways:

Phone: 1-800-421-3976
Facsimile: 1-480-949-1707
Email: info@poisonedpenpress.com
Website: www.poisonedpenpress.com

Poisoned Pen Press
6962 E. First Ave. Ste 103
Scottsdale, AZ 85251

CPSIA information can be obtained at www.ICGtesting.com
Printed in the USA
BVOW01*2315191214

380087BV00001B/1/P